Praise for
HITTIN' THE BRICKS

"Fantastic . . . a compelling story.
Noire does it again . . . and never fails."
—Urban Reviews

Praise for
HOOD

"A strong plot and carefully drawn characters
with classic motivations."
—*Publishers Weekly*

Praise for
THONG ON FIRE
Winner of the African-American
Literary Award for Erotica

"Noire delivers a captivating page-turner that will be hard to
put down. *Thong on Fire* is not just a book but a
literary journey that goes beyond the sheets."
—APOOO BookClub

"*Thong on Fire* is compelling and engaging, the kind of
story that, once started, is hard to put down."
—RAWSISTAZ

UNZIPPED

UNZIPPED

Noire

AN URBAN EROTIC TALE

ONE WORLD TRADE PAPERBACKS

BALLANTINE BOOKS | NEW YORK

A One World Trade Paperback Original

Copyright © 2010 by Noire

All rights reserved.

Published in the United States by One World Books, an imprint of The Random House Publishing Group, a division of Random House, Inc., New York.

ONE WORLD is a registered trademark and the One World colophon is a trademark of Random House, Inc.

ISBN 978-0-345-50879-9

Printed in the United States of America

www.oneworldbooks.net

9 8 7 6 5 4 3

Book design by Laurie Jewell

"In the projects of Manhattan, the Bronx, and Staten Island,
we grind real hard and we always wildin!
And don't forget Brooklyn, Mount V, and also Queens,
the streets of New York are never squeaky clean!"

—REEM RAW

WARNING

This here ain't no romance it's an urban erotic tale,
Payback is a bitch and Pearl's determined not to fail
It only took one night to lose her family to the streets
Until the guilty pay the piper Pearl will know no peace
For her there is no future until she battles her tortured past
Pearl worked herself a hardcore plan full of calculated wrath
A brutal crew of gangstas, all seasoned, not up-and-coming
Miscalculating a family's bond, they never saw her coming
Pearl rolled up in the cut and caught 'em sleeping one by one
It was a grimy murderous mission but she sure nuff got it done
So this here ain't no romance somebody's ass is gettin' whipped!
The inside man gets dealt with first 'cause Pearl has come unzipped!

IN THE BEGINNING . . .

Have you ever had everything you love snatched from you in the blink of an eye? Do you know what it's like to watch helplessly as those you cherish burn to a crisp in cruel, merciless flames? Have you ever been wounded in your soul and paralyzed with grief? Alone in this cold, cruel world without your loved ones to hold you close and wipe away your tears? Did you hear a mournful cry for street justice and realize that the only person left alive to heed the call was you? Did you shake off your terrors and your fears and get gully enough to hold court in the middle of the street? Did you dig deep down into the pit of your soul and find the heart, the courage, to be judge, jury, and executioner too? Walk a couple of blocks in my shoes, why don't you. Come on, feel what I've felt! Hurt like I've hurt, and cry like I've cried! Are you gangsta enough to do the things I've done? To grab the hood by the horns and get yours in? If you are, then sit down beside me while I take you to a little town called Harlem. Check out how a scared little ghetto girl found the courage to get her some get back. Come with me to a strip joint called Club Humpz. A grimeball spot deep in the cut where young chicks lose all innocence, and brutal hits are ordered without regard for family love. My name is Pearl Janay Baines. I lost my whole family at the hands of a cold-blooded killer, and this is how I got him back.

THE
CRIME

CHAPTER 1

IN DA CLUB . . .

Fridays were big baller nights at Club Humpz. While the music boomed and half-naked dancers worked that gushy all over the golden stage poles, a gorgeous young stripper thrashed around in the Jacuzzi and prayed.

Dear God . . . it's me, Diamond.

The bubbling water was lukewarm, and if it wasn't for the naked violence in the hands that were gripping her throat, it would have felt peaceful and relaxing.

God! Please help me!

She clawed at her attacker's arms, shredding his dark skin and drawing bright red blood as she fought to reach the surface. She opened her mouth and sucked in one snagging breath before she sputtered and choked and was shoved under the water again.

"Yeah, *bitch*!" he raged as he thrust downward and brutally slammed her head against the bottom of the tub. "I *told* ya punk-ass daddy 'bout playing with my doe! That niggah wanna sic them Alphabet Boys on me? He wanna fuck wit' my paper? I'm gonna rip out his *heart*!"

Mookie Murdock was a cold-blooded gangsta. A highly reclusive, but quick-tempered kingpin who usually did his dirty work from a distance, Mookie lorded over his territory with a brutal, iron fist, and nobody crossed him and lived too much longer afterward.

Bumping beats and loud laughter drifted in from Club Humpz, and as Mookie yanked her above the water's surface again Diamond drew a breath and screamed, praying like hell that somebody would hear her.

But the party was live and the capos and high rollers were too busy ballin' to be worried about one little hollering wet ho. They were sipping Krug and toking sticky, hooting and wildin' and throwing serious gwap up on the stage as they watched the jiggling asses of their favorite grinders.

The beautiful stripper gagged as her head was dunked underwater again. Dressed in a lime green thong, her firm, round breasts floated free and her curly brown hair drifted upward with the millions of bubbles being expelled from the jets.

Dear God . . . Please get me out of this one! I know I done did a lotta foul shit but I can change! I can change! Get me outta this and I promise this time I'll change!

Mookie snatched her head from the rolling water and Diamond snorted, inhaling liquid as he loomed over her. It was rare for Big Mookie to show up at the club, and even rarer for him to get his hands dirty or wet, but Diamond's father, Irish Baines, was special bizz, and this was one case the usually low-profile Mookie was gonna catch himself.

"I'm deading *all* y'all!" he raged, locking his elbows and leaning his three hundred fifty pounds of flab on her slender neck. "*Everybody* is getting laid down! Your faggot-ass daddy is next!

My boyz is layin' *fire* on his ass right *now*! They 'bout to burn his whole *shit* down to the ground!"

Mookie had a cruel streak. Slow death and horrific torture were his favorite killing tools. He liked his victims to suffer and curse his name before meeting their demise. He jerked Diamond's head from the water briefly and allowed her to take a few quick, ragged breaths, then he shoved her back under again.

Fire exploded in her nostrils and water filled her lungs. Twisting and turning, Diamond scratched at his choking hands as she fought desperately to come up for one more sip of air. She knew shit looked pretty bad for her right about now. In fact, if Big Mookie had come down to the club to deal with her himself then it meant shit was worse than bad. It was a wrap.

Diamond prayed.

God . . . Not today . . . please don't take me home today . . . it's our birthday . . . and I promised Pearl I was gonna be there . . . I'm so sorry . . . and so fuckin' stupid . . . please . . . I need my daddy and my momma . . . and Sasha . . . I got me a beautiful little girl . . . I wish I could be there . . .

Above the water Mookie was still raging and talking cash shit. "Your daddy think he can take a niggah like me down? Well that niggah don't know big Mookie! I'm 'bout to plant ya entire family! *All* of them fools gonna get rocked to sleep tonight!"

Mookie plunged her deeper under the water and squeezed her neck until Diamond gave up and went limp. She was drowning and there was nothing but watery bubbles available for her to breathe. She arched her back and her eyes flitted open. Her hands floated in submission as her lungs filled with water and her body spasmed uncontrollably.

Oh God . . . can you please help us? I can understand if you don't wanna save me . . . but please . . . save my baby . . . my mama . . . Please . . . protect my family . . .

CHAPTER 2

ACROSS TOWN . . .

Pain radiated through Irish Baines' skull as he struggled against his mental fog and the thick ropes that bound him to the chair. He coughed and choked and nearly strangled on his rage as blood spilled from his mouth and the pitiful sounds of his old lady, moaning from the floor, became muffled, then softer, then seemed to die out altogether.

Screams rang out from the little girls' bedroom and the world went foggy for a moment as his mind stumbled back in time.

Diamond! he panicked. *Pearl!*

His babies!

But as the children cried out, "*Pa-Pop! Pa-Pop!*" over and over again, screaming in fear and begging for his help, Irish realized that these weren't his twin daughters calling out for him. These were his grandbabies. Sasha and Chante. The two beautiful little seven-year-olds that him and Zeta had raised since the day they were born. These babies were his heart and his soul. And right now they were screaming and crying and begging for him to save their lives.

Irish was an OG and he knew the street code well. Shit, he'd helped write that muhfuckah. He'd come up scrambling in the back alleys of Harlem, and during his wild, hardhearted youth he had wreaked more hood havoc than a little bit.

So from the moment his front door had been kicked in by a posse of Mookie's hardbody goons, Irish had sensed how shit was gonna play out, and he knew it wouldn't be good. He'd heard noises outside and figured Pearl had turned Cole down and come home early, but the minute the front door caved in and he saw Yoda gripping his burner, Irish knew what time it was for real. This type of shit was chargeable straight to the game. It had been a long time since Irish had pulled a kick-door on a niggah without regard for life, property, or even retribution, but some things just never changed.

Irish blinked through the blood that was running into his eyes as he fought to see the young traitorous muhfuckah who was straddling his wife on the floor. Zeta was sprawled on her back, her beautiful mouth brutally sodomized, her bloody, pulverized hands limp beside her. She wasn't fighting or struggling no more, she wasn't even moving, and this scared the shit outta Irish.

"Zeta!" he screamed despite the blood-soaked gag tied around his mouth. He strained against his binds and his busted head exploded with the agony of a million firecrackers as his broken heart detonated with killer rage.

Them bastards had put a hurting on Zeta. Abused her and tossed her around like a common bitch, then violated her womanhood and shredded her mouth right before his eyes. Irish trembled, burning with cold fury.

This wasn't the way of men.

The way of true Gs who honored and respected the code of the streets.

Irish had taken his beat-down without a problem. He knew what to expect, and didn't give a fuck what Mookie's boys did to him because he could handle it.

The surprise had come in the way they'd handled Zeta, his woman. They'd smashed the tips of her fingers with a hammer, pounding through her nails and bursting her flesh open like grapes as she screamed out in shock and agony.

It had been many years since Irish had struck fear and elicited terror on the streets of Harlem, and he'd served enough time and seen enough treachery and brutality in the joint to convince him that life on the right side of the law was truly the only kind of life worth living. But even while he was out there on the streets living the lowest kind of life, when he was practicing the absolute worst sort of depraved, gutter behavior, there had always been some measure of manhood and principle in his game. Even the grimiest of rivals didn't fuck over an enemy's woman, and you damn sure didn't shit on little kids.

But these young heads today lived by no such rules. They had taken the game to a different level, one where no act was too dastardly or too foul, no boundaries were unbreachable, no victims were too young or too innocent, and absolutely nothing and nobody was untouchable or off-limits.

Irish shuddered. It was his fault that this madness and chaos had come down on his family. Zeta had begged him to move out of the old neighborhood years ago, when he was first released from the penitentiary, but he'd insisted on making a difference by trying to help young cats who were just like he had been, lost and in need of direction. He'd opened up an outreach center called No Limitz and devoted his life to thrusting his bare hands into ghetto cesspools and pulling out one degenerate black boy at a time.

And in return for his street dedication he was now sitting strapped to a chair in his own fuckin' living room. Grill busted, pistol-whipped, and gut stabbed, with his beautiful wife laying tortured on the floor and his seven-year-old grandbabies tied to their beds and crying for him to save them from their bedroom just down the hall.

"I'ma kill you!" Irish tried to scream. Tears of outrage filled his eyes as a tall, muscular thug called Yoda climbed off Zeta, then grabbed her by the feet and dragged her closer to the chair so her husband could see exactly what had been done to her with Mookie's infamous spiked iron dick. It was one of his favorite torture tools. Sometimes Mookie ripped his victims in the ass, other times he ripped them in the mouth or between their legs. Didn't matter. He ripped 'em.

"I'ma fuckin' *kill* you!" Irish screeched at the sight of his wife's brutalized, lifeless body. She was wearing her favorite yellow blouse and the jean skirt that she looked so good in. She had been tortured mercilessly and her naked thighs were smeared with blood. Her tongue protruded from her ripped mouth and her eyes bulged in her head.

Irish bucked in his chair in a futile attempt to attack. The excruciating pain of grief and helplessness surged in his body, and despite all the years he'd spent rehabilitating himself and trying to help others reconcile their past with their future, all Irish wanted now was bitter revenge.

"You're *dead*!" he cried, heaving his chair from side to side. Irish stared down at the battered body of the woman he had loved for damn near his entire life and let out a tortured roar. Piercing guilt, grief, and the burning desire for vengeance surged in him. "You backbiting little bitch-ass niggah! You're *dead*!"

Yoda laughed crazily, then called out to one of his boys who was in the back of the house. "Yo, Donut! Get ya ass up here, niggah!"

There were more of Mookie's cats moving through his crib, and Irish knew they were picking through his shit and stealing whatever they could carry out.

"Yo, D, y'all taking too fuckin' long!" Yoda complained as the girls shrieked loudly from their room. "You and Piff make some moves and shut them lil bitches down! Get that gasoline poured up in there. Make sure Tank lays a real good line right between them pretty little pink beds too, nah'mean?"

Irish began to pray.

Not for himself, but for his little girls. Above all else a man was supposed to protect and defend his family, and Irish had failed to do that. He closed his eyes and wept as he visualized his grand-babies tied helplessly to their twin-size beds, terror in their eyes as they reached out for each other in vain. They loved each other, Sasha and Chante did. They were cousins, but they were sisters too, and Irish and Zeta had raised them to share a bond that was even deeper than the one shared between their twin mothers.

The sound of their shrieks rose in the air and the smell of burning flames wafted through the small one-level house. The girls' screams were now rising to an anguished frenzy and Irish moaned as he felt their physical and emotional terror.

They were yelling each other's names now, and calling out words of love. Irish knew they were fear-struck and they needed to be close to each other for comfort. They needed to hold hands and wrap their arms around each other the way they did when they snuck into bed together to giggle and whisper childish se-crets at night.

Break free! he urged his granddaughters in his mind. The bil-lowing smoke was sure to kill them. Oh, the flames! *Break free!*

Irish knew death would come easier for Sasha and Chante if they could face it in each other's arms. But if he'd been unable to break free and save his wife, who he loved more than his next breath, there was no way those poor little girls could break free to save themselves.

And at that moment it was Irish who broke.

"Let 'em go," he sobbed in miserable defeat. His eyes touched Yoda's in broken submission, imploring mercy from a kid who was young enough to be his son.

"Tell Mookie I'm sorry. Tell him it's my bad. I'll give up everything. Call off the narcs, the AG, and them RICO muhfuckahs too. I'll close down my center and leave the block and never step foot back in Harlem again, I swear. He has my word. And Diamond can stay right here with him if she wants to. She ain't gotta leave. She can do whatever she wanna do up in that club and I won't say shit, I swear. Just let my babies go."

Smoke was spreading through the apartment rapidly now and the girls' screams were wild and heart wrenching. Irish wished he could cover his ears and block out the horrible sound of their beautiful voices.

Yoda looked down at Zeta's body on the floor, then touched the gat in his waistband and laughed, shaking his head in disbelief.

"Big bad-ass Irish Baines. I had you going, didn't I? You really thought I was on your team, didn't you? Well, I fucked ya head right up. I ain't on nobody's fuckin' team but my own!"

Yoda's ugly smile disappeared. "I used to hear legendary stories about your exploits when I was a kid, yo. They used to say you had ice cubes in your nuts. You was the *niggah* upstate, man! They still talk about how you wrecked shit on the tiers and cut the most brutal killers down in a vicious fashion. You call yourself counseling and mentoring young cats when they come through ya fuckin' bullshit little center, telling lil Gs how to be real men and live they fuckin' lives, and look at you now. Sitting here begging like a little bitch. Shut the fuck up Irish! Them babies ain't going nowhere but to hell with you and the rest of ya fam!"

"But they *kids,* man . . ." Irish moaned. "They just innocent little kids . . ."

"Fuck them kids!" Yoda snapped. "Mookie ain't tryna just dead you, man. He wanna teach you a fuckin' lesson. What the fuck was you thinking when you called in them blue boys? Your woman sucked Mookie's metal dick 'cause you *talk* too fuckin' much! So stop all that whining and respect ya inner G, muh-fuckah! Go out righteous! The same way you made all them other niggahs go out back in the day when the Glock was in *your* hand."

"Please," Irish begged, not giving a fuck if he sounded like a bitch or not. The smoke was getting worse now, and so were the little girls' cries.

"Tell Mookie he wins! He's the niggah and these here are *his* streets. We had a deal, Yoda. Me and you had us a fuckin' deal! But I ain't asking you to let me go, though. Leave me to die right here with Zeta, man. Just let my babies go . . ."

"I said *fuck* them babies!" Yoda exploded, kicking Irish deep in his stabbed gut. "You shoulda thought about them lil ugly bitches when you was doing all that talkin' to them Alphabet Boys, muhfuckah! And oh yeah," he said with a devious glint in his eyes, "deal or no deal, the next time five-oh goes looking for your trick-ho daughter they betta check the city dump 'cause that bitch is dead and rotting with the rest of Harlem's trash."

The roar that came out of Irish's mouth was beyond pain. There was no doubt in his mind that this backbiting, double-crossing bastard was speaking the truth and his youngest daughter had been snatched from this world. Irish howled so agonizingly that he sucked in the toxic smoke and choked on his cries.

Yoda coughed against the smoke too. He pulled his shirt up over his nose then backed away toward the door. Irish watched helplessly through the grayish haze as the come-up kid, who was once his most reliable inside man, jetted out the house and into the fresh night air.

I'ma get y'all back, Irish vowed as swirling gray terror swept over Zeta's body and rose like a cloud over his head. *All of y'all! Somehow, some kinda fuckin' way, even if I gotta do it from the pit of my cold fuckin' grave, I'ma pay y'all muhfuckahs back!*

Irish Baines squeezed his eyes and coughed as he struggled to take his final breaths. The last things he heard were the heavy footsteps of Mookie's hired killers running outta his house, and the pitiful sounds of his granddaughters' dying screams . . .

Somehow, someway, Irish thought as smoky blackness descended upon him, *I'ma get y'all bastards back!*

THE
JUDGE

CHAPTER 3

Pearl Baines was one of the more fortunate young girls to come of age on the cold streets of Harlem. Pregnant at fourteen by one of the slickest niggahs on the hustling scene, Pearl could have easily slid into the gutter just like so many other young chicks in her man-eat-dog town did. But Pearl and her twin sister Diamond had something that the average hoodrat in Harlem didn't have. They had a father and a mother who loved and supported them, and who bent over backward to provide them with a solid foundation to build their lives on.

Diamond had always been the bold and daring twin, while Pearl grew up quieter and much more reserved. Both girls had gone through a stage where they were hot in the ass and rebellious as hell though, and with bodies like theirs it wasn't hard to see why. The Baines sisters were straight Harlem stunnas, and they attracted mad sexual attention from young boys and grown men wherever they went, whether they wanted it or not.

Pearl had been born two minutes earlier than Diamond. They weren't identical, but there were a lot of physical similarities between them. For one thing, the sisters had bangin' bodies. They had been blessed with phat ghetto asses, devastating hips, and big round breasts that had sprouted fully and deliciously by the time they were fourteen.

And both of their faces were deceptively angelic, with perfectly proportioned features, innocent eyes, and sexy lips shaped explicitly for providing pleasure. Diamond had smoldering, cat-shaped brown eyes, while Pearl's eyes were a little lighter and even sexier. It was impossible to say which sister was finer, because both of them were gorgeous as fuck and they both knew it. But there were a couple of differences between them that were pretty obvious from first glance.

For one thing, Diamond's skin was lighter. She was a straight-up redbone with hints of natural blond curls in her hair that got even lighter under the summer sun. Pearl's skin was richer. Deeper. She was honey colored, a stunningly soft-baked tone that put you in the mind of sweet corn muffins just as they were beginning to rise.

Their differences didn't stop there though. The twins had personalities like night and day, with Diamond being the wild chick who craved dark excitement and couldn't help but heed the call of the streets. She switched her ass around on the avenue looking for the biggest high-post ballers she could find, and then jumped in their whips and rode with them all night, getting high, dancing in clubs, and enjoying life as the prettiest bitch in the hood.

But Pearl had a little bit more class about herself. She was a private person, kinda timid really, and she warmed up to strangers or new situations much slower than her sister did. Pearl had been traumatized as a child after living in several homeless shelters with her mother and sister while her father pulled a bid upstate.

Whereas young Diamond seemed to accept being surrounded by crackheads, winos, and dope fiends as a natural part of urban life, Pearl had been scared out of her skin by the harshness of her surroundings and had developed a shy aura of nervousness that had never entirely left her.

Their mother Zeta was a down bitch who rode hard for her family and did her best to protect her girls from the predators in the shelter and in the streets. Instead of sitting around waiting for her man to hit the bricks, Zeta used the system to her advantage and went to school to get her degree in social work.

Although her mother was loving and progressive, the streets were ever cold, and each night Daddy's Pearl prayed fiercely that her father would hurry up and get out of jail so he could rescue them from the human rats and roaches that scurried around Harlem looking for fresh victims each day.

Sure, Pearl had gotten older and partied and done her share of dirt in her wild teenaged days, and she was always down to get her gushy good and wet. But Pearl was no match for the fearless daring of her twin sister, and after getting pregnant at such a young age, Pearl had gotten her shit together and come to her senses.

Diamond had gotten pregnant too, and it wasn't hard to figure out why. The twins had come up surrounded by street niggahs with nothing but money, drugs, and sweet young pussy on their brains. Their father Irish Baines was legendary in the hood, and even though he'd crawled around in the gutter in his heyday, Irish had rehabilitated himself and opened an outreach center called No Limitz that attracted street-hardened young men from all over New York City.

Irish worked hard to reform those young hotheads. He believed they all deserved a second or third or even a fourth chance, and he never turned anybody away if they wanted to make a new start in life.

And that was how Pearl got hooked up with a shiesty young kingpin named Scotch Allen. Scotch had just established a small drug empire in East Harlem when he got knocked in a raid. One of the conditions for his parole was that he had to go into a rehabilitative program and stay there for two years.

Scotch was one of the few street nigs who had ever managed to outslick Irish. He was fine and built, and played his hustler's hand in stealth mode. Pearl was the only thing Scotch actually saw when he entered No Limitz. He spotted her high, shapely ass and his eyes zeroed in on it like two scalpel-sharp laser beams.

"Just lemme get the head wet," he whispered in Pearl's ear one afternoon as he nudged her knees apart and sucked on her sweet neck. They were humping up against a bathroom wall at No Limitz while Irish was in the main classroom giving his other protégés an exam. Pearl had been doing some typing for her father, and when Scotch saw her leave the main office and go into the ladies' room, he made sure the coast was clear, then jetted into the bathroom behind her.

Pearl was sprung. Scotch had been pushing up on her for a minute now, and even though she'd tried to play it off like she wasn't interested, her panties got soaked just from looking at his fine ass. He'd snuck in the bathroom and kissed her before, and once he'd popped her titty out her shirt and sucked and tongued her nipple until she came, but today was different. Scotch had gotten her jeans and panties down to her ankles and was massaging her wet clit with his rock-hard dick. Nothing had ever felt so good to Pearl before. It damn sure didn't feel like this when she mashed her clit up with her fingers—that was truth. Pearl had been schooled by her parents on all the tricks of horny young dudes, and she wanted to say no and tell him to stop. But Scotch was so damn gorgeous and his probing dick had her clit deliciously swollen and warm juices were running all down her inner thighs. Pearl's body tingled from her nipples to her knees, and there was nothing she could do except open her legs wider and let Scotch put out the fire that he had stoked up in her.

Pearl felt a brief surge of pain as her virginity was taken, but it was quickly replaced by the most exquisitely hot feeling of pleasure that she'd ever experienced. Her pussy slurped and slupped and clenched tight on his dick as Scotch drilled her gently up against that wall. His hands cupped her puffed out ass as his lips trailed from her earlobe to her neck to her nipples, and then back again.

Scotch was patient and attentive with the sweet young thang. He made her nut twice before allowing himself to burst, and they squeezed each other tightly and panted and moaned in desperate whispers as orgasms surged between them like electricity.

Scotch was all over her after that, feeding her dick 24/7. That shit was so good to Pearl that she made sure it was kept on the low. And when Scotch asked her to cover for him around the center here and there, she did it without question. Pearl didn't want a damn thing to interfere with the sweet words Scotch whispered in her ear or the sweet wood that he was putting between her legs.

So the whole time Irish thought he was showing the young'un how to strive for legitimate gains and walk in the light, Scotch was selling mad dope underground and laying deep pipe in Pearl's young pussy every chance he got.

But that wasn't all Scotch was doing.

He had parlayed his drug game into a highly profitable sex game too, and he had a string of young chicks turned out on the track, giving up the booty for big bucks and bringing him home the doe.

Hell, Scotch was so slick and charming that he was conning Irish, conning hoes, conning his parole officer, and conning Pearl too. But all that changed when Pearl found out she was pregnant, and then two months later her twin sister Diamond, popped up pregnant too.

By Scotch.

Pearl had hung her head in hurt and shame. The whole thing had gone down in such a grimy fashion that the embarrassment of it all still fucked with her. It was bad enough that your twin sister was going behind your back and getting her tip drilled by your so-called man, but the way Pearl found out made it even more painful.

At the tender age of fourteen Diamond had been getting high and running the street for months, staying gone for days at a time and worrying the shit out of their parents. Irish took it really hard that his daughters were so wild because he knew the streets and he knew the evil that lurked in the hearts of gangstas. He saw how the predatory niggahs at No Limitz sniffed around his daughters' asses, and it frustrated him that other than beating his girls down and locking them in a room, there was little he could do to keep them away from the lure of the streets.

Besides, he understood that shit. He was their father, and for over twenty years he'd been attracted to the street life too, so he knew the call of danger and excitement was coded in their blood right along with their DNA.

But Diamond had gotten real sick one day and had been taken to the emergency room. Irish was crushed to find out that his baby girl was not only pregnant, but that she had also come down with a bad case of gonorrhea.

"It's a good thing you brought her in," the doctor told them as Irish, Zeta, and Pearl gathered around Diamond's bedside. The cold streets of Harlem had run Diamond into the ground and she also had pneumonia and a high fever. "Certain sexually trans-mitted diseases can be very dangerous to a developing fetus, and your daughter is going to need specific treatment to ensure the health of her unborn baby."

Diamond had started crying so hard that her mother Zeta burst out crying too.

"Don't worry, baby," Zeta sniffled. "It's gone be all right. We're gonna take care of you and get you those treatments, Diamond. You and the baby are both gonna be all right."

"But you don't *understand*!" Diamond had moaned. She looked at her sister Pearl, who stood there with her hand on her five-month pregnant belly, and then ducked her head under the hospital blanket and mumbled.

"Pearl needs to get the treatment too."

Everybody in the room froze.

Irish moved first.

"Come again?" he said, moving closer to the head of Diamond's bed. "Yo, baby girl, I didn't catch that. Run that shit by me again?"

Diamond dug herself further under the covers and practically whispered. "I said, Pearl needs to get the treatment too."

It was Zeta who moved this time because Pearl sure as fuck couldn't budge.

"What you saying, Di?" Zeta urged, tugging down the covers so she could see her young daughter's face. "What in the world are you saying?"

Diamond broke.

"I *said*"—she flung the covers off and sat straight up in the bed—"*Pearl* needs to get the muthafuckin' treatment too, *goddammit*! Whatever fuckin' diseases I got up in my ass, they got in there the same way this fuckin' baby got up in there! And I got 'em from the same niggah I got this baby from too!"

All eyes were on Diamond as she spit out the culprit's name.

"I got it from *Pearl's* niggah! SCOTCH!"

CHAPTER 4

Forgiveness had not come easy for Pearl. Young and dumb, she had fallen deeply for Scotch's gaming lies, and had given her heart and her soul to him, not to mention full and complete access to her beautiful young body. Scotch was slick and fine, and he had sold her a silky bill of dreams by drilling her with tales of how much he loved her, and promises of how he was gonna get her out of Harlem and be her man for life.

Finding out about him and Diamond had been a painful blow for Pearl, but her reaction to their lies and betrayal had actually helped her discover something deep about herself: she could be a monster when she needed to. Pearl had lost her quiet demeanor right along with her mind as the humiliation of Scotch's deceit pressed down on her. For the first time in her life she allowed rage to consume her as she waited until Diamond was out of the hospital, then ran up on her in the street and kicked her fuckin' ass!

Diamond didn't have any wins when it came to her raging sister, either. She took her ass-whipping in stride because she knew she had it coming. Shit, Pearl was done being walked on! Done being scared to stand up for herself and for her proper respect. With her newfound courage she'd shaken off her tentativeness and went after a piece of Scotch's ass too! She'd taken a nice little slice of his neck meat, and he was lucky she'd fucked around and missed and cut him high when she was trying to cut him low.

Diamond had apologized over and over again, swearing all out she felt like shit for hurting and betraying her twin.

"I'm so sorry, Pearl. Please believe me. I can change. I swear to *God* I can. If you would just forgive me, Pearl, I can *change*!"

Pearl was straight disgusted with Diamond. Her sister had gotten down just like a regular Harlem chickenhead, just like the kind of gutter chicks that Pearl had grown to despise and had sworn she would never be. It was hard but Pearl went ahead and gave her sister the forgiveness she needed, but even after Irish Baines had seen to it that Scotch was dealt with in the proper street fashion, the knowledge of what her sister had done behind her back was still embarrassing and painful for Pearl.

But even through all of that, Pearl still loved Diamond. And while there was no doubt that her sister could be low-down and grimy, she knew Diamond loved her too. When they were younger they used to sing a poem of love and affection together every night before they went to bed, and over the years their feelings had remained strong. They had continued to sing their love words out loud, even as teens.

Diamond and Pearl, two hearts, one world.
I love you my Diamond.
I love you my Pearl.

There was nobody in the world who knew Pearl better than her twin, and even though their personalities were very different, their hearts had always moved to the same beat. But that didn't mean Pearl got down with everything Diamond did, or co-signed the way her sister shit on their parents, disrespected relationships, or cocked her legs open to strange men.

It had been late on a snowy Christmas Eve when Irish got a call that his youngest daughter had been dropped off in the lobby of a hospital because she was in labor. He hadn't laid eyes on Diamond in over a month, and both him and Zeta were worried about what she was doing out there on those mean streets. Prenatal care was just a joke to Diamond. Doing the right thing for the sake of her unborn child had never even occurred to her. Even though her sperm donor Scotch had been chased out of Harlem months ago, Irish had gotten word on the streets that Diamond had hooked up with some cat from the other side of town who was ten times worse than Scotch had ever been. Diamond had been seen dancing and drinking in all kinds of strip joints and clubs, wildin' like she wasn't even pregnant.

But regardless, it was too early for her to be having that baby anyway. Pearl was the one due to give birth any day, and as far as Irish and Zeta could tell, Diamond was only around seven months pregnant.

Worried by the call, Irish had woken up Zeta and Pearl, then bundled his wife and daughter into his late-model Cadillac and driven through the snow-slushed streets to see about Diamond and her unborn child.

When they got to the hospital's labor and delivery ward, Zeta broke down crying immediately. Pearl put her arms around her mother, and she wanted to cry too. The sight of Diamond was too fucked up for her to put into words. Instead of seeing an image of someone very similar to herself, a youthful fifteen-year-old expectant mother, Pearl's twin sister looked like a cold, wet, exhausted dog that somebody had kicked around and starved, then dragged through the ghetto streets for weeks on end.

"What the hell happened to you?" Pearl demanded, rushing over to her sister's bedside.

Diamond twisted and turned in pain, her hospital gown hiked over her stomach, her slender legs gaped wide-open.

"The same damn thing that happened to you!" she snapped, grabbing her sister's hand and squeezing it tightly.

"Damn" was all Pearl could say as she looked down at Diamond's small baby bump. She was naked under her hospital gown and her belly was barely big enough to even say there was a baby in it. Pearl reached for the sheet Diamond had flung off and tried to shield her twin's nakedness.

"Girl, cover ya ass. Daddy's standing right there," she said, eyeing the oddly shaped dark patch of skin directly below her sister's navel. It was Diamond's birthmark, and Pearl had one too, a mirror image of her twin's, in the exact same shape and size, and in the exact same place. It was the one thing they shared that branded them physically, and when they were little kids they used to stand belly to belly, laughing as their birthmarks lined up perfectly, as though they'd been connected in the womb at that very spot.

For years, no one, other than their doctors and their parents, knew about the odd birthmark the twins shared, and the reality of their situation came down on Pearl at that moment. That grimy fuckin' Scotch knew. He'd been banging both of them, probably kissing and licking Diamond's birthmark the same way he used to lick and suck and put hickeys all around hers. He'd shot babies up inside both of their young asses, and now Scotch was long gone from their hood, hopefully somewhere dead, and Diamond was about to give birth to her twin sister's betrayal.

The next several hours were hard for Pearl. She sat quietly and watched as her mother comforted Diamond through her excruciating labor pains. Wasn't no telling what the hell that wild girl had been doing in the streets, or who she had been doing it with. Diamond had probably been drinking, getting high, fucking strangers . . . Pearl sat there miserably, going back and forth between being mad about all the bad decisions her sister made, and hurting for Diamond as she actually felt her sister's labor pains. She could really feel them too. Physically. All in her back.

Pearl might have still been mad at Diamond for fucking Scotch, but she was scared too. Scared about what her own labor and delivery would be like, and hoping the doctors were right when they promised that the gonorrhea Scotch had infected her with had been cured in time, and that her baby was gonna be born healthy and strong instead of blind or deformed.

All of her fears and feelings really had Pearl going, and a few hours later, when Diamond was finally fully dilated and was being wheeled out of the labor room and taken into delivery, Pearl forced herself to kiss her sister's damp cheek.

Diamond grabbed her hand and pleaded with tears in her eyes. "I'm sorry, Pearl. For real. I am. I can change, Pearl. I can *change*. I love you. I'm sorry for everything, okay?"

Pearl couldn't say a word. That shit still hurt. It hurt her all over. She was sick of Diamond and all that "change" shit. Her sister always talked the game but she never walked it. Pearl just nodded as they wheeled Diamond through the doors with Zeta following closely behind the stretcher. She felt her father put his arm around her shoulder, then Irish pulled her close to him. His beard was scratchy as he kissed her forehead.

"It's all right, baby," her daddy told her. "Your sister fucked up. She betrayed your bond and it's still paining you. So whatever kind of way you feeling right now, it's cool. She earned that shit."

But everything wasn't cool in the delivery room.

An hour later Zeta came back to the waiting room with a grim look on her face.

"Diamond had a girl and she's doing fine. She popped that tiny baby out and didn't even need no stitches."

Pearl felt her heart banging around in her chest and suddenly she had to pee like hell. "H-how does the baby look?" she asked. If Diamond's baby was okay, with no deformities or disfigurements from the disease they'd shared, then that meant her baby was probably healthy too. "Does the baby look okay?"

"She's cute. She's real tiny, though. A preemie. But it ain't her weight that's bothering the doctors right now." Zeta turned to face Irish with a tear on her cheek. "Just like we figured, Diamond's been out there getting high. She lied her ass off every time I asked her, but she just admitted it to the nurse in there. She said she was getting high this morning when she went in labor, and the doctors think the baby might have crack in her system."

For the first time in her life, Pearl saw her father break down.

"A *crack* baby?" Irish said, his eyes brimming with enraged tears. "She told me all she was doing was smoking a little weed every now and then! Here I been busting my ass and fighting drugs in this neighborhood for over ten damn years just to have my daughter sucking on a pipe and giving birth to a *crack baby*?"

Zeta started crying too, and it was at that moment that Pearl knew that no matter what kind of grime her sister was into, there was no way in hell she could turn her back on her precious little newborn niece. Pearl hadn't even seen her yet, but already she loved her niece with the same fierceness that she loved the baby she carried in her own belly.

"Come on, y'all," Pearl said, trying to comfort her parents and get them to concentrate not on their pain, but on the important issues at hand. "We gotta focus on the baby now. Diamond can handle her own damn business. The baby is what's important. She's gotta gain weight and get healthy. If she's got crack in her system then social services won't even let Diamond take her out of this hospital. It's all about the baby, y'all. We gotta be there for the baby."

It would be a minute before Pearl found out that her speculation was right on point, because no sooner than the words were out of her mouth did a big gush of water erupt from her and begin streaming down her legs.

"You all right?" Zeta asked, reaching for her daughter as Pearl grabbed at her lower back and almost lost her balance.

"Dag, I'm wet. I'm peeing. I think my water broke . . ."

As her mother helped lower her to a chair, Pearl felt a hard knot of pressure swelling in her groin, and the gush of warm liquid drenching her pants was proof that some big things were about to get popping.

"Nurse!" Irish looked scared as he stuck his head out the door and called toward the nursing station. "Yo! Nurse! My daughter! Gimme some help in here!"

The next few minutes were a painful blur for Pearl as she was taken into an examining room right next door to the one Diamond had recently come out of. She held tight to her mother's hand, just as her sister had done, as she was examined and the labor pains surged through her young body.

Pushing out one baby would be more than enough for her, Pearl had vowed as she fought the wave of contractions that were thrusting her unborn child out into the world. She had locked eyes with her father just as they were taking her into the delivery room and it almost made her cry. She knew Irish had held high hopes and dreams for her. Instead of giving birth to a baby at fifteen, he'd wanted her to go big places and do big things with her life, and above all to escape the street trappings that had claimed so many people he loved. Pearl stared deeply at her father, and what she saw in his soul hurt her almost as bad as the labor pains.

"One day you're gonna be proud of me, Daddy," Pearl whispered as they wheeled her away. "One day I'm gonna make you real proud."

Irish Baines had smiled down at his daughter and said, "I'm already proud of you, Daddy's Pearl. I'm already proud."

CHAPTER 5

So as it turned out, two baby girls had been born into the Baines family in the early morning hours of Christmas Day, and both of them were just as beautiful as their mothers.

Pearl had been right about Diamond and the baby girl she'd named Chante. The hospital social worker had filed an immediate injunction suspending Diamond's parental rights and temporarily transferring them to Irish and Zeta. The only reason Diamond got out of there without getting arrested was because of her age, Irish's political connections, and the fact that she volunteered to leave the hospital and go straight into a drug treatment program.

Pearl had named her baby girl Sasha, and all her fears about what some nasty disease might have done to her baby flew right out the window the moment she saw her. Sasha was perfect. She weighed six pounds and two ounces, and looked just like Pearl, except her skin was a whole lot lighter.

"That's just her baby color," Zeta said as she held her newest granddaughter in her arms. She was full of joy at Pearl's baby, but that didn't stop her from worrying like hell about Diamond's baby, who was upstairs in the neo-natal intensive care unit struggling to kick a cocaine monkey off her back. She held sweet Sasha to her breast and kissed the top of her head. This baby was so much bigger and healthier than the other one. It was just proof of the difference between taking care of yourself, eating right, and getting good prenatal care, versus running the streets, abusing drugs, and drinking beer for breakfast.

Pearl took her baby home to her parents' house where Sasha was given the utmost love and care. It was several weeks before Chante was strong enough to leave the hospital and go home to join her cousin who the family realized, but never mentioned, was also her sister.

Two active babies made the small house come alive. Irish and Zeta agreed that even though their twins had been young and reckless to get caught up in the street drama and come home pregnant at such an early age, regardless of how and when their granddaughters were born, they loved them with every part of their hearts and would do everything under the sun to make sure that both girls had a good life.

"I'm glad you're back in school," Zeta praised Pearl when Sasha was only a few weeks old and Pearl was sitting right back in her high school classes where she belonged. "I just wish we could talk Diamond into going back too. The girl has a mind for numbers that's borderline brilliant, but she won't do a damn thing with it."

Pearl could only nod. Diamond was smart as hell, but sometimes being blessed with book smarts just wasn't enough out there on the streets. But Pearl, though, knew exactly what was enough for her. Getting pregnant at fifteen was a real wake-up call for her. She was grateful that her parents had taken both Chante and Sasha into their arms and under their care. Pearl knew other girls who'd had babies and were out there on their own with no man, no family, no friends or nothing to help support them. She felt lucky that she had the opportunity to jump right back into her life like she hadn't really stumbled at all.

The babies shared a room, and slept in cribs that were right next to each other. The room was decorated in pink and brown, with all kinds of cartoon characters and animated figures taped to the walls.

Being born addicted to crack had made Chante a cranky, sickly baby, but Zeta and Irish got up every night with both girls when they cried, chasing Pearl right back to bed when she tried to take Sasha off their hands or offered to help rock and soothe Chante so they could get a little bit of rest or time alone for themselves.

"Nah," her father would say, pulling the belt to his bathrobe tight as he fed one of the tiny babies in his big, strong arms. "Gone back to bed. You gotta be fresh for school tomorrow, Pearl. You need your sleep so your head can be right for them schoolbooks."

It made Pearl feel good that despite being so hardheaded and hot in the ass, her father still had high hopes and dreams for her. Him and Zeta were willing to support her and Sasha and do whatever it took to make it possible for Pearl to make those dreams come true.

But Diamond was another story.

About a week after having Chante, she had snuck out of the drug treatment program and was itching to get back out on the street.

"What the hell did you do?" Pearl had screamed on her sister when she showed up at the crib in a miniskirt on New Year's Eve. "You ducked outta the program? I thought the judge said you had to stay for thirty days?"

Diamond had shrugged and rolled her pretty eyes. "Fuck that judge. He don't know me and neither do those damned counselors in that program. Just because I hit the pipe a few times don't mean I'm no crackhead."

She peeped into the crib where Sasha lay sleeping on her side.

"Oh, Pearl! Look at my little niece. She is just too cute! She looks like me instead of you, though. Yo, you got a few ends I can hold?"

Pearl shook her head. "Nope. All my money gotta go for milk and Pampers. But your daughter is cute too, Diamond. While you busy sneaking up outta places, did you sneak up to the hospital to see Chante? They trying to wean her off that shit you was pumping into her system, you know."

A look of despair came into Diamond's eyes and Pearl could see how sorry and despondent her sister was. Their father had made it his life's business to fight drugs and crime in their community, and Pearl had been around street thugs and addicts her whole life. She recognized that hopeless, helpless look when she saw it, and right now her heart was breaking at the sight of it in the eyes of her twin.

"I don't know why the fuck I do so much stupid shit," Diamond muttered softly. She sat down beside Pearl and rested her head on her sister's shoulder the way she did whenever she had been bad out on the streets and was looking for comfort. "But I can *change*. I know I can! I ain't gotta lie to you, Pearl. You the only fuckin' one I ain't gotta lie to. Even when I was getting high I was hating myself. Maybe that's the reason I smoke that shit in the first place. Because I hate myself."

Pearl forced her anger down and took Diamond in her arms. There had been many times over the years that they had done that for each other. Opened up their arms.

"You ain't gotta hate yourself, Di," Pearl said. She rocked her sister gently, knowing that truly, no matter what happened, nothing, especially no man, could ever really come between them. "But you do have to get your shit straight, ya heard?"

"I know."

"Well stop *knowing* about shit and start *being* about it." Pearl had mad love for her sister, but she wasn't past telling Diamond when her shit got stupid neither. "And the first thing you need to do is stop all that bullshit talk about changing! You either gonna do right or you ain't, Diamond. People don't walk around 'changing' every goddamn day."

Diamond sat up straight and gave her sister a real hurt look.

"You know what, Pearl? You got a whole lotta shit with you! Everybody got something about them that needs working on! Just because you in school and stuff don't mean shit. I might be a fuck-up but you're selfish as *hell*, Pearl. It's all about *you,* all the fuckin' time. You's the type of chick who is strictly out for self. But you ain't no better than me, Pearl! We both got pregnant by a loser, remember? I didn't do a goddamn thing that you didn't do too! So instead of riding me for all the shit I do wrong, there's a lotta things you might wanna check and 'change' about your goddamn self."

Pearl listened to her sister vent and waved all that noise off. "Kill that drama, Diamond. This ain't about me and what I'm doing, it's about you and what you *ain't* doing! Don't try to flip the switch on me, because I'm living right and there ain't shit I need to change about the way I get down. But if you wanna be around your daughter then what *you* need to do is get your ass back to that damn program and stay there until your head is right and those people tell the judge you can leave."

Diamond had softened under the truth and nodded. "Yeah, I know. It's just that it's New Year's Eve and everybody else is gonna be out there partying and shit . . . all my friends . . ."

"*What* damn friends?" Pearl stood up and demanded. "You mean them trick bitches who hit the pipe with you while you was in labor then dropped you off at the hospital and left you by yourself? *Those* damn friends?"

"You know what I mean, Pearl. You ain't gotta put so much drama into it, damn."

"No, that ain't drama, Diamond. Drama is you wanting to get out in the street a week after dropping a damn baby! For real, girl, you got on a short skirt up the ass and your coochie ain't even closed up tight yet! That stank thang is still wide open! And look at your freakin' shirt! Your titties is still leaking milk!"

It took another fifteen minutes, but Pearl was finally able to talk Diamond into going back to the treatment center. Diamond had begged Pearl to just let her climb in her own bed and go to sleep, but Pearl wasn't having it.

"Hell, no! You ain't the one tired. *Mommy and Daddy* are drag-ass tired! They been up at that hospital day and night worrying about Chante, then coming home and trying to help me with Sasha too. The last thing they need is to find out you snuck outta rehab. Don't be giving them shit else to worry about, Diamond. They have enough on their shoulders. Just take your red ass back where you belong, and don't come back here until you got your head right."

Diamond had left to go back to the rehabilitation center that night, but Pearl wasn't stupid enough to put any money on where her sister had really gone. What she did know for sure is that over the next couple of years her mother and father gave her a series of opportunities that she just couldn't refuse. They encouraged her to put all her time and energy into school and to live her life just like any other young teenager who had college instead of dick on the brain.

Not only did Pearl study hard and get top grades in all her classes, she ran track, played basketball, and joined the school debate team too, and her parents bent over backward to make sure she had room in her life to do all the things that interested her without making her feel guilty as they raised her baby.

"Gone, Pearl. Go on and enjoy your life while you can. If we can take care of one," Irish would say, nodding at Chante, "then we can take care of two."

On weekends Pearl would try to make it up to them by doing laundry for the girls, washing and braiding their hair, and entertaining them on Sunday mornings while Zeta cooked a big dinner and Irish put on his glasses and sat at his desk going over work for his center.

Those were Pearl's special times alone with her daughter and her niece, and she loved watching them play and grow. Both of them were gorgeous, but Pearl's daughter Sasha was taller, and the quieter of the two. Despite what Zeta had predicted, she never did get much darker than her birth tone, and actually did look a lot more like Diamond than she did like Pearl.

Chante was still kinda tiny, but she was fast and bright and always into something. The girl was so quick you had to watch her or she'd be pulling stuff outta drawers, playing in the toilet, or putting something in her mouth that didn't go there. She was as cute as she could get, and the family found it funny that she looked just like her aunt Pearl.

Neither one of the girls looked like their daddy, Pearl noted with relief. She had stared into their cute little faces for hours, glad to see that Scotch's trifling ass was nowhere to be found in either of them. She still burned up just thinking about all them fuckin' shots and pills she took trying to get rid of the venereal disease that bastard had infected her and Diamond with. Their babies could have been born blind, twisted, deformed, all fucked up, or even dead! That shit had been so humiliating and embarrassing that Pearl had sworn she would never let another dick slide up in her raw until she was married, and so far she had kept that vow. Scotch mighta been her and Diamond's grimy sperm donor, but the Baines genes were strong as hell and that niggah hadn't contributed hardly a damn thing to his offspring.

The girls' baby years flew by, and before Pearl knew it she was graduating from high school. There had been a lot of cute dudes who tried to get her train to jump off the tracks, and she'd gone out a few times and gotten her sex thang rocked and her back knocked outta joint real good. Pearl attracted men like ants to a slice of watermelon and there was never a shortage on dudes who were eager to please her. She had a preference for dark-skinned guys with killer white smiles and hard bodies and could spend hours in bed on one sex session. Pearl didn't get her swerve on that often, but when she did get it she pulled all-nighters. She liked it slow, hard, and nasty. She had mad respect for a guy who could hold out a long time. Long enough so she could cum at least three times. Oral sex was a must for her too. If she went through the whole process of making sure a dude was good enough to get up in her stomach, she was damn sure gonna get her pussy licked first. That was a requirement!

But sex always took a backseat when it came to her family or to her education. For the most part Pearl had done her best to ignore the call of the streets and stay on point as she finished high school, and her reward had come in the form of a full academic scholarship to the University of Georgia.

"You doing the whole damn neighborhood proud," Irish had beamed and told his daughter. Him and Zeta had thrown Pearl a big-ass party at Studio Sass, and all the nigs from No Limitz had turned out to see his baby girl off to college. They had catered ribs and wings and buckets of potato salad from a local joint called Nastee's up the block, and even though Irish didn't tolerate no drugs, there was plenty of Krug and Cristal flowing, and of course chicks was sneaking all up in the bathroom hitting lines and blowing sticky like crazy.

Diamond was at the party too. Even though she was brilliant in school and had a damn-near photographic memory, there was no way in hell she could have graduated on time with the small amount of credits she'd earned. School had never interested Diamond much, although she was practically a genius in math. She'd gotten high almost every day between classes, dropped out after completing less then two years, and began living on the streets shortly after that.

Over the past three years she'd been in and out of the house, only coming back home to pull herself together when she was so far down in the gutter that she had nowhere else to go. At those times Zeta would run into her daughter on the streets somewhere looking tore down and shot out, and she'd cry and beg Irish to go fuck up whichever drug dealer was banging Diamond at the time, and bring her baby back home.

Diamond's street addiction was extremely hard on her family. Irish cursed himself for being a hustler and kingpin when he was younger and didn't know no better, and he swore that street shit was in his blood because his daddy had been a street niggah and so had both of his brothers. All three of them had lived by the street code and died by that shit too, getting popped in a blaze of gunfire while trying to defended a cache of drugs that they'd stolen from somebody else. When Irish saw how helpless Diamond was when it came to the lure of that kind of lifestyle, he never blamed his daughter. He always blamed himself.

"Congratulations." Diamond had hugged her sister and given her a card and a long-stemmed rose at the going-away-to-college party. "I always knew you would turn out to be somebody, Pearl. It was always in you. I know you prolly ashamed to be my sister, but I'm really proud to be yours."

There had been tears in Diamond's eyes, and Pearl had started crying too. She couldn't help but feel a little guilty and a little selfish for wanting to up and leave Harlem and everyone in it far behind. Pearl was grateful that her parents were willing to keep Sasha for her and told herself that there was nothing selfish about wanting to pull herself up out of the sewer. Shit, Harlem was no joke. Growing up on these city streets was enough to make any person with dreams and goals a little bit selfish.

"I love you, Pearl," Diamond sniffled. She wiped her nose with the back of her hand and Pearl cringed at the sight of her sister's grimy, bit-back fingernails and all the city dirt that was caked up beneath them. "I might do a lot of fucked-up shit," Diamond continued, "but it's all aimed at me. Never at y'all. I swear. No matter how low I get, I never get too low to remember how much I love my family."

Pearl sighed and took her sister into her arms as she heard a familiar melody playing in her head.

Diamond and Pearl, two hearts, one world.
I love you my Diamond.
I love you my Pearl.

Pearl had held on to those words while she was in college, because over the next three years Diamond continued to sink lower and lower. In her senior year Pearl got a call from a guy named

Vince who used to give her crazy-good head back when they were in high school. Vince was cute and had a stacked body like he inhaled weights for breakfast, but he was short up top under the cap, and would never make it much further than the block.

Still, he was a cool guy who was bent on Pearl, and he had spent years trying to get in her panties. But after giving birth to Sasha, Pearl was done fuckin' losers, so the most she would let Vince do back then was suck her titties a little bit, and a few times he'd pulled her panties to the side and licked her pussy gently until she came, but she'd always maintained control and sent him on his way with a big-ass bulge busting outta his pants. Vince had stayed in touch with her all throughout college, and now he was calling to tell her that her twin sister was raking in big doe pole dancing at a new strip joint that had just opened up.

"Yo, Diamond is the main attraction over at a spot called Club Humpz," he told Pearl. "Her stripper name is N'Vee and that jawn is so hot she got her own fuckin' set, yo! Niggahs gotta drop top dollas just to get a peek in the door, for real. I sweated five hunnerd on that gorgeous phat ass the other night, and if you anywhere near as fine butt-naked as ya sister is . . . shit I wish I had'a got them panties off in high school."

Pearl was worried about her sister, but she wasn't about to share this latest bit of news with her mother or her father. Zeta would only cry and wanna bust up in the strip club and drag Diamond home, and Irish would get mad and try to use all his street pull and political clout to try and shut the whole operation down.

Even though hearing shit like this hurt, there was really nothing Pearl could do to help Diamond. She had learned that a long time ago. There had been too many nights of tracking her sister down and pulling her out of whatever little drug spot she was holed up in, or sitting in the car while Irish rolled up on some niggah and cracked him in the dome and snatched Diamond out of his lap, to even count. The girl wasn't just a hopeless junkie, it was the ballers and the playas that Diamond was addicted to as well. The street life. The whips and the bling. The status and the sex. Those were the things that called out to Diamond's heart, so when Pearl had earned enough credits to graduate only three years after she started college, and her sister was nowhere to be found on her special day, she was hurt but she wasn't surprised.

Irish had driven the family down to Georgia in his spanking-new Caddy, and as they stood outside the large auditorium he took his daughter in his arms and held her close. "Daddy's Pearl. I can't even describe how proud I am right now. You did it, baby. You did it."

Irish had kissed his daughter's forehead before continuing. "And just so you know, Diamond came by yesterday and said she didn't have nothing decent to wear to your graduation, so I gave her a few dollars. She was supposed to buy some clothes and meet us at the house late last night, but she never showed up. We waited as long as we could, and I even swung by all the little cuts I know she likes to hang out in, but ain't nobody seen her."

"Your sister is trying her best to change," Zeta butt in. "She knows how important today is to you, and as smart as she is she knows she could have been graduating right along with you if she had just stayed in school. But don't be too hard on her, baby. I think she really wanted to be here."

Zeta couldn't meet the disappointment in her daughter's eyes. Instead, she nudged Sasha and Chante forward. "Look at their little lace dresses, Pearl. Ain't they cute? Sasha wanted to wear a pair of raggedy jeans and"—she nodded at Diamond's daughter, Chante—"lil mama over here had the nerve to ask her Pa-Pop to buy her a red miniskirt. Hmph. If she ain't her momma's child?"

Both girls had curls in their hair and were dressed in gorgeous little dresses with crinoline slips and lace embroidery at the hem.

They looked like perfect six-year-old angels. Sasha's dress was bright yellow and Chante's was baby blue. They wore white-laced tights and white patent-leather shoes, and carried matching white patent-leather little girls' purses.

Pearl had bent down and taken both of them in her arms. She hugged and kissed them, pressing her face deep into her niece's neck to hide the tears that had suddenly sprung to her eyes over the absence of her sister.

Why the hell you crying over her? Pearl chastised herself, forcing her heart to go cold. Shit, Diamond didn't show up for nobody and she wasn't never gonna change. Not even for her own daughter. What made Pearl think her college graduation was gonna be more important than Chante's kindergarten graduation had been? Diamond hadn't shown up for that event either.

Pearl smirked.

No matter how much shit her sister talked about doing the right thing, Diamond had made her choices and was living them out on the streets.

Some shit, and some people, just never changed.

CHAPTER 6

Two weeks after her college graduation Pearl headed to FBI training at Quantico, Virginia. She was one of fourteen females in a class of over two hundred students, and she had known from jump that it was gonna be cutthroat and madly competitive.

The first thing Pearl had done was put her family out of her mind, especially her baby girl, Sasha. She could become weak just by thinking about them, and she couldn't afford to have any soft spots in her armor because she planned to kick ass in this class and graduate all the way at the top.

The next thing she did was let it be known that she wasn't down with the rest of the females. She had peeped their game from the gate. Most of them were looking for somebody to latch on to to help drag their cute asses through the course. Pearl wasn't going for it. She wasn't that scared little Harlem girl anymore. These days she walked strong by herself, refusing to click up with anybody. If she hung out with anybody it was with a few of the smartest, strongest dudes in the class. She worked out with them, doing just as many push-ups as they did, and lifted crazy weights with them too. Every morning they ran together in a military formation and Pearl always got up front and set the pace. She had strong legs and mad stamina, and could run with those hard-body jocks until they were throwing up and ready to pass out.

When it came time to perform competitive chin-ups or climb the fifty-foot knotted rope, Pearl hoped her classmates wouldn't let her ass weight fool them. Bodacious booty and all, she showed her unique upper-body strength and lifted her body weight more times than any of the men, and she scampered up that rope like she had some monkey in her for real.

Social time at the academy was another matter. Pearl knew she was considered fine, but she didn't even speak to the idiotic men whose eyes got boggled watching her ass bounce when she walked by. They were too easily swayed and distracted, and that was a major weakness in Pearl's book. She shook her booty be-cause it rolled that way naturally, not because she was trying to keep a string of sweating dudes with hard dicks chasing behind her on the regular.

Overall, Pearl fucked heads up left and right at the Academy, and it wasn't long before the cadre and administrators took sharp notice of her exceptional skills. It wasn't every day that a beauti-ful black female from Harlem came through their doors kicking ass and taking names. Pearl had made a bold statement with her physical strength, work ethic, intelligence, extreme instincts, and competence. She won her class's master fitness award, shot ex-pert on all rifles and small-arms weapons, and when it came to hardcore tactics like non-traditional weapons employment, hand-to-hand combat, stealth operations, and evasive self-defense, most agreed that Pearl was one of the top students to ever come through the doors, black or white, male or female. As a result she received the Tip of the Spear award, which was the Academy's highest honor, given for valor, strength, and superior performance in all areas of training.

Getting the top award was dope and all, but it was right before graduation when Pearl got the big break that would set her up lovely.

"We're looking to fast-track a couple of agents for our Tactical Recruiting Program," the senior instructor told her. He'd called her into his office and Pearl was standing at attention, her gear sharp as hell, her banging body fit to fight, nails done, and not a hair out of place.

"I've been authorized two waivers for our Hostage Rescue Team. If you're interested, I can make sure one of the waivers has your name on it."

Pearl had breezed through the next two weeks and floated on clouds all the way through graduation. Hostage Rescue was going to be tough and scary, but she was living a new and improved life, and somehow she knew that type of danger and excitement would also be right up her alley. So she'd stayed on at Quantico for further training, which is how she met her best friend Carlita a senior agent and cold-case analyzer, and her boyfriend Cole who was one of the few brothahs in the Tactical Recruiting Program.

Pearl was the only sistah in the program, so of course she had all the chocolate boys jocking for her attention.

"Yo, mami," Cole had said to her during a break one day. They had been rappelling off the sides of staged buildings and kicking through windows to rescue mock hostages, and Pearl had laughed at the way he'd looked free-falling off the roof and over the edge. "What's so damn funny?"

"You." Pearl had shrugged. "You so damn funny."

"Oh yeah? So what's funny about me?"

"Hmph." Pearl had cut her eyes and turned away. The requirements for all FBI agents was at least a four-year college degree, so she knew he was educated, but still, this niggah was hood. She had picked up on his city swagger and saw straight through his New York bullshit. "Your ass was shook up there. Shook for real."

Cole had surprised her when he busted out laughing.

"Oh so you peeped that, huh? Hell yeah I was shook! Check it out, when I was little my wino cousin took me up on top of a building around my way, right? That drunk fool slung me over the edge and told me he was gonna toss my punk ass down straight into Linden Boulevard traffic. I ain't been right with roofs since. It ain't heights that mess me up, though. It's rooftops, I swear! The damn building ain't gotta be but one story high and my ass'll be up on the roof sweating and panicking like a muthah!"

Pearl had smiled. It was funny how all her old fears and anxieties seemed to disappear while she was training on her new job. She used to be scared to go up on the roof of her own building back in the day, shook at the heights *and* the bums, hoes, and winos, but now she rappelled off higher shit than that like it was no big thing. So she wasn't mad at Cole for being scared up there, regardless of his reasons. In fact, she liked a man who could push past his limitations and go for his.

They ate lunch together that day, and then slowly started making it a daily habit. Pearl liked being around Cole because he was a New York homey but he wasn't a thug or a baller in the true sense of the words. He was street, but he was also educated and he had goals and dreams. She wasn't sprung on him or nothing, but Cole couldn't hide the way he felt about her, and before she knew it Cole was cracking for some pussy like crazy.

The first time Pearl gave up the na-na was in her apartment after a date. Cole had taken her out to an art gallery and afterward they went back to her crib and ate some sushi. Cole ate a whole lot of stuff that night! Pearl had ended up moaning on her living-room sofa with her legs cocked open as she wiped pussy juice all over his grill.

And Cole couldn't eat enough of her stuff neither. His tongue had been everywhere at once as Pearl squirmed on the couch with warm cum running outta her slit like a faucet. She'd pulled Cole up to her and yelped as he slammed his dick into her, surprised at the power in his thrust. Sparks shot through her groin as he pounded her pussy meat like a real gangsta, tenderizing it as she arched her back and gripped the couch cushions in sheer pleasure.

Cole gripped her ass and thrust his tongue down her throat and Pearl tasted herself in his mouth. She sucked his tongue greedily, totally turned out as she enjoyed the sweet traces of her own pussy.

She'd flipped over eagerly at his urgings, her entire body trembling in anticipation as he lay her down on her stomach and spread her legs. Pearl almost cried as Cole nibbled softly on her ass cheeks, getting up in that booty with his kisses. By the time he slid the tip of his dick into her dark tunnel, Pearl was ready for him. She moaned and whimpered as he burrowed into her back hole, giving her just a little bit at a time, making sure she could handle it and was enjoying it as much as he was.

Pearl slid her hand between her legs as he thrust rhythmically behind her. She inserted her middle finger in her pussy and used her palm to rub and massage her tender clit. She rocked her hips forward and cupped and squeezed her pussy, then raised her ass up to meet Cole's slow, gentle thrusts. She did this over and over again as he rodded her ass out lovely. She finger-fucked herself deeply, driving her hips into the couch, then arching her spine and tooting her round ass up to meet Cole's back door plunge.

The orgasm that ripped through Pearl was so intense that it took her breath away. It lasted forever as it triggered Cole's orgasm and he pushed down and seated his dick deeply into her ass, shooting his hot load into his condom as he held on tight to her hips. Cole wanted to be up in her goodies 24/7 after that, and they became a couple and started to grow closer.

Pearl and Carlita had grown close too. Carlita was a sharp Hispanic chick from Miami, and a woman who Pearl looked up to with respect and admiration. She was quite a few years older than Pearl, but you really couldn't tell it. Carlita was tall and extremely fit, and she had excelled in so many FBI training courses and performed in so many high-pressure positions that it was hard to find someone in the Academy who didn't hold her in the highest regard.

Carlita had come up in a Miami slum, and she was all about the bizz. She had been married once, to an agent who had gotten his throat slashed while investigating a drug ring from Nicaragua, and instead of wallowing in pity after her husband's murder, Carlita had become tougher and harder and more devoted to fighting drugs and crime than ever.

The two women got close while on a hostage rescue mission at a local emergency room in D.C. A young nurse was going through a divorce, and her distraught husband had flipped out and come unzipped. Screaming that he was ready to die, he barged into the emergency room with his toolies out, blasting patients and doctors alike.

He shot four people and took seventeen hostages, including his wife and five babies. Pearl was one of the eight agents who were dispatched to the scene. As a junior agent she normally would have played a minor supporting role, but the plan was to have a couple of agents pretend to be innocent and nonthreatening nursing staff who were just coming on shift.

Since Pearl and Carlita were the only two women on the team, they got the job. The gunman was bonkers and he also had help. His younger brother had come to his aid before the police got there, and he was also armed as he helped control the terrified patients and crying babies.

It was a dangerous mission, but Pearl showed her ass. Dressed in nursing scrubs, her and Carlita had gained entry to the emergency room by crawling through the complex ventilation system, then came walking nonchalantly out of the staff's kitchen area like they were innocently reporting to work. The gunman had quickly thrown them to the floor and taken them as hostages too, which is exactly what the women wanted him to do.

Pearl had drawn strength from Carlita's confidence, and in moments the two agents found themselves flowing. They read each other's nonverbal signals and seemed to have a little ESP going between them. After assessing the situation, Carlita had used her eyes to indicate that Pearl should go for the younger brother and that she would take care of the husband.

The small backpack hanging from Pearl's back may have looked like an innocent nurse's bag, but in reality it was an FBI-issued Attack Pak. It contained weaponry and tools designed for taking an adversary down at close range, and that's exactly what Pearl did.

In the midst of the pile of hostages cringing on the floor, Pearl had slid her hand toward the small of her back and come out with a blow dart and a six-inch length of extendable tubing. After making eye contact with Carlita and confirming that they were still tracking at the same pace, Pearl placed the extended tubing armed with the deadly dart in her mouth and blew precisely, the ultrathin, toxin-coated mosquito needle embedding itself deeply in the younger man's neck.

He swatted at his neck like he'd been stung by a bee, and by the time he knew what hit him the incapacitating toxins were already paralyzing his muscles.

Carlita had used a miniature crossbow and toxin-tipped arrow on her target, and her aim was also true. Before the hostages knew what was happening, both women had leaped to their feet and taken the stunned gunmen all the way down to the ground, using the disabling hand-to-hand techniques that they both excelled at.

After that, Pearl and Carlita had been paired up on several missions. They had very similar instincts and worked well together, and while Pearl was impressed with how much Carlita knew, Carlita was also impressed by how fast Pearl learned, and how, for such a laid-back, shy young woman, Pearl attacked her targets with such determined ferocity.

They began spending some of their down time together, and Pearl found she really enjoyed Carlita's company. She had never had a close female friend like Carlita before, even in high school. Pearl had never gotten down with most Harlem chicks. She'd grown up around dudes at No Limitz, and her only real female friends had been her sister and her mother. Carlita was a lot older than Pearl and had more of a street edge on her, but she was easy to like because she and Pearl had the same high standards. They both loved intense action and hated slackers, and neither one of them had any use for chicks who used their looks and bodies to get through life instead of using their brains.

Carlita didn't have any kids, but she had raised her niece Zoe, who had gone to NYU and gotten a degree in sports medicine. One of Carilta's friends had hooked Zoe up with a job as an assistant athletic trainer for the New York Knicks, but Zoe's heart wasn't really into sports anymore. After her uncle's murder Zoe had developed a desire to do the same kind of meaningful work that Carlita was doing. Work that she felt would help take people like her uncle's killer off the streets.

As a favor to Carlita, Pearl had helped Zoe fill out her FBI application. She had even written Zoe a highly praising letter of recommendation, since family members were prohibited from endorsing potential FBI candidates.

Pearl and Carlita seemed to click on every level, but one of the few areas where they clashed was over Cole.

"He's not good for you, mami," Carlita complained. "Look at how he bitches up whenever we're about to hang out together! He's always all over you. Smothering you. Smelling your pussy! He doesn't want anyone else to spend time with you. You should have paid better attention in profiling class, girl. That Cole could turn into a stalker."

Pearl just laughed. Cole was harmless and Carlita was a street skeptic. It was true that he played her a little close sometimes, but Pearl knew how to shake a niggah off when she needed to. Besides, a position had recently come open in the violent crime and gangs section, and Cole had applied for it and gotten the job. They'd still be working out of the same field office, but they wouldn't be on a rescue team together, or all up in each other's grill every day.

"Okay." Carlita had given in with a knowing smirk on her face. "Keep riding ya big-dicked donkey, then. But I'm watching his ass, so keep him on a string, okay? Men like Cole are too damned insecure, Pearl, and that's never a good thing."

Pearl loved and respected Carlita, and she trusted her instincts too. Which was probably why she played Cole to the left every now and then, just to make sure he didn't get all up in her life like that. She had started limiting him to fucking her only on Wednesday and Friday nights, which drove Cole crazy and kept him sniffing around her all week long. And it was under these circumstances that Cole had driven her home for her birthday on the fateful Friday night that her entire world went up in flames.

CHAPTER 7

"Damn, girl! You working that sugar cone to death. Anybody ever tell you you've got the sexiest fuckin' lips on the planet?"

"Ssshh!" Pearl shushed Cole as she glanced around the ice cream shop then quickly lowered her head, hoping none of the hoodsters sitting around had heard him. This cat was so weak with his compliments that it wasn't funny sometimes. Pearl mighta been straight outta the heart of Harlem but she was no-body's hoodrat. She was a lady in the streets and she liked her pillow talk strictly on the pillow, even though Cole liked to talk nasty all out in public.

"Nah, nah, nah," he said, reaching for her hand across the small sticky table. "You ain't gotta be bashful. Learn how to take a compliment, baby. Your lips are sexy as fuck and they turn me on. I know you got a sophisticated image to protect and you don't like nobody else hearing all that, but I'll tell that shit to the whole damn world. *Pearl Baines got a crazy lip game!* My baby got the bombest lips in the entire universe! Which is why . . ." Cole said as he stood up and walked his pretty self around the small table until he was standing in front of her.

Despite her embarrassment Pearl couldn't stop her mouth from watering when she saw that big, hard bulge in the front of Cole's pants.

". . . which is why I want to be the only man to ever suck them pretty lips into my mouth and taste them."

Sucking lips wasn't the only thing Cole was good at.

Early that morning before they got on the road to come to New York, he had sucked her lips and a whole lot more than that. Pearl got hot just thinking about how King Cole had beat her stuff up real nice for her. They'd gone jogging at a nearby park just as the sun was coming up. Cole was in shape, but he had the type of body that could grow a belly real quick so he liked to run. Pearl liked to run too, and truthfully she could have outrun Cole and left his ass in the dust on one of her bad days, but she knew how fragile his ego was, so she usually held herself back and let him lead the way. They'd run for two miles down their favorite path, and instead of turning around at their usual point, Cole had grabbed her hand and pulled her off the road.

"C'mere," he'd said, yanking her toward the grassy treeline.

"Stop!" Pearl had squealed. "Where the hell are you taking me?"

Cole laughed, a sly look in his eyes. "Quit hollering, girl. You gonna get me arrested. Just relax," he said, pulling her deeper into the woods. "You trust me, right?"

Pearl didn't really trust any man deep in the woods out in the middle of nowhere, Cole included. But what she did know was that she was strong enough to kick a hole in Cole's ass if he tried to get special on her.

She let him lead her through a small clearing, and to her surprise they came out on another jogging path, right near a large wooden pavillion.

"How'd you find this?" Pearl asked as they ran up the steps and stood under the wooden rafters.

"Don't worry about it," Cole said, sitting down on the narrow perimeter bench. "I know how to find a whole lot of shit."

Pearl couldn't believe it when he pulled down his running shorts and his sand-colored dick was already hard. It was light brown and beautiful, with a nice mushroom head and strong veins running all along the sides. Cole jacked it slowly with his hand, then took hers and used it as a replacement.

"Yeah," he'd moaned. "Stroke King Cole just like that."

Cole lifted Pearl's shirt as her hand moved rhythmically in his lap. The morning air drifted over her damp breasts and her caramel-toned nipples stiffened in the breeze. Cole pulled her closer and rubbed them between his thick fingers, making her moan and squeeze her thighs together with pleasure.

"We're gonna get caught . . ." Pearl whispered, looking over her shoulder like a criminal, but her titties were singing and she damn sure didn't want him to stop.

"By who?" Cole muttered. "Ain't nobody else out here and both of us got badges, remember?"

Pearl didn't protest as he turned her around and yanked the back of her shorts down. He massaged her fluffy ass cheeks, then parted them with both hands. Pearl bent her knees and lowered her stuff onto his rod. It was thick and hot, and she had to wiggle her hips around just to get the head inside.

"Damn," Cole sighed. He balanced her heavy cheeks in the palms of his hands and helped support her until her pussy adjusted and opened up for him. He could tell Pearl was ready when she started moaning and her pussy got slick, coating his shaft as she raised and lowered herself to a nice slow rhythm.

Two seconds later Pearl was bouncing in his lap, taking dick like a champ, riding all nine inches of Cole's thickness, and making soft fuck noises with each thrust.

Cole gripped her slender waist and stared at all that ass as it jockeyed in his lap. Pearl had the most beautiful body he had ever seen. She was born to fuck, and she loved dick, and every inch of her body was the stuff of a man's dreams.

Cole slid his hands up her sides and squeezed her breasts. He slammed her down hard and thrust his dick up in her deep, loving the feel of her warm ass on his thighs.

Pearl's pussy was soaked. She squeezed her legs together and gripped the sides of the bench. Tooting out her ass, she rotated her hips in a tight hard circle, grinding her gushy all over his lap.

Cole moaned and nibbled at the skin on her back. He tasted the salt of her sweat and licked his lips, wanting more. Reaching around in front of her, Cole found Pearl's juicy clit and stroked it, coaxing the little man to jump outta his boat. He trapped her clit between two fingers and squeezed it gently, all the while deep-dicking her from behind as she swirled her hips around like a tornado.

Pearl felt a storm raging between her legs. Her clit tingled deliciously as her pussy clenched and throbbed. Right about then she didn't give a damn if the entire police department rolled up. Her breaths got shorter and she fucked back harder, loving the hell out of what Cole's fingers and dick were doing to her at the same time. She swallowed hard and tried not to scream, but one tore from her throat anyway. She couldn't help it. Cole was giving it to her nice and deep, and her gushy felt like it had a warm bubbly creek running through it.

They came at the same time, Cole biting softly into her shoulder as Pearl moaned and shuddered in his lap, squeezing her legs together and moving Cole's hand aside so she could massage her own clit.

When they were all fucked out they headed home slowly, holding hands the whole way. Cole walked back barechested and sweaty since Pearl had used his T-shirt to dry herself with. Pearl loved the way her body felt after being sexed so good. Cole had a bamming package, and the sexual chemistry between them was off the charts. Thirty minutes later they were back at Pearl's apartment and Cole had immediately gone in for round two. They'd taken a shower together and this time instead of going straight for his, Cole had kissed and licked Pearl exactly where he knew she liked it, and when she screamed out his name at the height of her orgasm, Cole didn't even try to get him a nut. He simply broke out in a big smile.

And now he was standing in front of her about to ask the most important question of his life.

"Pearl Janay Baines," Cole said, reaching into his jacket pocket as he stared into her eyes. He came out with a small box from a very expensive jeweler and flipped it open. "I already ran this by your pops and he gave me the go-ahead to slide this little shine on your finger, so will you marry me?"

Pearl was speechless.

Cole Jackson was from a Brooklyn political family that had tight connections and deep pockets. Although they'd both come up in boroughs of New York City, they'd met during FBI training in Virginia and worked together out of the D.C. field office. Pearl was on a hostage rescue team and Cole was an agent who investigated gangs and criminal enterprises. Pearl's family came to visit her in D.C. all the time, so she rarely came back to Harlem anymore, but there was a lot to celebrate this weekend, and her mother had wanted her to come home. Since Cole had a little surprise of his own planned for her, he'd offered to drive her to New York so she could spend her twenty-second birthday with her family.

But Pearl's twin sister Diamond hadn't shown up for their birthday dinner. Pearl had sent her a text the night before and Diamond had texted back promising to be on time for their family dinner, but by seven o'clock Diamond hadn't shown her face and was nowhere to be found. Pearl thought it was strange since Diamond's boy Menace had shown up with gifts for both of them.

"That damned girl," Irish had said with a worried look on his face. He sat at the head of the dinner table grimacing and drumming his fingers nervously as they waited for Diamond.

"It's all good, Daddy," Pearl said. She reached over and rubbed his arm. She hated to see her father pressed out about anything. "Y'all said Di's been doing better lately, right? I mean, her hands are all healed up and she's almost back to normal, right?"

Irish had grimaced.

"What the hell is *normal* when it comes to your sister, Pearl? Who knows what normal is for her! If getting both your damn thumbs and all eight of your fingers smashed up don't slow your stroll, what the hell will?"

Pearl's hands had actually throbbed and cramped up when she thought about how, a few months back, some thug niggahs had knocked Diamond on her ass and then slammed both of her hands in a car door. Every one of Diamond's fingers had been broken in at least two places, and both of her hands had stayed in casts for almost two months.

Pearl could definitely feel where her father was coming from. Loving Diamond was hard, and all of them suffered for that love. Pearl knew Irish took great pains to keep her as far removed from her sister's drama as possible. From the time Pearl had left for college, Irish had deliberately kept her in the dark about a lot of shit that went down, both with the running of his center and with Diamond's street capers.

"If you wanna work for the government one day then you can't be involved with all the shit that goes on around here, Pearl," Irish had told her. "You might get in a position where you need one of them top-secret clearances one day. Them folks will dig into your life and sniff out everything you did since kindergarten, baby. The less you know about the niggahs on these streets the better. That's why I want you to stay outta Harlem, Pearl. Ain't no telling how far you gonna go with your career, baby. Me and your momma want you to be able to go all the way to the top."

Pearl didn't always like being kept in the dark about what was happening at home, but when Irish made a decision about something it was almost impossible to budge him. It had been Zeta who had called to tell her that Diamond had gotten hurt, and Pearl didn't even wanna imagine the kind of pain and agony her twin must have gone through as those niggahs left her laying in a gutter with over twenty broken bones in her hands. Somebody had rushed over to No Limitz and told Irish that Diamond had been taken to Harlem Hospital by ambulance. Zeta had sounded like she was having a heart attack when she called Pearl and told her that her twin had been brutalized by a posse of street nigs.

Zeta had begged Irish to go to the cops, but Diamond had nutted up and played dumb and pretended not to know who had fucked her up so royally. Even Pearl, who only got bits and pieces of the story down in D.C., knew that was a lie. She figured her sister had finally stolen something from the wrong niggah, and breaking her fingers was his form of payback.

Pearl had really been looking forward to seeing her twin for their birthday celebration tonight, but with dinner getting cold, Zeta had insisted they sit down and eat, and said she would fix a plate and wrap it up just in case Diamond showed up hungry later.

It had been a long time since Pearl had eaten her mother's home-cooked Louisiana-style seafood, and she had dipped everything in butter and slobbed it down. And after dinner, when Cole announced that he wanted to take her out to get some ice cream, Pearl had been surprised as Zeta practically pushed her out the door.

"Gone, Pearl," her mother had insisted, grinning her ass off as she switched toward the door in her sexy little jean skirt. At thirty-nine Zeta was still beautiful and her body was fitter than most women half her age. She worked at a rape crisis center and could have passed for Pearl's sister instead of her mother, although she was wise and mature and had obviously come up on the streets. "Let that man buy you some ice cream, Pearl! Hell, that boy's daddy is *paid*. Let him buy you any damn thing he wants!"

"But Sasha and Chante might want some ice cream too," Pearl had protested, thinking of her young daughter and her niece. The two little girls looked and acted so much like her and Diamond when they were little, and like their mothers, they had also been born on the same day. "They can go with us, and I'll bring you and Daddy back some butter pecan in a cup too, okay?"

Zeta had waved her out the door.

"Nope. Sasha and Chante don't need no ice cream and they ain't going nowhere but to bed. This night is for you and Cole. Go ahead, Pearl. You can bring me and Irish back a whole butter-pecan cow if you want to, but you and Cole are going outta here by yourselves tonight."

And that's how Pearl ended up sitting in Baskin Robbins with the stupid look on her face as Cole Jackson slid a crazy-phat rock onto her ring finger that glinted under the lights and damn-near blinded her.

"Me?" Pearl asked like she was hearing voices. "You wanna marry *me*?"

"Hell yeah, pretty girl," Cole said quietly, and at that moment something about the way he was holding her hand with his hard dick all in her face was sexy as hell. It made Pearl feel truly wanted. "I love you, Pearl. And I wanna marry you and make you mine, and only mine, forever."

Pearl couldn't even answer as that big hunk of ice glinted on her finger. Like every chick from the hood she had grown up dreaming about falling in love and being swept off her feet by a strong, handsome man one day. And the fact that Cole had an education and a bomb career and didn't want to just bang her as a wifey, but had felt enough to put a ring on her finger, signified love and a whole lot more in anybody's book. But giving him an answer was still hard, because Cole didn't really know her, he only thought he did. When he looked at her all he saw was the wavy hair, the gorgeous skin, the dimpled face, and the sexy, round ass that most dudes saw. He only saw what Pearl allowed him to see. The big fat front that she put on for the world so she could hide who she really was.

Cole mighta been from Brooklyn, but he didn't know the hood like she did. He had no clue that Pearl had spent her early years timid and afraid and living in a rat-infested homeless shelter while her father pulled a bid in a cold upstate prison for committing vile acts of violence against his fellow man. He didn't see her as a scared fourteen-year-old guttersnipe who hid her fears and anxieties by running up and down the streets, wildin' with thugs and hoods until she messed around and got pregnant by a local drug dealer. Or the crazy young chick who, a few months later, found the heart to beat the shit out of her twin sister when she too had popped up pregnant by the same grimy drug dealer, a man who Pearl had later chased down and sliced up with a 007 flick knife.

The person Cole saw sitting before him today, the beautiful, confident, well-cultured, educated sister with the banging ass that he liked to ride deep in the middle of the night, was the reformed version of Pearl Baines. He saw the smart chick who had turned her back on both her drug dealer boyfriend and the streets of Harlem, and found the courage to leave the hood life far behind.

What Cole saw was a fighter and a survivor. The new-and-improved, strong, capable, and fearless Pearl Baines, totally reborn.

Cole was staring at her with a funny look on his face, still waiting for her answer. Pearl's lips moved but no sound came out. She had mad love for Cole and she really dug what they had going on. Even though Carlita swore all out that he was nothing but a controlling-ass future stalker with a big dick.

And in some ways Carlita was right. Cole *was* spoiled and possessive. He was a pretty boy, and he liked to throw his weight around when shit didn't go his way. But none of that mattered because Pearl had only met one man in her life who she even considered committing her heart and her life to. One man who had the street cred of her father, the intellect of her mother, and the courage of a thousand gorillas. And even though that man had once fucked around and betrayed her, no other man, not even Cole, could stack up to him in Pearl's heart or in her mind.

"I-I . . . umm, I—" She was struggling to give Cole an answer but couldn't find the right words, then suddenly she didn't have to bother as her cell phone rang and she snatched it off the clip, flipped it open, and pressed it to her ear.

"Hello?"

It was Menace.

The sound of his voice made Pearl's heart bang in her chest.

It had been crazy sitting across from him at the dinner table earlier that evening. Pearl always stayed as far away from Harlem as she could, so she hadn't seen him in a minute. She had shot him mad shitty looks over dinner and flirted with Cole like his dick belonged on a hot dog bun. Menace tried to act like he wasn't sniffing her vapors but Pearl knew he was bent. That gaming-ass nig had had the nerve to bring her a gift that looked professionally wrapped, and Pearl had smirked as he held it out to her with a smile on his face.

"Happy birthday, Pearl," he'd said, and even though her eyes were flashing daggers at him, Pearl's heart had swelled up like a balloon in her chest. They had moved in different directions in their lives, with Menace leaving Harlem after graduate school and going to work for a major financial management firm before opening his own company in Philly, and Pearl booking out of Harlem for good as she headed off to college to study pre-law. She hadn't thought about him in a long time, and she told herself that she hadn't missed his low-post ass neither. She remembered her father mentioning that Menace came back to Harlem a few times each month to put in work at the center, and according to Irish and Zeta, the young man could do no wrong.

Pearl knew different, though. That nigga could be as wrong as two left fuckin' feet. But no matter how hot Pearl was with Menace, being in his presence still gave her a thrill. He was a physical bomb. Tall and fine, he still smelled good and wore his gear like it had been designed especially for him. Standing there looking like a chimmee-chimmee-cocoa-pop, Pearl could tell Menace's hard, dieseled body was still as black and hard and swollen with perfect muscles as she remembered.

"You gonna take your present or what?" he'd said as she left him hanging with his gift extended in his hand.

Pearl smirked and heat flashed in her pretty eyes. This stunt had a lot of shit with him, giving her a gift. When she was a kid he used to surprise her with something dope for her birthday every year, but ever since she'd cut him off and stopped speaking to him he'd stayed away on her special day.

"Um, you sure that's for me? You sure you ain't mistaking me for Diamond, right? I mean, we are *sisters,*" Pearl said, stressing the relationship. "*Twins,* remember?"

Menace had brushed her shitty act off his shoulders like dust. "I got a gift for both of y'all. I figured since your moms was nice enough to invite me to your birthday dinner it would be cool to bring y'all a little sumthin'."

"I gotcha damn sumthin'," Pearl had muttered, taking the gift and throwing that shit under the table. She didn't know what was in the pretty box and she didn't give a damn, neither. All she was gonna do was toss it in the trash without opening it anyway.

Menace had been real quiet during dinner, but Pearl had shown her ass. She'd sat right across from him and made sure he saw her leaning all over Cole, laughing in his face and rubbing her big titty on his arm. She'd let Cole cut her steak and shrimp scampi into small pieces, then she'd slid a few bits into his mouth and squealed real loud when he sucked and tongued her juicy fingers.

Menace broke out the door the moment they were finished eating, and Pearl couldn't help grinning as she helped her mother clear the table and load the dishwasher. That niggah had looked real jealous in the face watching her rub all over Cole and lick his earlobes, and she had laughed stupid loud as he jetted off their porch like he was mad as fuck.

And now, an hour later, Menace was on the phone, in her ear, yelling something crazy that didn't make a bit of sense.

"My *what*?" she shrieked. "My house is on *what*? On *fire*?"

Pearl had no memory of running the three blocks back to the house her parents had lived in for the past eighteen years. She had been a state-champion sprinter in college and could run just as fast or faster than most of the men in her class at the FBI training academy.

Today she ran in a designer skirt and spiked heels, with Cole galloping along like a puppy, faithfully by her side. Fire trucks and police cars were already rolling up on the front lawn as they arrived, and an ambulance was speeding toward them with its lights flashing wildly.

Smoke billowed from the roof and the windows as Pearl ran right up on the lawn, her eyes darting around the crowd of onlookers, anxious for a sign that her family had made it out of the flaming house.

"Where's my baby?" Pearl screamed to nobody in particular as firefighters and police took up their positions and got ready to do their jobs. "Where's my daughter? My niece? Where are my parents?"

A line of firemen were running past her carrying hoses, and one grabbed Pearl's arm and shook his head.

"Stand back, ma'am. Please wait across the street. If there's anyone in there we'll get them out. It's too dangerous for you over here."

Pearl heard an eerie sound and froze. Every mother's nightmare had suddenly become her reality. From deep inside the house, beyond the smoke and flames, Pearl could have sworn she heard a plaintive cry, softer than a kitten's meow.

Her knees sagged as she imagined the worst, her child trapped inside the smoking box of flames, calling for her, wanting her, needing her.

The muffled cries rang out again and Pearl's whole body strained toward the house.

She fought against the fireman's arm. "D-d-did you hear that?"

He shrugged and tightened his grip, manhandling her as he tried to turn her around and push her across the street. "I didn't hear anything. It would be impossible to hear anyone in there anyway. Please stand back!"

Pearl dug her heels into the ground. "I heard my daughter crying! My *baby* is in there!"

"Stand ba—"

"Sasha!" Pearl broke free and darted toward the house at full speed, determined to get to Sasha and Chante. The young fireman lunged forward and snagged the back of her blouse and Pearl went straight gorilla.

She whirled around and side-kicked the man below his right knee, cracking his shin. The blow was so powerful and unexpected that his lower body halted as his upper body continued moving forward on momentum. Two fingers jabbed in just the right spot between his jaw and neck finished the job, and the firefighter went down like he'd been shot in the head.

An overweight veteran police officer noticed the action and lunged for Pearl, catching her by the shoulder. She rolled swiftly with his motion, using the hand-to-hand-combat techniques she'd excelled at in the Academy, then lightning fast she slid her fingers down his arm until she clenched his hand in a firm grasp, then twisted his thumb sideways while cocking his wrist and snapping it backward before he knew what had hit him.

The cop yelped and swung on her wildly with his other hand, and Pearl blocked the blow and drove the flat of her palm deep into the meat of his throat. He coughed and grabbed at his crushed Adam's apple and staggered a few steps before bending at his knees and gasping for air.

Pearl ran toward the house like a speeding train, and she didn't even see the smoke or the danger that stood between her and her family. Her baby. Her niece. Her mother *and* her father. Every fuckin' body she loved was trapped in there. All she knew was that she had to get inside to save them.

Pearl had almost made it up on the porch when another cop rushed her. This one yanked her by her hair and Pearl screamed and lifted her chin fiercely, snapping her head back so hard she broke his pointy nose and temporarily blinded him.

Three steps later Pearl was at her parents' front door. The outer screen door was still intact, but the wooden interior door had been kicked in. Smoke was pouring from the house and the heat on the porch was way past intense as it nearly drove her back. Pearl's lungs felt like they were bubbling and the skin on her cheeks and forehead was getting scorched. She had just reached for the blistering screen door handle when it hit her.

A spiny Taser barb was launched. It bit into her left shoulder and the pain of fifty thousand volts of electricity shot through every inch of her body. Pearl lost control of her physical functions as her back arched and her muscles stiffened in shock.

"Pearl!" Through the fog of her pain she heard a man's voice screaming out her name, and it wasn't Cole's, but Menace's name that rose to her lips. But then another trigger-happy NYPD officer got in on the action and hit her with his stun gun too, and this time Pearl fell face forward into a painful oblivion, with only the sound of her daughter's phantom cries echoing in her ears.

CHAPTER 8

Mookie Murdock leaned back on the sofa as the pretty young hooker planted a trail of wet kisses along the sagging skin on his neck. They were alone in the living room of the phat penthouse apartment Mookie rented off Central Park West, but as usual, a crew of his manz were on guard just down the hall.

The girl had done a slow, sexy striptease for him earlier, and Mookie had enjoyed the sight of her luscious brown skin and flawless, perfectly proportioned body. She was beautiful and sexy, a combination that was an awesome sight to the reclusive overweight gangsta.

Mookie moaned softly as she rubbed her small hands over his nakedness, but even his hard dick and the anticipation of getting it juiced and gargled wasn't enough to obliterate his ever-present embarrassment.

Mookie Murdock was *not* one of the beautiful people, and no amount of money or power could change that unalterable fact.

Weighing in at 375 pounds, Mookie detested his obese, bulbous body. He had spent his entire life as the ugly fat kid on the block, and whereas his mind had always been superior to most people's, his body had remained his hideous and humiliating burden to bear.

Back in the day before he got his gangsta on, Mookie used to stand in front of the mirror and cry as he gazed at his fluffy breasts, his bulging stomach, his ham-hock thighs, and his gnarled, knocked knees. It actually hurt his eyes to look at his ashy, ugly self, and he'd feen for a physique like those he saw in men's magazines and on the hardbody playas who ruled the streets with a chiseled swagger.

But while Mookie had never managed to change the way he looked at himself, he had learned that wielding money, power, and brutality could change the way other people looked at you. He could never be comfortable in a normal relationship with a chick, but he paid good fuckin' money for his monthly shot of neck pussy, and his manz was supposed to school the skanks on the proper way to look at him before they got anywhere near his door.

Because there were only two things Mookie wanted to see in the eyes of any man or woman: adoration or fear. Bitches that were lucky enough to get close enough to gaze into his close-set eyes had best look at him with the proper street respect, and if they didn't . . . well, fear was something Mookie got off on too.

The big-hipped ho who had been hired for the night was young but she was skilled. She snaked her hand around his waist, and Mookie felt his blubbery love handles jiggle repulsively. Using his elbow to knock her hand away, he lay back and panted as she cupped his full breast and sucked his nipple between her eager lips as she ran her tongue back and forth across his tingling bud.

"Suck my . . ." Mookie panted, humping into the air. His

wide-waisted pants were billowed on the floor around his ankles and his green-and-white-striped drawers sported a crusty shit stain in the crotch. "Come on, bitch . . ." Mookie moaned. "Suck my dick . . ."

He watched closely as the girl planted wet, smacking kisses down his flabby chest and over the great mound of his stretch-marked belly. But by the time she got past his navel Mookie knew the bitch hadn't been schooled properly.

Anger rose in him as he watched her lift his jellonious gut in the air and frown slightly as she peered down between his plump, ashy thighs. Mookie saw it all in her eyes as she pinched his narrow penis between two fingers like it was a nasty worm. She shuddered and held her breath so she wouldn't have to smell him, and Mookie had to stop himself from wildin' out and flying her fucking head.

It was there, he'd seen it. He was absolutely certain. It was right there in her eyes. It was only there for a brief second, but it was there nevertheless.

Disgust.

Revulsion.

The bitch had looked at his grotesque body like she was gonna throw up, and then she tried to play it off with a smile as she parted her lips and went to work licking the pre-cum from his mushroom-shaped head.

Mookie was mad. Furious. He didn't even want her neck pussy no more.

"Bitch!" he exploded. "Who the *fuck* you lookin' at like that?"

He grabbed the ho by her waist-length hair and mushed her face down into his funky groin.

"Wh-what I do wrong?" she shrieked as Mookie slammed her head into his knees and thighs. "Please, Mister Mookie! What I do?"

"Oh, you *know* what the fuck you did!" Mookie roared, knocking the young chick to the floor as he jumped to his feet. Mookie moved fast for a big guy. His dick jiggled below his sagging stomach as he waddled across the room with his feet still stuck in his pants. "You know *just* what the fuck you did!"

Mookie went over to a corner of the room and unlocked a small footlocker that held the tools of his trade. This bitch was gonna catch a bad one. For real.

Furious and light on his feet, Mookie waddled back to the sofa in a flash.

"You got a problem with my dick?" he demanded.

The girl shook her head back and forth so hard and fast that her lips flapped from side to side.

"Well, I got me another joint for you to suck right here, baby doll," Mookie said, brandishing a medieval-looking tool that put terror in the young girl's eyes as she scooted backward on her ass like a crab. "Yeah, if what I got don't do it for you then I got something you gone really like. And the next time you look at Mookie Murdock it ain't gone be with nothing but *respect*!"

Mookie clamped his massive hand around the back of the girl's neck and squeezed so hard that it almost paralyzed her.

"Yeah," he said as her mouth flew open and she tried to scream. "Suck it, tramp!" Mookie barked, plunging his spiked metal dick past her teeth and lips and ramming it down her throat. "Ge'head, bitch!" he screeched, his voice high and his face contorted in ugly rage. "Suck Mookie's big hard dick!"

The girl screamed as her lips tore and the roof of her mouth was shredded. She bucked backward in fear and pain, and Mookie's real dick got hard just from the look of stone-cold terror that was radiating from her eyes.

He slid his monster grip around to her throat and applied more deadly pressure.

"Hold still, ho. And suck this fuckin' dick! And if you ever wanna see the fuckin' sun rise again . . ." Mookie's voice was just a deadly whisper as he jerked and twisted the barbed metal rod, mercilessly tearing her flesh and loosening her teeth. " . . . then you better suck it *good*!"

The first time Mookie had elicited fear in the eyes of a grown man it had sent a thrill through his body that almost made him nut. The dude's name was Onion and he was Mookie's first cousin. Onion had thrown some loaded dice during a cee-low game in a crowded bar, prompting Mookie to lose a big pot of cash to a small-time chump. Mookie had nutted the fuck up, dragging Onion outta the gambling room and slinging him behind the bar counter, raging and muscling the skinny dude up as he turned on the blender that was used to make daiquiries. Mookie had pushed the button for crushed ice and made a nice strawberry daiquiri right outta Onion's hand, making sure he ground the shit outta those same fingers that Onion had used to toss those hot dice.

Mookie had been working for an old street hustler called Capo back then. Capo had been one of those fly, pretty niggahs when he was in his prime. He'd had the kind of solid, muscular body that chicks craved for and men slaved for. But Capo was an old head now, one of the few gangstas who had survived the streets long enough to reach senior-citizen status in the game. After years of stacking his cream and running his empire with his eyes cocked at every angle, Capo was heading to Florida to relax and live the good life in the sun, and he was turning everything he'd amassed on the streets over to Mookie.

"It's all yours," Capo told Mookie, glancing around at his stomping grounds as he climbed into his brand-new Mercedes sedan. He had two foxy young bitches in the backseat who were retiring from the game right along with him. "I done gave you everything I could give you and I didn't hold shit back. I gave you the secrets to my success just as if you were my very own son. But watch out, Mookie," Capo warned. "You and me are more alike than you think. When I was a young man I was real handsome, ya know? Had chicks all over me and niggahs hatin' like hell. My good looks mighta got me into a whole lotta pussy, but they got me into a whole lotta trouble too. I had to learn to lay low, Mookie. Learn to stay outta sight. The less I was seen, the less I was envied and hated.

"You gonna have the exact same problem if you ain't careful too. You's a dirt-ugly black muhfuckah, Mookie, and it's hard for you to hide, ya feel me? A muhfuckah ain't gotta see you but one time to remember you for life. And I ain't tryna disrespect you or your feelings either, that's just the truth. Remember that shit you pulled with Onion in that bar that time? Man, don't you never let nothing like that happen no more. I don't know what you was thinking that night, but you went about ya shit all wrong, man. All wrong. You played a stupid man's game, Mookie, and I know I schooled you better than that."

Mookie nodded. Capo was a don, and Mookie knew he had learned the art of stackin' chips from one of the best.

"Dig," Capo went on. "The only reason I've stayed outta the joint and I'm alive to take this ride down 95 with enough cream to see me to the end of my days is because I got real smart real fast, son. You gonna have to get smart too, Mookie. You gonna wanna keep a low profile, man. Real low. Stay off the streets and for God's sake, stay outta them goddamn clubs. Lay low and hustle above the radar. I'll say it again because it bears repeating: you got an unforgettable look to you, my man. You ugly, Mook. Believe that. Whether it be a rival or a Roscoe, you gonna be re-membered everywhere you go."

Capo's seat belt slid out automatically from its retractable holder, and when he turned the key in the Mercedes' engine that baby purred like a pussy-stroked bitch.

"Remember," he warned again with a stern look. "Seldom seen, seldom heard. That's the secret to staying on top in this game. A niggah like Onion cross you and you wanna get at him? Cool. You a G. Teach him his lesson. But let your goonies put the work in. Don't invite dirt to grow under your own fingernails. And never, ever, be so flagrant with your shit that somebody can draw a line back to you. Always keep your crew in the middle, Mookie. Dead center between you and the dirt. Otherwise, it's like shittin' where you sleep, ak. A big no-no.

"So unless you wanna leave footprints for the feds to follow, let that dumb shit with Onion be a lesson learned. Fuck around like that again and it won't be long before them Alphabet Boys come knockin' for you."

Mookie couldn't do a damn thing but stay silent and listen. For the last five years he had been a good pupil and had learned the trappings at the knee of his teacher. Mookie knew he was bad ugly, but he was also smart enough to know the value of street wisdom, and if anybody had some to give away it was damn sure his man Capo. And right now he was properly checked and chas-tened because he knew Capo was spittin' some straight-up gospel truth in his ears.

And truth was the only thing that could keep him free, Mookie knew. The way he'd handled that shiesty fuck Onion was more than dangerous. It was plain dumb. Wildin' out in public like that was an engraved invitation for five-oh to walk dead into his crib and grab a chair.

But Mookie was a rager by nature and the streets could get the best of the most temperate of niggahs in this game. A muhfuckah was always gonna try you, and Mookie knew that. Shoving Onion's hand into a roaring blender had been plain wrong. Yeah, that niggah had got what he deserved for flipping loaded dice, but the situation should have been dealt with far more discreetly, Mookie admitted. He had been trained by one of the best gangstas to ever rule the streets of Harlem, and if he wanted to follow in Capo's footsteps and retire to Florida as a rich old man, he was gonna have to do like Capo said and stay low in the trenches.

Although Capo had left New York for good, his words forever rang in Mookie's ears. Mookie followed his boss's street mantra like it was a religion. He stayed away from the usual street haunts and played it low-key whenever he was out and about. He had enough bank to floss and shine, but instead he dressed down in bland colors and the kind of nondescript shit that made fat men seem invisible. He bought a fly whip but he put it in one of his cousin's names, and he always rode in the backseat, where the windows were tinted. He did the same thing with the sweet penthouse apartment he rented in Midtown, he eased in and out like a furry little mouse and was seldom seen and seldom heard.

In short, Mookie played his shit smart. He surrounded himself with a crew of strong-hearted niggahs who had been loyal to him and Capo for years, and he built a fortress around himself that was damn near impenetrable.

Day in and day out, Mookie practiced what Capo had preached. He built his empire up until he was the moneyman behind the local strip clubs, controlled the local drug flow, ran a prosperous stolen-identity ring, and bankrolled the largest gambling operation that Harlem had ever seen. Mookie dipped two fingers into every moneymaking pocket known in the hood, and licked every pie that even looked like it might be sweet.

And to protect himself from both the come-ups and the take downs, Mookie did just like Capo had told him. He rode real low and developed vices that didn't require him to be on the front line all the time in order to enjoy them. Sure, Mookie socialized sometimes and he loved himself a nice shot of neck pussy every now and then, but the thing he loved most required an un-shakeable courage, a bold confidence, and a whole lot of sweet green gwap.

Mookie was a man who studied the odds and who lived for the game of chance.

Mookie Murdock was a gambler.

CHAPTER 9

But sometimes it's the very thing you love so much that has the power to throw you off your game, and when it came to his number one vice, Mookie just didn't fuck around.

Sure, he had mad bank rolling in from multiple sources like the gully clubs, his drug operations, and the strung-out chickenheads he kept on the poles and out on the track, but Mookie wasn't overly impressed by any of that. Those things were just a bunch of spokes on the hub of his core business. He fronted the money and ate the bulk of the profits, but he paid a competent crew to handle all the day-to-day runnings of those routine business ventures and he rarely got personally involved.

To Mookie, it didn't matter how much cream he skimmed off somebody else's back, it was just business. But the bank he earned from his gambling skills . . . that was *passion*. Gambling doe was real special in Mookie's eyes because it was all him. It was doe that he amassed like a man, from the strength of his keen intuition and from the heart it took to put his money where his mothafuckin' mouth was. That kind of posture required intestinal courage and commanded mad respect in gambling circles. Not many betting men had such keen logic on when to hold and when to fold, but Mookie had developed a sixth sense that told him exactly when to push forward and when to fall back. Odds that looked long to other men looked like opportunities for great reward to Mookie, and he always placed a bet with the full expectation of profiting immensely from his wins.

And that's why fuckin' around with stupid niggahs was so dangerous for Mookie. He had slipped up and exposed his throat twice since taking the reins from Capo's hands. And each time it had been a hard stumble. A major mistake. He had messed around and lost control behind that thing that was closest to his heart, allowing himself to be exposed to the regular fools on the street and the feds as well.

The first time had been at a racetrack in New Jersey.

The night before, Mookie had had a most vivid dream. In his dream he was shooting pool at an old Harlem joint called T.C.'s Place, and all kinds of crazy numbers were spinning around on the colorful balls as he racked them. Mookie had woken up in a sweat. Like his grandmother, Mookie was heavily into signs, and he'd reached for a notepad he kept next to his bed and immediately written down all the numbers he'd seen on the little pool balls. He had taken the first and last letter of each number and played scramble with them until they spelled out a name. And when Mookie saw that one of the long-shot drivers on the track that day had a similar first name as the one he'd deciphered from his dream, he was pumped. It was a sign, sure as shit.

But his man Gallon who usually placed his bets musta been feeling himself that day. He fucked around and put Mookie's shit in all ass-backward. He bet on the car driven by a cat named Jason instead of Jase like Mookie had told him, so instead of sitting in the stands and basking in the thrill of the win as his long-shot driver came around the track and crossed the finish line first, Mookie was treated to the agony of defeat as he came up empty-handed and lost a gwap behind some dumb niggah's stupidity.

"You gone fuck around and kill him" was the warning his right-hand manz Yoda gave him as Mookie leaped over chairs and down two rows to choke the shit outta the fool who had caused him to lose his bank. "You got eyes on you, Mook," Yoda warned, glancing around at the curious crowd of racing fans. "You got a whole lotta eyes."

Mookie didn't even hear that shit. The spectators sitting in the row Mookie landed in screamed and scattered. They didn't know where the fuck this mad black gorilla had come flying out of the air from, and they knocked each other down trying to get away from him.

"Yo, that's your cuz, man," Yoda said quietly. "He's loyal, yo. He been grinding for you a long time, Mook."

Mookie was blinded by his rage. All he could feel was the tremendous pain and disappointment of losing a bet. He put all his weight on Gallon, bending him backward over the seat and strangling him as people in the crowd frantically called for security and looked on, stunned.

Mookie was on a mission. He squeezed Gallon's throat until that niggah's eyes bulged out and foam started leaking from the corners of his mouth.

Above him, Yoda stayed cool as he watched his boss wild out. He gave a fuck about Gallon, but the po-po would be there in a minute and his job was to keep Mookie out of hot water.

"Yo, go get the whip!" Yoda barked at his boy Donut. "Drive that shit right over there on the other side of that fence and ram that bitch. Make a hole, niggah! Right next to these fuckin' bleachers!"

Yoda turned his attention back to Mookie. "Yo, Mook, Gallon is fam, man. His moms took yours to the hospital when she got sick, remember? They was sisters, man, and your moms died in her arms. That old lady did right by you, Mook. That's her son, dude."

Mookie kept right on squeezing. It was true that Gallon was his cousin and that his moms had been good to Mookie, loving him, feeding him, and clothing him when he was a kid. But these days Mookie was strictly about his fuckin' money, and none of that family shit meant a damn thing stacked up against his gambling loss.

By the time Mookie came to his senses, his cousin was slumped over backward with his mouth gaped open and a thin stream of blood running from his nose.

"Get up, niggah!" Mookie eased off the man and punched him hard in the gut. He looked around the stands, wondering why the fuck everybody had their eyeballs all up in his grill.

"Gallon! Man, you know I was just playing with you. Get the fuck up you dyslexic muhfuckah!"

But Gallon wouldn't get up. He couldn't.

He was dead.

For a brief second Mookie felt a hint of remorse. Him and Gallon had come up together in the same house when they were kids. As tykes they had slept on opposite ends of the same raggedy sofa. They'd taken baths together, and ate off each other's plates. Gallon had slipped up on Mookie's instructions, but he was steady and loyal. Mookie was gonna miss him. But that's what the niggah got for fuckin' up his bet. Mookie could overlook a whole lot of things, but making him lose a bet was unpardonable.

Mookie had barely made it outta the race arena before the boys in blue were on the scene. Yoda and his boyz had hustled him down the bleachers and over to the fence where Donut had driven the front end of Yoda's Hummer through the fence's wiring. The crew from Harlem stuffed Mookie's jiggly bulk into the whip and burned rubber, getting the fuck outta there before security was on their asses.

The second time Mookie lost sight of Capo's warning it almost cost him far more than the loss of a loyal family member. Mookie had caught a fever for casinos, and one in Connecticut in particular had stroked his passion.

For every security system in a casino, there was a slickster who spent valuable time and brain energy devising a scheme to beat the house. Mookie loved everything about gambling except losing, and he had no problem stacking the deck to make sure the odds were in his favor. Of course he did all the usual shit that dirty gamers do, like bribing officials and paying key players to throw matches and games, but the world of casino gambling was an exciting challenge for Mookie, and he looked forward to pitting his game against the house's best operational defense and seeing who came out on top.

Mookie had a sharp mind and knew he could outslick a dealer, but there was no way he could show up in a casino and not be watched like a hawk or remembered long after he had won a big bank and gone home. He'd put one of his manz on the task of scouting out a couple of loyal chicks who had superior brains and could stay cool under pressure. One such jawn came highly recommended due to her street knowledge and her brilliance with numbers. Mookie was eager to set her up as a card counter at the blackjack table and use her to tip the odds in his direction.

The first time Mookie watched the girl practice on video he

was damned impressed. Her eyes flitted around the table virtu-ally unnoticed. If you didn't know she was a plant designed to produce a certain outcome, you would have thought she was just one beautifully lucky bitch.

Six weeks later Mookie was highly pleased with the results this chick was getting at the tables. She didn't get stupid with it or nothing, just made small, reasonable bets that didn't invite too much attention. Mookie respected that shit. The bitch was fine and she was a natural with numbers. Even though he could tell she was a dabbler, she didn't look run through and her mega win-nings were proof that she was keeping her concentration up while on the job.

Shit went on grand like this for a minute and Mookie was thrilled with his wins, but then suddenly the bitch fell off. One of his boyz thought she mighta been getting high before work, causing her to lose focus and slip up at the table, but Mookie wasn't trying to hear that shit. Game recognized game, and after a week of straight losses Mookie knew what time it was.

And man, that ho caught a bad one.

Stealing from any niggah in the game was some risky biz, but skimming off Mookie Murdock's table winnings was a cardinal fuckin' sin. The ho prolly could have gotten away with fuckin' with his money stream from any other revenue without a whole lot of fanfare, but dippin' in his gambling pot was a big no-no.

A little surveillance and investigating uncovered the fact that the chick had sticky fingers *and* a greedy heart. To Mookie's fury, she had gotten down with the dealer to shut him out of his wins. The bird was losing on purpose at times, and winning big at oth-ers, then splitting the ends with the dealer without giving Mookie a cut.

Mookie blacked the fuck out.

He rolled up on that trick in daylight right on 125th Street.

He jumped outta his whip in the middle of the street and crashed his tool across her face.

"Bitch, you can either take one in the dome," Mookie said, cocking the burner and pressing it against her temple as she cringed and clung to a parking meter for dear life, "or you can pay me with them sticky-ass fingers you got."

It really wasn't much of a choice.

Seasoned hustlers flinched on the sidelines as Mookie held his Glock to the chick's head and dragged her into the middle of the street, where he had left his car running. He forced her to stick her fingers in the small crack between his whip's body and the door as the chick screamed and begged for mercy.

Blood flew everywhere as Mookie made sure her hand was jammed in the crack real good, then slammed the car door closed with every bit of his massive strength, swinging it so hard that the impact shattered the glass in the window along with most of the bones in the girl's fingers.

"What about that thumb?" Mookie demanded at the top of his lungs as the poor girl shrieked and gripped her bloody hand to her chest. You could tell the pain was excruciating by the way she heaved and vomited all over herself, but Mookie gave a damn about all that. "You throwing up and shitting all over ya self and I ain't even get you good yet, baby," Mookie told her. He shoved the barrel of his piece into her ear and not a soul on the streets doubted that he would pull the trigger. "Stick that thumb in there now."

Not every gangsta had the stomach for this type of thing, but Mookie Murdock did. He actually enjoyed it to the max. He saw the way some of them bitch-ass posers who was supposed to be hardbody were turning away from the scene in disgust. They pro-lly felt sorry for the dumbass girl, but not sorry enough to open their traps and take her fuckin' punishment!

Mookie damn near sliced the girl's right thumb off in the car door, and then he went to work on her left hand. By the time he had gotten his money's worth she was a mess. With both of her crushed, rapidly swelling hands pressed to her chest, the chick stumbled over to the curb and fell down in the gutter, slumped over. Passed the fuck out. Her hands mighta been all fucked up, but at least she still had her life. And she could thank Mookie Murdock and his generous spirit for that.

"Time to fly, boss," his manz Donut had said, urging Mookie toward their whip as a small crowd of concerned Harlemites gathered around the unconscious girl.

"That's domestic fuckin' violence, yo!" somebody hollered from a nearby window. "Call the fuckin' cops!"

Mookie took his time getting in the whip. He didn't give a fuck who they called. Putting a bird in her place wasn't a federal offense. He kept mad pockets lined in every precinct in his perimeter, and there wasn't much the local authorities could do to Mookie Murdock.

But it wasn't the local boys who would prove to be a problem.

"You gone wanna lay low for a minute," warned a quiet voice in the backseat as they whipped down the streets of Harlem. "There's bound to be some dirt kicked up behind this shit."

Mookie had shrugged. "That scheming bitch is nothing. Street grime. Just another slimy ho like all the rest of them out there."

Reclining in the comfort of the backseat, Yoda nodded his agreement.

"Yeah. She's dirty all right. Been that way for a long time. But she's also something else, ak. She's Diamond Baines, yo. Irish Baines' daughter."

Not a damn thing changed about Mookie's demeanor on the outside, but inside he was silently apologizing to Capo and cursing at himself for once again losing his head and putting his whole operation at risk.

Mookie knew all about the OG Irish Baines. He had been watching Irish and all that bullshit he was conducting over at his boys center for a minute now, and his manz out on the streets had been steady scooping up all the leftover kids that Irish couldn't rehabilitate.

Fucking Diamond up was a mistake, Mookie soon realized. It wasn't even the money that had sent him into a rage when he found out the trick bitch was skimming. It was the loss! Mookie Murdock didn't lose fuckin' bets! Not on shit that he'd set up to work to his advantage!

Intuition told Mookie that trouble was coming. Diamond was a piper and a fiend, and it prolly woulda been better just to get one of his boys to give her a hot shot and be done with the thievin' bitch. But both the gambler and the gangsta in him had driven Mookie to make a public example outta Diamond's ass on the streets where everybody could see it. He bet the next bitch he sent to that casino on a special job would think long and hard about fuckin' over Mookie Murdock. Those jawns didn't realize that those faggot-ass dealers couldn't protect they ass. Diamond had actually come out lucky. The dealer she had gotten down with had bucked when Mookie's manz went to teach him a lesson, and ended up rotting under a piece of cardboard in a deserted alleyway.

Yeah, the bitch had been lucky indeed.

CHAPTER 10

But luck didn't have shit to do with the aftermath that followed. That old niggah Irish had been outta the game for so long that he'd forgotten a cardinal street code: you don't get in bed with the Feds. That do-gooding cat had taken Mookie's retribution personally, and a little birdie tweeted the news in Mookie's ear that thanks to Irish he was being watched by the Alphabet Boys and investigated for illegal gambling, tax evasion, money laundering, and racketeering.

Mookie was enraged, but he felt a little remorse too. Not for hurting Diamond—he could have easily murked that bitch and thought nothing of it. Nah, Mookie was down on himself for violating Capo's cardinal rule and blowing his fuckin' top in public. He'd shined a light on himself and brought attention to his operations on a level that was now out of his control.

Mookie knew what was coming next, and when his manz found a bug under his couch and strange cars were seen parked outside his crib at all times of night, it wasn't hard to figure out who was riding him. Them Alphabet Boys followed Mookie everywhere, and he took them on a guided tour through the streets of Harlem every chance he could. Sometimes he would order his driver to just drive around town for the fuck of it. They wouldn't get out of the car, they wouldn't even stop anywhere. They would just ride. Mookie was just letting those muhfuckahs know that *he* knew.

The surveillance didn't last long because Mookie was one boring muhfuckah. He went to bed early and slept late. He seldom went to any clubs, especially those he owned, and he used his crew as a buffer between him and every kind of transaction that went down.

In short, Mookie looked real clean. He smelled clean too.

But appearances could only take you so far, and when the Feds started connecting the dots between Mookie's preciously guarded stolen-identity ring and his offshore bank accounts, the shit hit the fan all over Harlem.

Like his street daddy Capo, Mookie had been stacking paper for his retirement. But unlike Capo, Mookie didn't plan on waiting until he was old as dirt to break out of the game. But now, with Irish orchestrating the Feds on his ass, everything Mookie had worked for was at risk. He could fuck around and lose his entire bankroll just because some old-ass washed-up G couldn't keep his daughter in his fuckin' yard.

The more he thought about it, the madder Mookie got.

And when Mookie got mad, shit happened and it happened in a major way. Deciding to get rid of Irish Baines was a no-brainer. That niggah had flapped his lips and sucked federal dick, and there was nothing street about that. Mookie sent his goonies to take care of Irish in a way he thought was most fitting. He'd show Irish what a dick down the throat could do to you. That niggah wanted to bring the heat down on Big Mookie? Well Mookie would light a fuckin' bonfire under his natural ass!

Irish Baines didn't know who he was fuckin' with. But by the time the smoke cleared over his property Mookie was sure the old head had figured that shit out. Mookie had laughed like fuck as his manz Yoda described how Irish had cried and begged just like a bitch. Yoda had made sure Irish's woman sucked Mookie's metal dick real good, and he'd had even less mercy on the two little future hoes they'd found crying together in their bedroom.

Yeah, Mookie's boyz had dealt with Irish in a brutal, gutter fashion, and the whole time they were handling Irish, Mookie was across town at Club Humpz handling the thievin' bitch who had started it all: Diamond.

Yeah. All them Baineses had been served. It wasn't business either. That shit was personal! Chaos had been coming down on his empire because of Irish, and Mookie was glad that niggah and his family were burned and gone.

Problem solved!

Mookie was happy as fuck. Without Irish pushing the issue the Feds had eased off somewhat and moved on to cases that were much easier to trace and prosecute. And now that Irish was nothing more than hood dust and that bullshit little center of his was on the rocks, Mookie's business revenue was about to pick up lovely.

CHAPTER 11

The first few weeks after the murder of her family members were pure hell for Pearl. She was staying at Cole's apartment because she wasn't capable of being alone. Carlita came by to check on her every day after work, and her niece Zoe called Pearl with words of sympathy and support several times a week. Pearl hadn't heard a word from Diamond since the night before their birthday, nor had her twin shown up at the funeral or at the cemetery to see their loved ones put in the ground.

It was hard for Pearl not to go crazy thinking about where Diamond could be or what could be happening to her, but it was even harder to accept the fact she'd never hear her mother's sweet voice again or never again be able to call on her father for wisdom or advice. But the hardest thing was the knowledge that she'd never kiss or hug her daughter Sasha again, and that she'd never have a chance to explain to her child why she hadn't been more of a mother to her during her short, beautiful life.

The funerals had been heart wrenching. Twice Pearl had lunged from her seat and tried to climb on top of her mother's closed coffin. And twice Carlita and Zoe had broken into tears as several men held Pearl down while she kicked and screamed that her baby girl couldn't breathe down inside that fuckin' box!

And now, no matter where she was or what she was doing, Pearl just couldn't get Sasha's cries out of her ears. Her daughter's spirit haunted her from the grave. Pearl just couldn't stop seeing Sasha's beautiful face or hearing her choking, anguished pleas for help as she suffered a cruel and heartless death that no child should ever have to bear.

Pearl also went through anguished bouts of guilt that were sometimes far more painful than her unbearable grief. She would fall to the ground on her hands and knees, wailing and screaming with her entire being racked with guilt and convinced that her selfishness had contributed to the murder of her precious little girl. If only she hadn't left home! If only she hadn't wanted to *be* somebody and have a fuckin' future! If only she had stayed her ass in Harlem where the people she loved were, somehow she might have been able to protect and defend her family!

From head to toe, Pearl was an emotional wreck. She lost insane weight and her pretty hair started falling out in clumps. She couldn't work and she couldn't eat. Sleep eluded her night after night as she trembled and moaned and cried out, tortured by a child's horrible screams that no one else seemed to hear.

Pearl's emotional torment was unspeakable, and it was definitely unbearable. She had gone from a scared, nervous kid to a wild teen and had finally evolved into a highly capable young woman, yet she had failed at the one task that should have meant more to her than anything else: being a good mother to her daughter.

Cole was there for her 24/7. He fed her soup, bathed her tenderly, held her when she cried, and soothed her through the murderous, smoke-filled night terrors she fought against in the midst of her dreams.

In fact, if it hadn't been for Cole then Pearl would have probably died from grief. The FBI had placed her on a leave of absence from the Hostage Rescue Team immediately following her family's murder, and they had even sent an agent to a Harlem precinct to inquire about her sister's whereabouts.

"They don't have any information listed about Diamond," Carlita told Pearl after accessing the file. "But it looks like somebody up in higher headquarters put out some feelers based on a request by your father. I couldn't get access to the complete file, but one of our governmental agencies was investigating something on your father's behalf. Unfortunately, there's nothing at all here about your sister."

Pearl was devastated. It was like Harlem had opened its filthy mouth and swallowed Diamond whole. No matter which grimeball hole in the wall the cops searched, Pearl's twin was nowhere to be found.

Pearl was emotionally busted. The leave of absence the FBI had insisted she take was definitely needed because she was in no condition to work anybody's high-intensity job, not even at a desk answering phones. The FBI psychiatrist said she was in a severe depression brought on by extreme grief, and he prescribed her an antidepressant and something strong to help her sleep through the night.

But a couple of weeks later Pearl woke up in the middle of the night sweating in a cold panic. Sasha was crying and screaming for her in her dreams, and Pearl was reliving her worst nightmare. It was the night of the fire all over again. She was running out of Baskin Robbins and her high-heel pumps clacked on the concrete like drums in her ears.

Her legs were stroking, she was moving like a track star, and when she turned the corner and glimpsed her house, thick smoke and vicious flames were already shooting from the windows. Getting past the firemen was real easy in Pearl's dream. She moved in slow motion and she took two of them down without breaking a sweat. The po-po were something else though. She fucked the young one up real good, the one who had Tasered her first. The second one got more than a broken nose for touching her fuckin' hair, and Pearl left him on the ground trying to push his eyeball back inside of his skull.

She was almost at the front door, but moving in dream speed. She felt the heat and the smoke but she wasn't gonna let it stop her. She reached for the white-hot door handle and felt bits of her palm flesh sear off and stick to it, but she yanked it open anyway and fled inside, pushed on by the desperate sound of her little girl's cries.

She passed by her father Irish in the living room, and hesitated only briefly when she saw that he was beat down and bloody and hogtied to a chair. Pearl's legs were long and strong as hell in her dream, and she bound into Sasha and Chante's room in just three steps, yelling for the girls through the smoke as loud as she could.

"I'm coming, Sasha!" Pearl screamed to her dream daughter. "Hold on baby! I'm coming!!"

But just as she rounded the corner and burst into the blistering pink-and-brown room whose walls were already scorched black, Pearl stopped short, frozen in grief by what she saw.

Sasha stood next to her burning bed tapping one flaming foot on the floor. Her melted eyes were narrowed and her arms were crossed defiantly in front of her. She was pissed off and burning, and loose flesh was sliding off her like thick candle wax.

"You got time for every goddamn thing except *me*," Pearl's

dead daughter accused her from a mouth that was held together by crispy, burnt lips. "Why you running your ass up in here now? You shoulda been here for me the whole time, *Pearl*. But you left us here to die 'cause you was too busy thinking about *yourself*."

Then right before Pearl's eyes, Sasha's whole body began turning to liquid. It started at her feet and she melted to the floor, first to her knees, and then up to her waist, and then her shoulders and finally her head. The entire time her little girl was screaming, "*You left me, Pearl!* You made sure you got outta the hood, but you left me here to *die*!"

Pearl cried out and fled from the dream room as Sasha's lips still moved accusingly in her puddle of human wax. She heard Irish moaning as she ran toward the front door and stopped when she saw her mother's brutalized body near his feet. Zeta was dead. Streaks of blood were on her thighs. Her beautiful mouth was busted; bloodied and torn apart. Irish was strapped to a chair and he was on fire. Flames were coming out of his mouth, his nose, and his eyes.

"Them muthafuckas got us!" her father gurgled in her dream, spitting fire as he tried to shake the flames from his head. Pearl screamed again and ran toward the door.

"Get 'em back!" she heard Irish yelling behind her. "You get 'em back, Daddy's Pearl! You pay them muhfuckahs *back*!"

Pearl screamed out loud and bolted upright in the bed for real. She was sweating and crying and could have sworn she tasted burnt flesh in her mouth. Her heart ached with grief, and the rage in her baby girl's bubbling eyes and the ringing of her father's last words in her ears caused her more pain than she had ever imagined possible.

She called out for Cole and found that she was alone in his apartment. He had left a note beside her on the bed saying he'd gone out to get something to eat and would be right back.

Pearl was alone and she knew what she had to do.

There was no way in hell she could live like this and there was no other way to end it.

She reached under Cole's pillow and found his service revolver where he always left it when he was off duty. She thought about sticking the barrel in her mouth and eating some lead but she just couldn't do it. That shit was too foul. Brains would be spattered all over the walls; blood and goo would be everywhere. Somebody would have to come behind her and clean all that shit up.

The same thing went for cutting her wrists or jumping off a roof. Too much fuckin' drama. She wasn't about leaving a whole bunch of mess behind for some poor fool to deal with. Pearl eyed the medicine vials on her night table. The FBI psychiatrist had prescribed the pills for her but they hadn't done a damn bit of good. Her muscles were weak, but she managed to open both canisters. She shook out almost all the tablets from each one. She poured the tablets into her mouth and chewed them into a foul-tasting goo.

"Oh, Sasha," Pearl moaned as she went into the bathroom, then climbed into the dry tub and stretched out flat. She was weak and exhausted and all she wanted was for the nightmare that had become her life to finally end.

"My *baby*," she muttered, her heart aching and grieving as she visualized her dead daughter. "Oh God . . . my *baby*."

Tears rolled from Pearl's eyes as she closed them and waited for the drugs to take effect. "I'm so sorry, baby girl," she whispered. "Chante. Daddy. Mama. Diamond. I'm sorry y'all."

CHAPTER 12

Cole walked the rainy streets of D.C. without an umbrella or a hat.

From the moment he had asked Pearl to be his woman for life, nothing but clouds had hung over their lives. He didn't even feel the rain as it slid off his head and rolled down his neck. He was a big dude, and his feet kicked up waves in the puddles of the cracked pavement as he walked through the hood trying to figure out what to do about Pearl. He had to find a way to bring his baby back to life so she could start acting right again and they could get on with their relationship.

He stopped in a local pizza joint and got two hot slices and an order of buffalo wings to go. He stuffed the bulging paper bag under his jacket as he walked back out in the rain and headed to his small apartment where Pearl was waiting. He was tired as fuck, but there was no slowing down in sight. Ever since Pearl's family had died there had been no fun, no hanging out, no home cooking, and definitely no fucking.

Cole was a brother with needs, and the sooner Pearl came out of her funk and got her shit together the sooner he could get them met. The past few weeks had been real hard on him. He worked a twelve-hour shift every day then rushed home to take care of Pearl, who mostly cried her days away. She slept on and off, screaming from nightmares so loud that it scared the shit outta his neighbors.

It was all that crying that had gotten her sent home from the job.

The Bureau had given her two weeks of bereavement leave to bury her people and take care of bizz up in New York, but two weeks didn't even put a dent in the amount of time it looked like Pearl was gonna need to get back on track.

For one thing, her sister Diamond had been missing since the night of their birthday, and now that she had been found at the county landfill just two days ago, Cole was hesitant about hitting Pearl with the devastating news about her twin. What good would knowing do her? Nah, Cole wasn't with it. As bad as Pearl was grieving, hearing about Diamond's death would fuck her head up even more and push her completely over the edge. Wasn't no telling how long it would take her to get over that shit. After the way she had spazzed out at the funerals, Cole wasn't about to lay no extra trip like that on her.

"Yo, Diamond is dead," the dude calling Pearl's cell phone had said flatly. Immediately, Cole had gotten swole and sought to protect Pearl. From the devastating news about her sister, and from the ass-clocking muhfuckah delivering that shit.

"Shawty caught a bad one," the dude went on. "They holding her body at the county morgue. They had to ID her through dental records, man, 'cause there wasn't enough of her left to get a fingerprint from to find out who she was."

There was a long pause on the line, and Cole saw no reason to fill it, 'cause even though he felt real sorry for Diamond, Pearl was his baby. He wanted her on her feet living life, not wrecked out and crying all day in no bed. Pearl had told him all about this slimy cat Menace and how he had been fucking Diamond over the years. Fuck this niggah! Cole was strictly out for Pearl. Let this punk on the line look out for the twin he had been jocking for.

"They said she was all fucked up, man," Menace said finally. "But even in her bad condition they could tell she had broken bones all in her neck . . . some niggah musta strangled her or something . . . somebody's gonna have to go claim her body so she can be buried. I guess Pearl needs to know that."

Cole smirked. "Why the fuck do Pearl need to know?"

"What?"

"I said, why Pearl gotta know? She's already pressed the fuck out. She don't need no more bad news."

"Man, what the fuck is you talking about? That's her *sister* layin' in the morgue dead, yo! Her fuckin' *twin*! They pops raised them to be tight, niggah! To look out for each other! Hell yeah she needs to know!"

Cole just shrugged. He gave a damn about all that. "Yo," he told Menace, "you was boning Diamond right? Sliding up in that? Then you go take care of her body. Handle that shit. I'm fuckin' Pearl, and I'ma make sure *my* baby is straight."

Pearl! Pearl!

Wake up, Pearl! Stay with us, baby!

It was almost as bad as her nightmare, the pain and confusion that had suddenly gripped her. She was shaken violently, her face slapped by large, rough hands. From a great distance she imagined she heard Cole yelling, then talking to someone frantically, begging them for help.

She was lifted and jostled. Then she was stretched out flat and being bumped along, moving fast. Hands dug deep into her stomach, pressing toward her backbone, and a sharp-tasting liquid was forced down her throat.

Pearl gagged and fought back, but she was weak.

There were lots of people above her. Loud voices. Sharp commands and murmured words of concern.

She tried to turn over on her side. Wanted to sleep. They flipped her onto her back again and jammed a tube up her nose. It scraped the back of her throat and snaked down into her stomach. Cold liquid whooshed quickly through the tube and flooded her insides. The sound of suction assaulted her ears. Pearl choked as she tried to cry out. She couldn't catch her breath.

She was so tired. Just wanted to sleep. Forever. *Forever!*

Pearl! *Pearl!*

Cold fingers lifted her eyelids.

Bright lights pierced her brain. Her stomach lurched and she gagged, spewing up the foul-tasting liquid they'd forced into her belly.

There were so many people around, so many voices floating within her fog, but one voice in particular Pearl heard loud and clear.

Why? a woman asked with deep concern in her voice.

Pearl opened her eyes to the blurry image of an elderly white nurse leaning over her. She had a full head of gray hair and eyes that crinkled in the corners.

Why would such a beautiful young woman do something like this to herself? the lady wanted to know.

Cole's deep voice washed over Pearl as he answered.

She lost her whole family and she's been sad, he said. *She's hurting. It's hard on her . . . she's grieving so bad till I guess she just don't wanna live no more . . .*

Through her haze, Pearl watched as the old white nurse leaned over her again. Somewhere in the background little Sasha cried out for her mother, and Pearl squeezed her eyes closed tightly and willed her soul to fly free from her body.

When Pearl opened her eyes again, it wasn't the old nurse whose face floated above her.

It was the face of her dead father.

It was that old street niggah Irish Baines, who once upon a time had handled the most vicious of gangstas in a brutal fashion. Irish gazed down at his daughter as she lay on that hospital gurney, racked with grief and trying her best to join her family in death and he told her, "I know it hurts, but you gotta be strong, Daddy's Pearl. I don't want you to be sad no more, you hear me?" Pearl listened intently to her father, and the words firing from his mouth caused her to become straight-up unzipped.

"Daddy wants you to get *mad* now, baby. Daddy wants you to get *even!*"

CHAPTER 13

Pearl had endured a lot during her hospital stay. She'd been admitted to the psych ward and placed on suicide watch for almost two weeks. After being forced to take antidepressants and sit through endless hours of nuthouse counseling, by the time Pearl was discharged she had developed a new sense of purpose, an objective, and a plan.

Getting rid of Cole had been harder than faking out her psychiatrists. Shaking that clingy niggah off was like trying to kick a tribe of fleas out of a pissy carpet. Carlita had been right about him. Cole was possessive and controlling, and the only thing he gave a damn about was keeping Pearl right next to him so that the next man couldn't get close to her.

"You need to chill with all that packing," he had told her as she tossed a few items of clothes into a suitcase. He had followed Pearl to her apartment even though she'd told him she wanted to go home alone. Pearl ignored him and kept on packing. She didn't know why she was bothering to take most of her stuff anyway. She had paid her rent up for the next two months and she was gonna need a whole new wardrobe for the kind of role she was about to play.

"You got a damn good job here, Pearl," Cole went on. "You got people here who care about you. Even Carlita thinks you should stay here!"

Pearl nodded. Carlita *did* want her to stay in D.C. But Carlita had also done everything within her power to make sure that Pearl would be safe and successful when she left. Carlita had used her security clearance to help Pearl access a file on another New York family who had been killed in a crime that was almost identical to hers, and had done countless other things to help her. So, while Carlita *wanted* Pearl to stay, she understood why her young friend had to go.

"Just holla if something heavy goes down," Carlita had told her. "If you need help kickin' ass I'll jet to Harlem in a blink, girl. Me and Zoe are both ready to get strapped and get it started."

Carlita and Zoe were true friends and they were gonna support Pearl regardless, through thick and thin. But Cole's selfish ass had kept the heat on at his end.

"Yo, Pearl. All that 'I gotta get away and find myself' bullshit sounds real suspect to me. You ain't never been *lost,* baby. Your life is right here. *I'm* right here. This is where you belong."

Pearl was grateful to Cole for standing by her side and holding her up through the funerals and stuff, but gratitude wasn't gonna stop her from doing what she had to do. Wasn't nothing in the world gonna stop her from accomplishing the mission that was in front of her, but there was no way to break that down for Cole in terms that would make him understand it:

"This ain't about you or a job or the FBI, Cole. It's about me. I already told you that a thousand times."

"But you ain't really telling me much of nothing!" he exploded. "Why don't you try telling me exactly what the fuck I've been asking you, Pearl! Where are you going? Who are you gonna be with? Why can't I come with you? How fuckin' long are you gonna be gone?"

Pearl scooped up a row of expensive toiletries and perfumes off her dresser and dumped them into a plastic carry bag. She kept her back turned to Cole as she placed her few good pieces of jewelry into a satin travel pouch, then hesitated briefly before sliding Cole's icy engagement ring off her finger and setting it on top of the bare dresser.

Pearl sighed and refused to answer him. It was Cole's fault she was leaving anyway. She had been laying in bed beside him as he watched SportsCenter on Sunday night when it hit her. A plan for retribution had rang out in her head just as clear as a bell, and she had Cole to thank for hooking her up with all the important details.

"Aw, man!" Cole had said as the SportsCenter announcers cut to a commercial break. Cole was drinking a beer and shaking his head at something being said on the screen. "Patrick Ewing is hosting a Summer Jam Basketball Classic at the Garden. That's the kinda shit I miss about New York," Cole complained. "Every fuckin' thing that's hot happens in New York in the summertime. I ain't bitching or nothing. D.C. is working for me and I got you here, but New York is the place to be. LeBron is about to suit up for the Knicks, and Pat's name is still ringing big bells. The Classic is a major draw. Every high roller in the country is gonna be swarming on the city that weekend. Hell, forget about the game. The pregame and after-game parties alone are gonna be off the chain."

Pearl had been laying there, listless and uninterested, but suddenly her ears perked up and her curiosity was stoked.

"What you know about the after parties and all that, Cole? What kind of high rollers go to summer basketball games?"

"Yo, girl, my father was a hoop star before he was a politician, remember? I grew up around all kinds of professional sporting events. It ain't just about the game, Pearl. It's about the *business* of the game. The whole atmosphere. The shine. The tricks, the drugs, the betting, point shaving, and game throwing. Nigs be ballin'! There's a whole underworld of activity going on at major events like these. The Bureau keeps moles on the job trying to tamp that shit down. But it's hard to infiltrate those circles because the criminal elements are loyal and they grind it like they live it. To the bone."

Pearl had nodded, and then sat up straight in the bed, listening to him intently.

Ever since her suicide attempt she had been haunted. Not simply by her family's murder as she once was, but by what her father commanded her to do from the depths of his cold, smoke-filled grave.

Get them muthafuckahs back, Pearl! Irish begged her each night in her dreams. *Don't get mad, Daddy's Pearl. Get even!*

And with her father's voice urging her on in her head, Pearl stayed quiet and listened as Cole painted a colorful picture of a three-day ballin' extravaganza complete with big money rollers, sex, drugs, gambling, and some of the slickest hustlers and kingpins in the nation. It sounded like a real good time to Pearl, the kind of place where sleazy muthafuckahs like the men who had deaded her family in cold blood would fit right in.

Less than forty-eight hours later she was in her apartment packing her shit and Cole was damn near crying.

"You still ain't answered me, Pearl. Where you going, girl? And why you gotta leave? Shit is perfect for us here. *Why?*"

Pearl finally turned around to face him. The only person she had trusted with any details of her plan was Carlita, and Pearl hadn't even told her everything, just enough to gain her support. Carlita hadn't liked the thought of Pearl placing herself in danger. She thought Pearl should let the authorities do what they did best.

"Let the New York police take a crack at it, Pearl," Carlita had pleaded. "I know they don't give a damn about most black and brown people, but you should at least let them try. If they can't find those bastards in the next few weeks then I'll roll up in Harlem with you and help you swole some heads. But give the police the opportunity to at least look."

Of course, Pearl wasn't trying to hear that. What she needed Carlita to do was help her gain access to FBI resources that could make her mission a success. Because of her seniority and experience Carlita's security clearance was much higher than Pearl's, and there were documents that she needed her girl to access on her behalf, and weaponry items she needed to order using Carlita's clearance code.

And just like Pearl had expected, her girl had been down for her 100 percent. Carlita understood how it felt to lose someone you loved, but even the loss of her husband didn't compare to the horrific murder of Pearl's entire family. After finding out some of the dirty details of what had been done to Pearl's family in their last minutes on earth, Carlita had promised to help her friend anyway she could.

Which was why Pearl couldn't understand why Cole couldn't give her that same kind of love and respect. His whole attitude was about me, me, me. Like a spoiled fuckin' two-year-old who was about to fall out because he couldn't get what he wanted.

Pearl kept her voice calm and low when she spoke to him, and there was real sadness in her tone.

"I don't have a whole lotta answers for you right now, Cole. I could make something up, but I'm not trying to lie to you. I could bullshit you and say I'm heading east or north or south, but how would it matter? I'm outta D.C., Cole. That's what's real. And I don't know when I'll be back."

"Man, just tell me you ain't going back to Harlem!" Cole exploded. "Tell me you ain't going back to get with that niggah Menace! Damn, girl! Just tell me that."

Pearl gave him a look so cold it sent a bullet through his heart.

"I don't know how you was brought up down there in Brooklyn, Cole, but Irish and Zeta Baines raised me better than that. I already told you about how Menace got down with Diamond. No matter how grimy my sister trolled behind me, I don't *fuck* behind my sister. So don't put it on me if you're used to slummin' with guttersnipe feather flyers in the BK with no morals or no character, because that ain't me."

Pearl wasn't moved an inch by the look of pain on Cole's face. She had decent love for him and would always appreciate what he had done for her, but there was no room for love or softness or gratitude in Pearl's heart right now. Today, her heart was ice-cold and her mind was already hundreds of miles to the north, squarely in the city of New York. Right in the heart of a gritty little town called Harlem. A place where cutthroat killers raped and tortured women and terrorized and burned up innocent little kids who were tied to their beds. A place where violent wars were waged and good men suffered brutal deaths.

A place of retribution, reprisal, reckoning, and revenge.

Harlem, USA.

THE
JURY

CHAPTER 14

D.C. didn't have shit on Harlem in the summertime. Somehow, if it was ninety degrees in the nation's capitol, it was damn near a hundred on 125th Street. It was like that with the other boroughs too. Brooklyn, Queens, Staten Island, even the Bronx. Out of all the hot spots in the city of New York, Harlem was always the hottest. In temperature and in the level of crime and drama that played out on the urban streets.

Flying into a New York airport was nothing like it used to be. Instead of finding Irish and Zeta there holding hands with Sasha and Chante, Pearl was all alone as she looked out into a moving sea of strange faces.

Keeping her head high and her emotions in deep check, Pearl walked briskly through the corridors and past baggage claim, then exited the airport and caught a taxicab and gave the driver a Harlem address.

She sat back as the New York streets sped past in a blur, grateful for the small stream of almost-cool air that wheezed from the car's vents. Pearl was keeping it low profile today. She had pulled her hair back into a simple but stylish bun and wore a pair of black slacks and a plain pullover cotton shift. The back of her arms stuck to the taxi's plastic upholstery and Pearl fanned herself with her crumpled boarding pass. Harlem summers had always been back-alley humid, and the intense heat kept tempers high and corner boys, winos, and crackheads amped up and fighting mad.

When the taxi pulled up outside the address Pearl had given him, it was a long moment before Pearl could make herself get out of the man's cab. A big knot of fear had formed in her chest, but when a child's painful voice cried out in her mind, Pearl fought to slam the voice straight out of her head as she begged her wounded heart to shut down and go ice-cold.

Pearl paid the driver then retrieved her small suitcase from the trunk. She stood looking down at the sidewalk, hating Harlem. She hated all of New York. Her world had ended here, and if it wasn't for the commanding voice of her father she would have never stepped foot back on these foul, dirty streets.

Pearl raised her eyes and forced herself to take in the devastation as she stared at the scorched remainders of her family's small empire. It had been burned down to the ground. There were still traces of an acrid smell coming from the gutted house and pieces of yellow crime-scene tape stuck to a pillar on the porch. A few stray beams and some melted roof tiles were scattered about, and the foundation was still there, but everything else was gone. Either it had been destroyed by the fire, washed into the gutter by the firemen's hoses, or picked over by the human vultures who crept by in the dark of night to see if there was anything left of value to steal.

Pearl just stood there, transfixed by the sight.

Mommy! Mommy! Help me, Mommy!

And then she lost it. Her heart exploded in grief as she sank down to her knees right there on the busy sidewalk. She wailed out loud as thick plumes of smoke seemed to snake up her nose and a blurry vision of her mother's tortured body and her daughter's burned flesh filled her mind.

Get up, Pearl! a loud, strong voice commanded in her head. Harlemites were walking past her on the sidewalk, most of them so used to seeing strange shit on the regular that they didn't even give her a second glance. *Get your ass up, Pearl! You've got work to do, baby. You got a grind to get on!*

Crouching on the sidewalk, Pearl breathed deep gulps of car exhaust–tinged air into her lungs. She fought the terror and grief that was trying to cripple her, and hung on to her father's commands with every ounce of strength she had.

Oblivious to the traffic and the pedestrians, Pearl's body shook with sobs until she was depleted and could cry no more. And when she finally rose to her feet, her back was straight and strong and she was filled with her father's love and his presence.

She dried her tears. Daddy's Pearl had business to handle. With a resolute look in her eyes, Pearl pulled her suitcase along the cracked sidewalk littered with trash, broken bottles, and crushed beer cans, and prepared herself to get shit done.

Pearl had fully expected her father's rehabilitation and outreach center to be closed and shuttered with its solid metal grille, but to her surprise the doors to No Limitz were standing wide open and several young men were inside seated at computer stations.

A huge plaque hung in the entryway, and reading it helped Pearl feel her father's presence:

THERE ARE NO LIMITZ ON A SOUL EMBOLDENED
AND A MIND INSPIRED.

Irish had placed the plaque there on the day the center opened, over fifteen years earlier. He had cut the wood, sanded it, and engraved the words himself, and every black or Latino kid who had ever walked through his doors had been made to recite and memorize the words and strive to understand and internalize their meaning.

Pearl stood in the doorway staring as a tall, gorgeous dude with a deliciously buff body and smooth cocoa skin walked up and down between the rows of terminals and chairs, stopping to answer a question here and there or to give technical computer support as needed.

He was a fifth-degree black belt, a tournament-winning elite martial artist, and one of the strongest, finest men she'd ever seen. Pearl knew from experience that he was an intellectual when it came to business, a powerful and unselfish lover in the gushy, and a straight-up gorilla out there on the streets.

Menace Brown had come to No Limitz at the age of fourteen under her father's guidance. Irish had taken the young criminal under his wing when he was just a pup, and Menace had pledged his loyalty to Irish and looked up to him like the father he'd never had.

Three years older than Pearl, Menace had once been a studious corner boy who slung trap for a major kingpin in Washington Heights. His mother had died from the AIDS virus when he was ten, and he'd never even known his father.

As young as he was, Menace had taken care of his mother all by himself in her final days. He'd fed her soup from a spoon, washed her gaunt, feverish body, brushed her thin wisps of hair, and prayed with her for strength and salvation.

Even though they'd been poor and couldn't afford the basic necessities, Laila Brown had loved her boy, and what she couldn't give him in material things she made up for by fortifying him with her love and her wisdom. It was Menace's father who had infected her with the virus while she was pregnant with him, and ever grateful that her baby had not been infected, Laila had used the tragedy of her hard life to teach her son what it meant to be a real man.

But her death rocked the boy off his foundation and left him angry and filled with rage. Alone and left to fend for himself, Menace had become one of those fearless, hopeless street kids who ran rampant through the projects kicking up chaos as he struggled to deal with his anger and survive the only way he knew how. With a stomach that was always on empty and the courage of a grown man, he pulled stick-ups, kick-doors, and shakedowns every chance he got, and even the baddest old heads agreed that he was a true menace to society.

Laila had done her best to instill the proper values in her son during her short lifetime, but the streets were cold and hard, and despite her many life lessons, when she died there was no mama in the hood to guide or discipline him. Menace ran with a crew of several other street kids and all of them got on the grind for the local kingpin and started slinging rock from various city corners.

By the time he was fourteen Menace had earned the best territory out of all the young pups on the trap. He'd amassed a stable of regulars who liked to cop from him because he was quick and discreet, two valuable traits on the trap. He worked tirelessly but was quiet and serious, and didn't drink, smoke, fuck hood-rats, or hang out with a crew unless stacking gwap was involved. As a result, he turned high profits and earned enough cream to stack some of it away for a rainy day.

It was a hot summer night when the jakes rained down in a

major drug bust, sweeping through the dank streets and rolling corner boys left and right. Menace followed procedures exactly the way he usually did. He had just re-upped his supply and turned over his doe, and when the jakes jumped outta their cars, Menace took off running to his usual drop spot, where he always stashed his weight until the coast was clear.

But shit didn't go the way it usually went. He had just loosened a brick on the side of the house and slid his package into the gaping hole when three grown men jumped on him from behind. They were a bunch of roscoes who had been casing his spot for a while, and knew exactly where he went to stash his shit during a raid.

Menace was a big, strong kid, but he was still just a kid. He fought furiously, scoring big blows, but eventually they got the cuffs on him and it was a wrap. The next thing Menace knew he was locked up with a bunch of other felonious young heads, and the cops were trying to pin about twenty other crimes on him. He'd stayed cool under questioning and kept his gangsta up, because the lowest thing you could be was a snitch, and Menace was far from that. He *was* a minor though, so he bided his time and waited for the authorities to slap him on the wrist and send him back to foster care. But the judge was tired of seeing him rolling in and out of his courtroom, so he got clever and sentenced Menace to a youth-outreach program instead.

Irish Baines showed up in court to collect young Menace, and instead of being the old do-gooder community activist Menace had expected, he was a big, killer-looking nig who looked like he had once been quite a menace to society himself.

Irish had taken him to a local group home and set about trying to reprogram the hood life out of the boy while there was still time.

"Two rules," Irish had told him after making sure he got

something to eat and showing him to his bunk. "Stay away from them drugs out there and finish school. You somebody's son, young man. Somebody's black prince. There ain't no limitz on a soul emboldened and a mind inspired! I don't know what your story is or where you been, but I'm sure your mama didn't raise no fool to be wildin' in the streets and wrecking shit like no animal."

Irish was no nonsense and had a legendary rep, and Menace respected that shit. More than that, he respected the way Irish walked the streets, all man, yet he rapped about progression and education instead of pimping bitches and slanging blow, and somehow all that positivity coming out of Irish's mouth was exactly what Menace needed to hear at that stage in his life.

He dug in and went to school and actually studied and learned. For the first time in his young life Menace had an older male influencing his mind in the proper manner, and along with the lessons that Irish was forever laying on his young pup, there was love and respect flowing between them too, something Menace had never gotten from any man before.

Menace idolized Irish and wanted to live his life in a way that would make the older man proud. Through his unselfish devotion to black kids who started life with two strikes against them, Irish had snatched another young'un from an endless black hole of despair, and young Menace Brown would never forget it.

CHAPTER 15

Over the years Menace grew bigger and wiser, and his loyalty to Irish grew stronger as well. He was serious and respectful, and Zeta Baines treated him like her very own son. He had a good relationship with the twins, Diamond and Pearl, too. At least until they got to be teenagers and started feeling themselves. Both twins were stunnas and had gorgeous faces and phatty back pockets, but Diamond was real extra with her shit, baller-crazy and always offering to lay some na-na on Menace like he was stupid enough to take it.

It came as no surprise to him when both girls ended up getting pregnant at fourteen, but it was scandalous when they both got pregnant by that ill niggah Scotch, who was supposed to be Pearl's man. Irish had come a long ways from his days of wildin' in the streets and fuckin' niggahs up, but when it came down to his daughters it was a real short trip back to the trenches. Menace had gladly helped Irish beat Scotch down and toss him off in a gutter. And after Irish battered that niggah until he cried like a bitch, they gave Scotch the choice of either leaving Harlem for good or turning up dead in a Dumpster full of trash. He made the right choice.

But even with Scotch run up outta Harlem it didn't put no dent in Diamond's show. Diamond had a lot of book smarts but she couldn't be pulled outta the clubs unless they were on fire. Menace hated to say it, but the girl was a street skank. She was on a never-ending baller hunt, slumming around in local clubs and rolling with some of the grimiest niggahs on the Harlem street scene. Diamond spent more time servicing niggahs on her knees than her father could have stomached, and even though she was gorgeous and had mad cats sniffing up her ass, she grew fixated on the one thing that she damn sure couldn't ever have: him.

Menace just wasn't interested. He was turned on by a different kind of woman. A shorty with style and class, somebody who was going places and wanted more than just some dick out of life. But Diamond was tryna slide all over Menace's pole. He ducked and dodged her hot ass more than a little bit, and it wasn't long before Irish peeped what was going on and ordered his youngest daughter to back off and leave his pup alone.

Menace was relieved. Not because he couldn't handle a chick like Diamond and lay some bone on her that would have her sprung for life, but because he wasn't interested in what she was offering. He saw straight through her act and understood that the only thing she felt she had of value was that trap door between her legs. Diamond was just like a lot of other young hood chickens who did all kinds of shit to get his attention. She didn't trust her brain so she relied on her body, and giving up the ass was the only way she knew how to get some validation in her life.

But Pearl was a lot different.

Yeah, she had gotten pregnant out there fuckin' with shiesty nigs like Scotch, but she had much more gloss on her glow than her sister did. Men flocked to Diamond because her shit was wide-open, but Menace had always thought Pearl was the finest of the two and had more smarts and substance than her sister could ever possess.

Like her twin, Pearl had a crackin' body, but she had a brain on her too. She was shy and intellectual, and Menace liked the way she took her time to think about shit before jumping off buck wild like most chicks did. Pearl had goals and dreams and she loved and respected her father down to the bone. Even though she'd had a baby at a young age, she'd learned a lot from the experience, and Menace could see that having Sasha in her life had made Pearl grow up fast and become a better woman.

But while Pearl had always had Menace's respect and admiration, she would never say the same thing about him. At one time the two of them had been vibing. Hard. They'd spent a lot of time together at the outreach center, and Pearl always flocked to him whenever he was at the house. When Menace moved into his own crib, Pearl was one of the few people he would let up in his space. Menace was staying in a rented room above Nastee's back then, and Pearl used to come up with her schoolbooks and watch movies and study algebra and physics too, especially if there was something going on in class that she didn't understand.

Menace was a star in math and science, and once Irish had gotten him enrolled in school again he'd taken off, busting out classes so brilliantly that it wasn't long before he was in his right grade and ready to graduate. He'd enrolled as a freshman at Manhattan Community College while Pearl was still in high school, and she looked up to him like he was the smartest cat in Harlem and knew everything under the sun.

She'd swung by his place one afternoon while he was practicing karate katas and sat cross-legged on his bed, transfixed as he put his sweat-covered muscular body through a series of complex empty-hand and weapons moves.

He had pushed his little bit of furniture to the edges of the room and stood in the center of the floor and performed martial-arts attack and defense movements that were sharp and fluid, brutal and precise. Pearl had sat there watching him intently, and he was conscious of his half-naked body and the way his tight stomach and bulging chest and arms were affecting her.

She came over to him at the end of his session while he was stretching and put her warm hand on his chest.

"I wanna learn how to move and fight like that," she said, stepping closer to him. Her fingers slid down his damp stomach until they were resting lightly on the band of his sweatpants. "Can you teach me?"

Menace knew what time it was. Pearl mighta been young and timid, but she was already a woman. It was all in her eyes, Menace saw; the attraction and the awe, that hot physical thang that told him Pearl could be his right then and there, if only he would allow her to be.

He'd swallowed hard, his dick on mega-rock. He had honeys chasing him up and down the block and could get up in some wet gushy whenever he wanted to. But none of the birds he knew were anything like Pearl. None of them affected him the way she was knotting up his drawers and swelling his heart right now.

He didn't remember who moved first, but moments later he was devouring her mouth, sucking her tongue as she moaned and slid her fingers up his sweaty back, pulling him closer. Menace's dick was swollen in his pants as he rubbed up against her trying to get closer to that sticky stuff. He lifted her slightly as he pulled her to him, cupping her bold ass and rubbing her through her jeans.

Somehow they made it over to his narrow bed and Menace took it up a level by sliding his hand under her shirt and palming her right breast. It was firm and thick, her nipple a tight little pebble that seemed to grow under his fingers.

Laying her down and lifting her shirt, Menace sucked all around her thick breast. The bulging top, the underside, everywhere. When he finally took her nipple between his lips, Pearl moaned and spread her legs slightly, letting him know she wanted to be touched down there too.

Tonguing her down, Menace unbuttoned her pants and slid her zipper down. He felt heat on his hand as he dipped his fingers between her legs, probing her hot pussy as she moaned again and opened herself wider to him.

Menace stood up and took off his sweats. His dick was black and strong, and so damned erect it nearly touched his navel. Pearl wiggled her hips as he helped her out of her pants, then she sat up slightly as he pulled her shirt and bra over her head and flung them on the floor.

"Yeah," he said as he stared at her naked beauty. Pearl had it. She had it all. From top to bottom she was a stunna and a work of art. Her body was strong and firm, and she was phatty exactly where it was necessary.

Menace dropped to his knees and tapped her leg so she could scoot to the edge of the bed. He gripped her curved thighs. He slurped at that pussy like a drowning man, licking her soft pink slit and swirling his tongue around on her clit.

Pearl was loving it. She was open and ready, purring like a cat, the honey in her spot bubbling over and spilling out on his sheets.

"Get the plastic," she told Menace as he gripped himself and stood up, guiding his dripping dick toward the center of her caramel thighs. Damn that pussy tasted good. He was ready to slide all up in that. He left the bed and walked naked over to his dresser and got some plastic from his top drawer. He stood with his back to her, fingering the smooth package and wrestling with his dick and his conscience.

This was Irish's daughter he was about to bang.

Pearl wasn't no ordinary chick who he could roll in and outta his sheets, nor did he want to. He wanted to be with her. To know every inch of her and take damn good care of her. He wanted Pearl to be his.

Seconds later, Menace was back at his bed, wrapped up tight and ready to put in work. He stood staring down at the creamy package of goodness laying on his sheets. Menace dug the shit outta Pearl, and tasting her on his tongue was the sweetest thing he had ever done. She wanted him too. The way she wrapped her long legs around his waist and rode him as he entered her, her hands stroking his arms, her mouth latched on to his nipples, was proof of that.

They fucked slow and deep. Menace pulled out a couple of times just so he could love Pearl all over. He kissed and licked everything on her, including the soles of her feet. Pearl kissed him all over too. She lay down on the bed as he stood over her and sucked his dick into her mouth. She gripped his long black shaft with the rim of her lips, and tickled the head with her tongue.

Slurping and purring, Pearl opened her throat as Menace fucked into the warmth of her mouth. She had never tasted anything like his sweet black licorice in her life, and she would have been happy to suck him off all night.

But Menace had other plans.

He extracted his joint from her mouth and ran the head lightly over her lips. Tickling her chin, he slid his dick down her neck and over to her right breast. Rubbing the wet head over her nipples, Menace fucked her beautiful plump titties, teasing her sensitive nipples and dripping pre-cum all over them until they were hot and slippery.

Pearl gasped and moaned as her breasts got even fuller and her nipples hardened into miniature stones.

"Beat 'em up . . ." she panted, squeezing her legs together and pumping her hips into the air as her clit surged with need. "Beat these titties up!"

She lifted both breasts toward him as Menace gripped his dick and lightly slapped her nipples back and forth with his mushroom-shaped crown. With her breasts moisturized with his slick pre-cum, Menace held his dick like a bat and slapped and rubbed, slapped and flicked Pearl's nipples, slapped and fucked into her breasts until she came, arching her back and crying out his name.

Menace was in total control as he pushed Pearl's legs open wide and entered her. He fucked her with gentle passion and desperate need, making sure he covered all her spots and hit the back of her pussy with firm, deep strokes. He made her cum long and hard, time and time again, and he felt absolutely complete when he finally sucked hard on her neck and busted inside of her, his whole body trembling with love spasms, his heart beating fast against her soft, sticky breasts. Menace had never felt better in his life. Rocking with Pearl was more powerful than anything he had ever imagined.

But a few minutes later he felt guilty as fuck too. Irish was his street daddy. He trusted him to do the right thing by his daughters. And in the aftermath of the sweet love they had just shared, Menace grew cold on Pearl as deep shame crept up on him.

What kind of man, what kind of *son*, was he? He'd trespassed against Irish and repaid his kindness by fucking his daughter, even if she did have a big place in his heart. There was no way he wanted to be dicking Pearl under the radar. His debt to Irish was too big for that. His loyalty too deep. It had taken every bit of his gangsta, but Menace had sent Pearl packing.

"Rise and fly," he'd told her coldly as she lay naked and intertwined in his sheets. The pain and confusion in her eyes was a pretty good match for what he was feeling in his heart.

"Time to go, Pearl. I got me a phat hottie on her way over here, baby, and Shawty ain't no joke. Rise and fly."

If Menace had never experienced the wrath of a chick who'd been tossed, he felt it that day. Pearl hadn't jumped bad or talked shit, or even cursed him out, but the stunned, wounded look in her eyes had almost killed him. She got up and put on her clothes quietly, and when she walked out of his door, for the very first time since the day he'd buried his precious mother all those years ago, Menace cried.

CHAPTER 16

Pearl had cut his ass off after that. There were no more study sessions, no more late-night movies, no deep conversations, not even any admiration. She walked around him giving off hostile vibes like she had no respect for his humanity. Menace knew he'd hurt her young, tender heart, but he also knew it was necessary. Maybe later, he consoled himself. Maybe when she was older and out of her father's house, and after he'd repaid Irish for his kindness and had something more to offer his daughter than sweet kisses and a stiff dick.

Menace tried to forget about Pearl, concentrating instead on his work at the center and graduating from college. Yeah, they crossed paths a lot still, but Pearl wouldn't even look at him and she damn sure didn't speak. He tried to stay cool with her anyway, afraid that Irish or Zeta might notice the sudden tension between them, but the only one who really seemed to notice was Diamond.

"You two been fucking?" she asked one day as he rang the bell and Pearl answered the door. As soon as she saw it was him she'd slammed the door shut and sauntered her pretty ass off toward her room.

Menace had pushed the door open himself, and shook his head as Diamond grinned from the sofa where she was playing with Sasha and Chante.

"What's up with all that?" she said, giving him a devious look. "You got sweet little Pearl flossing? Walking around here slamming doors and shit, like she pay the rent?" Diamond giggled and crossed her long legs. "Yo, Pearl acting like you mighta gave her some of that."

"You trippin'," Menace had told her.

"No I ain't. *Pearl* is trippin'. I'm just trying to find out why."

Menace shrugged and tried to play it off, but a guilty conscience is a real bitch.

"What you doing here anyway?" he shot back grilling Diamond hard. "Somebody stole all the poles out the club? That's why you finally came around to check on ya shorty?"

"Don't be worrying about my shorty!" Diamond laughed as Menace walked away looking guilty. "My daughter is well taken care of!"

If Menace thought Diamond was gonna stop there, he was wrong. She had a grimy heart that fucked up heads. While Menace knew her and Pearl were close and the entire Baines fam had mad love for each other, there was some twisted shit in Diamond that had her feening hard for the street life. And no matter how much Irish talked and counseled her, she was attracted to the gutter and didn't seem to mind living in it.

Plus, Diamond was manipulative and slick. She was so fuckin' hot and had the kind of body that busted straight outta her clothes. Menace was a man, and of course he saw and appreciated her bold curves and stacked frame, but there was nothing about Diamond that made him want to lay pipe on her, and he didn't have no problem breaking that shit down to her a few days later when he was doing some work at their crib and she bust up in the bathroom with him while he was taking a piss.

"Yo," he said, still leaking and holding his dick as she barged in on him without even knocking. Diamond was naked except for a small hand towel that barely covered anything, and she made sure Menace got a good look at her big round titties and strawberry nipples. "Why'ont you chill the fuck out, girl? Get out. Be gone! Can a niggah piss in peace?"

"I didn't know you was in here," she said, grinning. Her hips were bodacious and the triangle between her thighs sprouted soft, neatly trimmed light brown hair. "I'm 'bout to take a shower. Wanna wash my back?"

The yellow bitch was bold, Menace gave her that. Irish and Zeta were right down the hall in the kitchen and Menace could hear them talking. He stuffed his limp dick inside his pants, then flushed the toilet and moved toward the door.

"Cover that pussy up, Diamond. You up in ya father's castle right now. The strip joint is down the street."

Diamond wasn't even insulted. She laughed as she stepped in front of him, blocking the door as she peered down at his crotch.

"You's a piper, Menace. You got a big dick on you. It's nice and fat, even when it's soft."

Menace gripped her shoulders intending to move her out of his way, and that's when Diamond made her move.

"Yeah, niggah!" she broke free and gripped his neck. She pressed her titties into his chest as she humped her naked pussy all over his thigh. "I been wanting some of your shit for a long time!"

Menace leaned back as she tried to kiss him and she nipped at his chin and licked her tongue across his cheek instead.

"You crazy!" he said as Diamond plastered her body to his, still grinding. He tried to push her away and ended up with a big soft titty in one hand, and the phat curve of her humping hip in the other.

"Sssh . . ." she giggled, trying to stay glued to him as he fought her off. Still attempting to kiss him, Diamond locked her lower leg around his and squeezed his thigh between hers, moaning as she rubbed her clit all over his pants. "Daddy's gonna hear us . . ."

The words weren't even outta her mouth good when a shadow fell across the bathroom door. Menace looked guiltily past Diamond and straight into the blazing eyes of her twin.

"Fuckin' trick niggah!" Pearl muttered and shook her head in disgust. Her angry eyes raked over Diamond's naked ass as Menace gripped her by the hip and arm.

Pearl smirked and shook her head. "I shoulda known you wasn't shit."

CHAPTER 17

Pearl stood in the doorway of No Limitz watching Menace as the pain he'd caused her in the past came alive in her heart and replayed in her mind. She hadn't seen him since her family's burial. He had been a pallbearer for her father, and had gone up to the podium with countless others and testified about what a good man Irish had been.

Pearl had barely made it through the service. It was held in a large chapel in a funeral home because Zeta's church didn't have room for four caskets. Countless people had turned out to pay their respects and see the Baines family off, some coming from as far away as Europe. Irish had had a real long arm and an extremely giving hand. He mighta done the criminal thing during the first half of his life, but he'd cleaned it up royally during the second half, and nobody could deny the good that he'd brought to the people of his community.

Pearl had been freaked out at the sight of the closed caskets being rolled down the aisle, too horrified to imagine what the bodies inside must have looked like. Cole had to hold her up as large posters of her family's smiling faces were placed on top of the caskets. Pearl had fallen out on the floor at the sight of Sasha's school picture from the second grade. Her baby had just lost her two front teeth and she looked sweet and angelic in the photo that rested on her hand-carved, snow-white coffin.

And the burial had been even worse than the funeral.

The cemetery was quiet and Pearl had felt like she was moving through a thick gray haze. Her ears were buzzing as the preacher prayed over the bodies for the last time and the sympathetic mourners expressed their condolences into the grief-filled air.

All four bodies were being interred in the same burial plot, and when someone handed Pearl a bunch of roses and led her over to the edge of the grave, Pearl did more than throw the flowers down into the open pit.

Her baby was down in there! And so was her loving mother. Pearl reached out to toss the flowers, and in that instant something came over her and she wanted to jump down in that hole right along with them.

She didn't even remember moving, but Pearl found that she had broken free of the gripping hands that had tried to hold her back. She plopped down on her butt and tried to slide into the open grave where her whole family was waiting.

"Baby, *no!*" mourners screamed and cried out as they lunged for her. The preacher sent loud prayers toward the heavens, and Pearl kicked her feet and dug her fingers into the fresh, soft earth, wishing she could go to sleep and let it cover her too.

She was hauled out of the grave dirty, screaming and crying. One of the ushers got in and hoisted her out while another usher grabbed her arm and dragged her over the edge of the hole. Pearl lay at the edge of the grave and tasted dirt in her mouth. She plunged her face down into it, praying it would fill her throat and nose and choke the breath from her body so that they'd leave her right there where she belonged. Right there with her precious family.

Pearl was out of her mind with grief, and one of the church mothers knelt down beside her. She brushed the dirt from Pearl's face and urged Cole to call an ambulance. Pearl remembered very little after that. She had been whisked off to the hospital and sedated, so she didn't get a chance to talk to Menace at all. He had gone back to Philly without coming up to the hospital, and Pearl was so deep in her grief that she hadn't even noticed.

Seeing him here now was a surprise. A good one, Pearl reluctantly admitted, but still a surprise.

Menace was the last physical connection that Pearl had to her past. He had practically grown up in her house and was her only living tie to her family, and that alone meant so much to her. Everything about him was familiar, and the firm but understanding way he handled the street-hardened youngheads sitting at the computers reminded Pearl why her father had loved and trusted him so.

"What are you doing here?" she blurted out the moment Menace was free. Their love-hate relationship had lasted for years and Pearl had gotten in the habit of spitting harshly at him whenever she spoke.

And Menace had some shit with him too. He'd been wrongly accused and he refused to take any heat from Pearl, so he bit back every single time she attacked.

Pearl mean mugged his ass. She knew he'd seen her standing there the whole time, but he'd igged her until he was done talking and had dismissed the young'uns for the day.

"'Sup, Pearl," he finally responded. "I'm in here running shit. What it look like?"

His voice was deep and butter-smooth, and every time Pearl saw him she couldn't help but notice how much he'd matured since the day her father took him in. Menace had graduated from Manhattan Community College and gone on to Columbia University, where he studied finance and economics. He'd gotten a prime job, then opened a financial consulting firm, all while still putting in work part-time at the center for Irish.

Being around the young'uns and staying close to the streets had kept Menace hard-nosed and hood certified, but he was also a thinking, well-educated black man, the kind of cat that Pearl and many other black women found intensely attractive.

But even with all his accomplishments, his rugged, handsome face, and that ferociously sexy body that could break concrete, Pearl couldn't forgive him. She let that shit he was talking slide right off her then rolled her eyes and gave him the shitty face.

"How long you been back in Harlem?"

He shrugged. "A minute. I went to the cemetery on Tuesday, and I came by and opened up the center day before yesterday."

Pearl swallowed a knot of sorrow, remembering the taste of grave dirt in her mouth. She wasn't strong enough to go back to that cemetery yet. It was too soon. Not yet.

"Well, I remember telling Cole," she said, shaking her sorrow off, "to make sure this place was locked up tight after the funerals. Who gave you permission to bust up in here and open it again?"

Menace stared at Pearl for a quick second, then shrugged again.

"I didn't need no permission, Pearl. And I didn't bust the place open neither. My name is on the lease and I got a key. Your pops made me a partner in the bizz years ago, but your selfish ass was prolly too wrapped up in your own dreams to notice."

"I was busy in *college*, Menace."

He shrugged. "I went to college too, yo. But I ain't the type to stray too far from my fam. I got my degree and then stuck around out of gratitude for the man who raised me. That's more than you can say."

Pearl got heated. The only reason she had stayed away for so long was to better herself, and who the hell was this gaming niggah to cast judgment on her anyway?

"Look, I didn't come by here to kick shit around with you—"

"So," he cut her off with a hard glint in his eyes, "why your lips still flapping then?"

Pearl eyed him. His fine face was tight and he was giving her the killer glare.

"What the hell is wrong with you?" she said, squaring up to him. "Why you looking at me like you got some mafia in you? I'm the one who should be catching a damn fever! I'm the one who lost my whole fuckin' family!"

Menace closed the gap between them in two strides. He got up in her face and Pearl got ready to fuck him up. This niggah mighta been a hand-to-hand martial arts champ in the tristate area, but he'd never seen Pearl get down.

But when he grasped her upper arms and pulled her close enough that she could smell the cologne coming all off his neck, fighting him was the last thing on Pearl's mind.

"*We* lost our fuckin' family, Pearl! *We* lost them! Irish was the only daddy I ever *had*. And Zeta was so good to me she woulda made my dead momma smile. You so fuckin' *selfish*, you know that? It's always about *you*. I lost just as much as you did in that fire, Pearl. Just as fuckin' *much*!"

Even though her heart was bamming in her chest, Pearl forced herself to calm down. She knew all about the love that Irish and Menace had shared. Each of them had found something in the other that they'd been lacking, and even in her anger Pearl didn't wanna shit on that. Their relationship had been too important to Irish for her to diss it, and Pearl knew her father would have been upset with her for that.

But it pissed her off that even after all this time she still had conflicting feelings about Menace. What they had shared in his rented room on a rainy night so long ago had been magical and special. There was no fuckin' way he coulda been faking all that hot loving he had put on her, or lying when he whispered all those sexy words of love in her ear. No other man had ever made Pearl jump for the stars or kiss the sun the way Menace had, but the way he had dished her off afterward, and the shocking vision of him standing in her family's bathroom humping with her naked twin sister chilled Pearl down in her soul. While her heart told her one thing, her logic told her something altogether different, and Pearl knew she was eventually gonna have to choose between the two.

"I know you loved my family, Menace. And I'm not trespassing on that."

She swallowed hard and looked deep into his brown eyes. He was still gripping her arms. Their bodies were touching and she could feel the heat and electricity that flowed between them, even when they were mad.

"So let me go, Menace. I ain't got no beef with you. I came back to see if I could find my sister and to settle some family business. That's all. I didn't come here looking for no fight. I came looking for Diamond."

But Menace didn't release her and he didn't move away. He stood looking down at Pearl as their midsections kissed and her sweet lips almost grazed the hard muscles of his chest. As mad as he was, Pearl had him wide-open. He was bent on her, and it took a lot of effort and control for him to ease off when his dick was straining and his heart was thumping. All for her.

"Pearl," he said, his voice soft and low. There was no anger left in his eyes. Only love and pain. "I don't know how to say this in a way that ain't gonna fuck you up . . . but its something I know I gotta say . . ."

Pearl stepped back, alarmed by what she saw on his face.

"Say what??"

"Diamond is gone, baby. She's long gone. Her body was found at a dump site a couple of weeks ago and they're holding it at the city morgue until a family member claims it."

It took Pearl a second to understand exactly what he was saying, and when she did she broke all the way down.

"Diamond is dead? And you didn't tell me?" she wailed, her heart shattering in pieces all over again. Grief slammed into her chest, and then extreme anger surged through her whole body and before Pearl knew it she had slapped the shit out of Menace and gut-punched him too.

"Pearl," he whispered.

Her fingers were poised for a jab and moving toward his exposed throat when he caught her hand and stilled it in his big fist.

"I'm sorry, Pearl," he whispered gently, pulling her close. There was nothing but love and compassion in his arms as he rested his chin on top of her head and rocked her. "I know it's a shock, and I tried to tell you as soon as I found out . . . but ya man didn't want you to know. He was blocking. He answered your phone and said finding out about Diamond would kill you 'cause you wasn't strong enough to take it."

Pearl allowed herself to melt into Menace's chest.

"Nobody told me!" she wept pitifully. "Nobody told me a

goddamn thing!" Diamond . . . Diamond . . . she had come in this world with her twin and Diamond had left it without her. "Oh my God . . . *Diamond* . . . where is my sister? I wanna see my goddamn sister!"

Menace shook his head. He knew that was impossible. Diamond had been found surrounded by tons of rotting trash. Her body had decomposed and been picked over by bugs and rodents.

"I can take you down to the morgue but there's nothing to see, Pearl. Whoever killed Diamond tossed her in with the trash and sanitation took her to the city dump. Like I said, I wanted you to know. I tried to call you but ya man was blocking hard . . . *he* didn't want you to know."

Cole. A cold anger seeped into Pearl's heart. That selfish motherfucker. Carlita had called it right about him. She'd tried to warn Pearl about fucking with possessive-ass men like Cole.

"They eat your pussy real good *one time* and think they own you forever," Carlita had joked, and in Cole's case she was dead-on.

Pearl knew Cole had kept her away from her sister on purpose. He was small-minded and jealous of Menace, no matter how many times Pearl told him they hated each other. Cole just wanted her all to himself, no matter what it cost her.

But grief quickly overwhelmed her, blocking out her anger. Deep in her heart Pearl had known something bad had probably happened to Diamond. Her sister had her faults, but there was no way in fuck she would have missed that heartbreaking family funeral if she had been able to make it. With all the grieving Pearl was doing for the girls and her parents, she had pushed her fears for her sister into the subconscious of her mind and hoped for the best.

All that horrendous pain came rushing back to the surface now, though, and Pearl slid down Menace's body as her knees buckled and she cried loud, gut-wrenching tears for her twin.

"I'm sorry, baby" was all Menace could say as he lifted her to her feet and stood strong with her close in his arms as he tried to comfort her. "Cry if you need to, Pearl. I know it's hard baby, but it's gonna be okay."

Pearl cried until she was cried out. She was grateful when Menace led her to the small bedroom Irish had furnished in the back of the center and laid her down. He took off her shoes then slid in next to her and held her in his arms. He kissed her hair and rubbed her back as he murmured soothing words in her ear.

Pearl could only lay there and whimper. She was drunk with grief, but also feeling safe and warm, secure in the arms of the only man she had ever loved.

CHAPTER 18

Later, when her tears had finally dried up, Pearl had gotten up to pee and wash her face. When she came back in the room Menace was sitting up on the bed waiting for her.

"You okay?" he asked gently.

"Yeah," Pearl snapped. She hated herself for breaking down in front of him. For being so weak when she had big things to do. "I'm straight. You can leave now."

"Nah," Menace said, standing up and getting his attitude on too. "This is my shit, not yours. *You* can get gone."

Pearl sighed, but she couldn't raise her eyes to look at him. "I'll be gone after I get what I came for, Menace. I need time to go through my father's papers. I need to take a look at some of his files."

"For what?"

Pearl sighed again. "I have to find out what my father had going on when he died. Who he was dealing with, what kind of dirt he was trying to clean up. Those criminals murked my family for a reason, Menace. Either my father had something on them, or he found out something they didn't want him to tell. They didn't kick in the door and burn down the house just because he was helping young dudes come up proper. Something else was going down. Something shiesty. I need to know who my father was dealing with, and what he was after."

Menace shook his head. "If your pops wanted you involved with that kinda grime he woulda put you on, Pearl. Irish always protected you from the slime. Just let shit rest, okay? The guilty will get theirs, no doubt about it. Just go back to D.C., where you got a good job and a good life. Leave the thug life for the thugs like me to figure out."

Pearl exploded. She couldn't believe the shit he was talking.

"Somebody killed my whole fuckin' family, Menace! You expect me to just accept that shit and not try to find out who and why? Them niggahs is probably walking up and down the street real chill right now! Looking right through the front door and laughing at us, 'cause they know they got away with murder! You might be able to lay down on that, but I can't."

It was Menace's turn to explode.

"I ain't laying down on a goddamn thing! You don't know shit about me, Pearl, or shit about what I do! Irish was my street daddy, and you can believe I got eyes and ears out there just waiting for a niggah's head to pop up so I can slice it off! What you think I came back here for? I'ma find out who shit on your fam, but it was your pops who trained me. I was a soldier in Irish's army! He warned me about charging in all crazy for get-back, Pearl. He taught me to think when I was dealing with shit on the streets 'cause Irish got his payback by saving just one more kid, by snatching one more black boy outta the gutter. That's how your father handled shit, Pearl. He hit back like that."

"That was back then," Pearl said as she heard the words her father had spoken to her from the grave.

Get even, Daddy's Pearl! I want you to get even!

"Daddy mighta felt that way back then. But everything is different now. Like I said, I need to get in his office. I wanna check out a few things."

"Look, I shut my business down for a month, just to come here and find out who killed your father, and to figure out what I'm gonna do with the rest of my life. I ain't got nothing but time to piece shit together. If there's anything in Irish's files that links back to his killers, trust me, I'll find it and handle it. So go home, Pearl. Go on back to ya little fairy-tale life in D.C. with that soft, comfy niggah Cole."

Pearl stared at him hard, and all the pain and determination she felt was contained in one look.

"I'm getting in that office, Menace. With or without you."

Menace shrugged. He had seen that look of do-or-die determination before. In the eyes of Pearl's father. He reached into his pocket and tossed her a key.

"Then I guess it's with me, then. If there's any information in those files, then we'll have to find it together."

Seated at her father's desk, Pearl spent the next three hours going through the file cabinets in his office. Irish had been even bolder and badder than she'd known. Like Menace had said, Irish had always taken great care to shield Pearl from all the shady shit that went down in Harlem. He was wise and forward thinking like that, and didn't want nothing that was going down on the Harlem street scene to jump up and bite Pearl later.

Irish had explained that Pearl might one day need to qualify for a top-level security clearance, and he didn't want anything about his former life of crime or his current business rivals to stand in the way of her dreams.

Pearl had been happy to stay out of Harlem as much as possible at her father's command, but that meant she knew very little about what had been going on in his life that might have made somebody want to murk him. The things she was learning about her father right now made her head spin. Irish had a few top contacts at the Bureau, and for a moment Pearl wondered if he had done something or pulled a few strings to help her get into the FBI Academy.

She read through the folder eagerly, and to her amazement her father had been meticulous with his shit. Irish had kept detailed notes and handwritten files on his enemies and their ventures. While fighting for his community he had been in recent contact with his high post political connects all over New York, New Jersey, Connecticut, and Philadelphia.

One name that kept coming up in Irish's notes over and over again was some cat called Mookie Murdock. Irish's log revealed that he had asked one of his connects to watch Mookie closely, and there was a detailed file on him and his crew, complete with several color photos labeled with names, and brief notes on each person's habits and criminal characteristics.

Seeing the underworld through her father's eyes, Pearl learned that Mookie was a local kingpin who was responsible for all kinds of ill shit concerning drugs, gambling, identity theft, and racketeering. But unlike other urban linchpins, Mookie was a virtual recluse. He kept himself out of sight and almost out of mind.

"What do you know about a dude named Mookie Murdock?" Pearl asked Menace without taking her eyes off the file.

"That nig's nasty bizz," Menace said, frowning. "Your father hipped me to him a little bit. Mookie runs a lot of shit, but primarily he's a gambler. They say he's one of the fiercest primetime underground betters in the tristate area. Mookie puts grand stakes on sporting events, boxing matches, horse races, football, and basketball, but he don't just stop there. He'll bet on anything as long as the odds are good. And from what your pops said, Mookie don't just bet like no ordinary hustler, either. He gambles *big*. Real big. But always from a distance. A niggah like Mookie likes to keep clean hands, so he gets his manz to do all his dirty work."

Pearl absorbed that info as she read through the file further. Irish's notes indicated that Mookie ran an illegal numbers game, took wagers under the table at the racetracks, and had a slew of trainers and professional athletes, especially boxers, who were in his pocket and got paid good money to throw games and matches.

And from the rest of the stuff Pearl read, it seemed like Mookie also had a distinct cruel streak running through him too.

"So that's why Diamond got all her fingers smashed . . ." Pearl bit her lip and mused as she read a copy of a letter that her father had sent to a federal law enforcement agency some months earlier. In the letter, Irish described an incident where his daughter had nearly had her fingers cut off after pulling a scam in a Connecticut casino for a man named Mookie Murdock. Pearl remembered Diamond getting fucked up and ending up with both her hands in casts, but Diamond had given her so many bullshit versions of how it happened till Pearl couldn't keep the stories straight.

But it was all right there for her to read now in black and white. Irish's letter said that Diamond had been caught skimming some illegal casino bank, and as a concerned private citizen and community activist he was pressing the authorities to investigate the business dealings of Mookie Murdock.

Even good men had their limits, and Pearl's father had had his. Irish hadn't so much as thrown a cigarette butt on the sidewalk for over fifteen years. He was truly a reformed man. But if Mookie thought Irish was gonna lay down on what had been done to his child, he was dead wrong. Irish didn't fuck around when it came down to his daughters, and he'd vowed to put a stop to the kinda shit that Mookie had done to Diamond and what he was doing to their community in general.

"Mookie had some dealings with your father a while back," Menace told her. "He offered to skim a little cream off the top of his profits if Irish would turn his head and look the other way when he saw Mookie coming, but you know your pops wasn't about none of that."

Pearl's eyebrow shot up.

The dealings with Mookie were just one more thing she didn't know about her father. She felt like a little blind mouse, bumping into all kinds of shit in the dark.

"Yeah," Menace continued. "Irish despised that fuckin' bottom-feeder. Your pops wasn't the look the other way type of niggah, so him and Mookie stayed battling hard for the young souls in this hood."

Pearl couldn't help but ask.

"Do you think Mookie mighta had something to do with killing my family?"

Menace shrugged.

"I can't say, Pearl. I mean, that shit definitely crossed my mind, and even before the funerals I put some feelers out there to see what I could find, but Mookie's shit was locked up real tight. Your pops was surprised when Mookie fucked Diamond's hands up out in public 'cause he ain't the type to bring attention to himself. If Mookie was behind the murders then he sure cleaned up quick as shit because I couldn't find a speck of dirt nowhere near his ass."

Pearl nodded as she listened to Menace and studied Mookie's photograph. He was one ugly muhfuckah. She heard Menace talking but she wasn't sure about all that. She knew how her father got down when it came to his girls. The brutality that

Mookie had orchestrated on Diamond was all Irish needed to declare an all-out war on his beastly looking, overweight adversary.

Yeah, Pearl finally sighed. Judging by the file, war had certainly been declared, but from where Pearl was sitting it looked like Mookie had won. While Irish had used his life experiences and motivating personality to keep his boys coming back to No Limitz so they could escape the ghetto and do something positive with their lives, Mookie had been busy sliding the young'uns designer gear and expensive sneakers he got from professional basketball and football teams. He'd dress them up real nice and tight and put a little gwap in their pockets, then put them on the corner to run numbers, sell tan goods, and keep their eyes open for fresh young pussy meat. It was a constant struggle between good and evil, but Pearl was proud to know that no matter how much ground he lost, her father had refused to bow down in defeat.

In fact, as Pearl read on she discovered that before his death, Irish had found himself an inside man in Mookie's organization. Together, they had been working hard to clamp down on Mookie's most lucrative source of income: his gambling ventures. Irish had called a friend who worked for the federal authorities and they got hot on Mookie's trail and forced him to go even deeper underground than usual and wait for shit to cool off.

But things hadn't cooled off, it seemed. If anything, all that heat focused on his gambling and intricate identity-theft operations had been burning the shit outta Mookie's black ass.

Pearl wondered. Could the Feds have been hounding Mookie so hard that he'd decided that the only way to get the heat off his ass was to light a fire under Irish's?

Pearl thought back to her conversation with Cole about Patrick Ewing's Summer Basketball Classic and tried to fit all the pieces together. According to her father's notes, Mookie normally ran his gambling operation from a distance. But Cole had told her that high-rolling parties at major events like the Basketball Classic drew a lot of vice-related activity, including prostitution, liquor, and gambling.

Pearl figured she probably needed to get next to Mr. Mookie Murdock and take a closer look. With the type of betting crowds that Cole said showed up for major sporting events, Pearl figured Mookie would be all over any opportunity to stack some paper during the Classic weekend. Hell, he was so big-time that he'd probably take his entire operation mobile. A capo like Mookie would sponsor all the pregame and after parties, and provide all the hoes right out of his own stable. And he'd have his finger on every dime that was wagered too, Pearl bet. Yeah, a moneymaking weekend like this would probably be straight up Mookie's alley.

But getting up close and personal with Mookie might be easier desired than done. If her father's files were right, Mookie was hardly ever on the front lines of any of his operations, and getting next to him was damn-near impossible unless you had come up with him on the streets. Pearl guessed that's where her father's inside man had come in. He might have been the pathway for the Feds to get some inroads to Mookie, and he was probably scheming on some sort of takedown or coup.

Pearl read everything in front of her at least twice, and by the time she was finished, a whole lot of puzzle pieces had fallen into place. She was organizing the files into a time line and planning to go through every scrap of paper one more time with an eagle eye and a fine-toothed comb, when she remembered something.

"You ever heard of a place called Club Humpz?" she asked Menace, thinking about that call she'd gotten from her high school lover Vince some time back. He'd told her that Diamond was doing some heavy dancing and stripping up in there and pulling in big bank.

Seated at his own desk, opposite of Irish's, Menace nodded.

"Yeah," he said and leaned back in his chair. "It's up there on the Ave. Your sister was hung up on that joint. It's Mookie's place but Yoda Green runs it day to day."

Pearl nodded. "My father wrote a lot of notes about some inside man at Mookie's club who was giving him backdoor information. Somebody who was close enough to Mookie to flip on him. I wonder who it was?" Pearl said, nodding toward a ledger in her father's handwriting that detailed his contacts and activities with the man with no name.

"Yeah, the inside man," she said, tapping the document that Irish had left behind. "If Mookie sent somebody to kill my family, Yoda Green might know exactly who it was. If I can hook up with Yoda then maybe I can find out who this inside dude is."

Menace looked at her. "Like I said, your sister spent a lot of time slumming over at Humpz, so I know your father despised those niggahs and had no respect for them. But don't take your ass over to that club trying to do nothing without me, Pearl, ya heard? Them niggahs will be all over you. I told you I got my feelers out on the streets. Let me deal with Mookie and them, aiight?"

"Hmm . . . ," Pearl said like she hadn't heard a word that came out of his mouth. "You used to play a lot of basketball, Menace. Tell me what you know about Patrick Ewing's Summer Basketball Classic."

"What the fuck do basketball have to do with keeping you safe, Pearl?"

"Just tell me what you know about the Classic. Please?"

"I know it's hot." Menace shrugged and said, "They pull some of the best young talent in the nation together. East Coast teams against West Coast teams. Even with the refs taking bets and shaving points, them young dudes bounce that rock."

Pearl nodded. "Yeah, but what goes on outside of the arena? Before and after the games are played?"

Menace frowned. "The usual shit. Niggahs go to fancy hotels to party and drink, chase hoes, listen to music. Of course they got plenty of drugs flowing up in them hotels, you know that. But they also gamble big-time, chicks do apple bobbing and big-booty contests, and give celebrity lap dances. You know. The kind of low-post shit that happens behind the scenes at every professional sporting event."

"I bet Mookie's gonna be at that Basketball Classic. I wonder if I could get up on him while he's there," Pearl said. "You know, find a way to get close without him knowing it."

"Don't fuck around, Pearl," Menace said, narrowing his eyes. "Gimme a couple of days. I might be able to dig up some shit in that direction."

"I didn't say you, I said me."

Menace got swole. "Yo, Pearl! I'm telling you, don't go up in there without me. They'll eat ya ass out. They got police, politicians, and all kinds of Harlem law enforcement in they back pockets, girl. You been rolling with the FBI for two minutes and now you think you bad enough to fuck with Mookie Murdock? Well, what you got, huh? Tell me what the fuck you got?"

Right then and there Pearl's mind started clicking and calculating like a computer. Instead of reliving her worst nightmare and trembling under the weight of her dead daughter's accusing cries, Pearl was visualizing strategies and tactics, developing a plan of action, readying herself to implement her sophisticated line of attack. There wasn't a drop of fear in her at that moment. No grief either. Only a cunning, calculated wrath that was focused strictly on the bizz at hand. The bizz of gettin' even.

Pearl narrowed her eyes and glared at Menace, thinking, *This niggah must not know about me.*

"I got a plan," she said finally, glaring coldly into Menace's eyes. "I got me a plan."

CHAPTER 19

Walking out of No Limitz, Pearl's mind continued to whirl as she pulled her suitcase behind her on the dreaded streets of Harlem. Her initial plan had been to come back to New York and find out anything she could about her sisters' whereabouts and the murder of her family, but now that Diamond was dead and she was onto Mookie Murdock, it was time to move forward and do what needed to be done.

The inside man her father had written about was now her first target. No matter what Menace said, after reading through Irish's folders Pearl was convinced that Mookie had ordered her family's hit. If she could find that inside man and convince him to help her the way he had been helping her father, then she could figure out how to go about attacking Mookie from the inside.

She walked the city streets, just soaking up the depressing sights and the rotten flavor of Harlem. A lot had changed since she used to run these streets. Old houses had been abandoned or torn down, and quite a few brownstones had been renovated. Old businesses had closed their doors and new ones had opened.

Still, she had to admit that there was no place on the face of the earth like Harlem. All the storefronts, the bodegas, the brownstones, the project buildings and tenements . . . it was a place of hard times and sorrow. A melting pot of danger and excitement. Young girls walked around looking lost and turned out by the age of fourteen, and almost every young dude of color looked like he was posing to have his face plastered on a wanted poster.

Pearl walked past the funeral home where her family's homegoing services had been held.

Her heart quaked. She had suffered like hell on these streets and her family had been murdered here. Once she did what she came here to do Pearl didn't give a damn if she never saw or smelled Harlem again. The earth could open up and suck the whole damn neighborhood down a shitty drain as far as Pearl was concerned.

She pulled her suitcase along a few more blocks until she found what she was looking for.

Club Humpz.

It looked harmless in the daytime, but Pearl knew shit would be live and popping come nightfall. She eyed the chained doorway with her bottom lip trembling. She was gonna get up in Club Humpz. Get up in there and do some damage. Pearl knew Diamond had walked through those same doors countless times, but who knew if her sister had ever walked back out?

Pearl continued to walk the city streets for over an hour. She stopped at a pizza shop and ordered a slice, then sprinkled crushed red pepper flakes all over it before tearing into it like she used to do when she was a kid. When she was done, she bought a MetroCard, hopped on the 4 train, and headed downtown to Grand Central Station.

Once there, she walked through the terminal until she found what she was looking for. Glancing around to make sure there were no fiends scoping her, Pearl opened her suitcase and pulled out the clear plastic bag that held her jewelry, credit cards, and driver's license, and stashed it in a long-term locker. It was Tuesday, and Pearl knew the Classic wouldn't begin until Friday. If she handled her business properly, by Sunday it would all be over. A killer would be dead, her conscience would be quieted, and Irish would have his revenge.

Pearl put enough money for the locker to hold it for six days, and then she joined the throng of fast-moving New York pedestrians as she headed toward the cheap motel off Forty-second Street that she'd made reservations for earlier in the week.

The Sunset Motel was one of them funk-nasty hot-sheet joints.

Located on a side street lined with metal garbage cans that swarmed with bold, hungry city rats, there was an ancient marquee outside whose letters had fallen off long ago, and hoes and junkies staggered in and out the door in droves.

Pearl stepped over an alky who was passed out in the doorway, and she didn't even flinch when the smell of rancid piss hit her so hard it made her eyes water. She lifted her small travel bag over the skinny, sore-infested man, and wondered briefly where his people were and why the fuck they'd left him out on the mean streets of New York all alone.

After checking in and paying with cash, Pearl took the stairs up to her room. She had specifically requested a second-floor unit, and even if they had placed her all the way up on the tenth floor she wouldn't have trusted the raggedy elevators. They sounded like subway trains moving down the dusty shafts, and Pearl had no intentions of getting stuck in a hot, pissy box and having to break her way out.

The room was unlike anything she had ever seen. Menace had asked where she was staying but there was no way in hell she would have told him about this place. Even during those early years when her, Diamond, and Zeta lived in a shelter while they waited for Irish to finish his bid and come home and set them up proper, life hadn't been quite this bad.

There was a lumpy-looking bed in the middle of the floor covered by a blanket that was so old and thin, you could see straight through it to the dingy sheet below. The pillow was about a half-inch thick, and the faded flower pillowcase looked older than the blanket. Pushed against a wall was an antique dresser that had once been very beautiful. Pearl trailed her finger through a quarter inch of dust and saw that with a good stripping and refinishing it would probably be worth some pretty good doe.

The bathroom made the rest of the room look like a palace. The sink was discolored from years of dripping water, and a crumbly rust stain ran from the faucet to the drain. Pearl wrinkled her nose. A huge, nasty-looking water bug sat at the base of the bowl, its antennae waving in the air as its bulging eyes stared left and right.

Pearl held her breath and glanced over at the toilet. It was old as hell and a foul smell was coming up from the pipes. There was no toilet tissue on the roll, and a stiff, tough-looking hand towel hung over a rack, right above an old used bar of Ivory soap.

It was perfect, Pearl thought. Exactly what she needed.

An off-the-path spot to rest her head and cool her heels. It was raggedy, but she didn't plan on spending a whole lot of time here anyway. She'd be too busy handling her business and working on her plan to dig Mookie's black ass down in the dirt where he belonged.

Taking only her wallet with her, Pearl left the room and locked the door behind her. A pretty young ho with pink bows in her hair was giggling near the elevator as a trick pinned her up against the wall and gripped her ass and slobbered all down her neck.

Pearl gave the girl a sympathetic look as she stepped past, then pushed through the exit door and ran down the slimy steps. She crossed the lobby, dodging working girls and their johns. A few white men in business suits gave her questioning looks, wondering if she was available for an hour, but Pearl shook her ass right past them. She knew what time it was. Mr. Baker, the highly paid corporate lawyer, was supposed to be at a business lunch or out conferring with a client, and instead he was spending his lunch hour in a grimy little pussy pad, getting his dick sucked by a desperate Forty-second Street ho for twenty dollars a nut.

Pearl walked the streets until she found a Duane Reade drugstore. She purchased bleach, liquid laundry detergent, one can of Raid, four large beach towels, and some air freshener. On her way out the door she saw some large folding chairs on sale, the kind that come in a canvas bag that can be folded and carried over your shoulder, and she grabbed a couple and went back to the cash register and paid for them too.

Back at the roach motel, Pearl opened her suitcase and pulled out the items she had brought along especially for this mission. She stripped out of her traveling clothes and took her regular little pink panties and bra set off and balled them in a knot, thrusting them down into the bottom crevices of her bag.

Quickly she stepped into a bright yellow thong and matching bra set, and wiggled her juicy ass into a pair of cutoff jean shorts that made her phat pussy print look like a delicious camel toe.

Next she pulled a tight white tank over her head that was cut low in the front and the back, and made her golden skin look bronze and beautiful. Her arms were tight from endless push-ups, and her stomach and back were sexy and toned.

Pearl slipped on a pair of five-inch sandals that she'd seen her sister wear in a different color, and strapped them around her deceptively slender, feminine, shin-breaking ankles.

The dainty little rhinestone earrings she was wearing had to go, and Pearl opted for a pair of gold hoops that set off the angles of her face, then she raised her ponytail higher on her head and teased the ends of her hair until a curly bush hung down past her neck.

It took her five more minutes to get her makeup right, and after misting her body with the same brand of perfume that Diamond used to wear, Pearl was set. She stood in front of the dresser and looked at herself in the cracked mirror and was astounded by what she saw.

It sure as hell wasn't Pearl Baines, FBI Special Agent, who was staring back at her. It wasn't her twin sister Diamond either, a hot Harlem stripper also known by the club name N'Vee. No, the hottie reflected in the mirror was somebody altogether different. She was Daddy's Pearl. A trained FBI agent, a heartbroken mother, and a daughter on a mission. She was Daddy's Pearl, and for those low-life ballers and hustlers who had picked the wrong family to hit, the chick in the mirror was about to become their worst nightmare.

THE
EXECUTIONER

If prime pussy was what you were looking for, then Club Humpz was the place to be on Friday and Saturday nights in Harlem. Located next door to a gambling joint, Humpz specialized in showcasing the finest bitches in the Greater New York area, and Tank Parker, one of the managers, pimped each one of them with deadly control.

With three stages, nine poles, and six dance cages, ass got flung to all four corners of the club nonstop on the weekends. Tank was an ex-NFL star wide receiver who prided himself on choosing bitches who could make a niggah nut just from looking at them.

A firm ass was essential to landing a job at Humpz.

And it wasn't just the fact of having a lot of junk in the trunk, neither. All Tank's bitches sported an organized trunk. There were no jellyrolls or nasty stretch marks or patches of cellulite or cottage-cheesey dimples to be found on any of his strippers.

The same thing went for the tits. Tank liked them high and tight. He even went as far as measuring the distance between a stripper's nipples and her navel, and if that shit came up too short, he tossed her down the steps and straight out the back door.

Tank was out taking care of some business for Mookie, but Yoda Green was sitting at the bar on Thursday evening when the doors to Humpz banged open and a sexy, honey-colored chick strode in. She was tall and had killer legs that were not only toned and muscular but were also shapely as fuck, like an artist had penciled them onto a canvas.

"Who dat?" Yoda said, nodding toward his boy Donut, who was holding down the bar.

"All hoes come in through the back door!" he heard his nig Krazy Kevvie yell as the jawn entered.

Miss Tight Body pushed past Kevvie and cursed him out good. Kevvie wasn't used to bitches spittin' back at him, and Yoda coulda sworn the bouncer's oversized left eye got even bigger as his hand swung back to crack her.

"It's cool, Kev," Yoda hollered quickly. "Let her through, man, and be cool."

Donut Johnson looked up as the girl sashayed in. Her banging hips swayed slowly from side to side as she took her time heading in their direction. It had been a minute since he'd seen a body as tight as hers. He could tell from the front that she was packing a hammer in the back, and he knew she would rake in big doe just by wrapping her strong pretty legs around a pole.

"Can I help you, sweet stuff?" Donut said as she walked up and leaned on the bar. The bitch was bad. He coulda stuck his whole arm down between her titties. Her cleavage was just that deep.

She grinned and Donut's dick jumped on rock.

"Yeah. I'm looking for the boss. I need a job."

He stood up and grinned right back at her.

"Is that right?" he asked, rolling his toothpick around in his mouth as he looked her over with mad appreciation. "Yo, climb up on that stage right there. Lemme check you out."

The chick laughed and turned around to do what she'd been told, and Donut's breath got caught in his throat. She was a gangsta. Her waist was petite and V-shaped, and them ass cheeks were perfectly round and phatty, like her pockets held two bouncing-ass ghetto basketballs.

She stood on the stage grinning at him with one hand on her vicious hip. Her smile sparkled and her eyes danced with playfulness.

"Turn around . . . ," he commanded hoarsely. "Lemme check out that ass back there again . . ."

The chick rotated her body slowly, rocking her lower half in a deliciously sensual motion that kept her upper body straight while her bangin' bottom did a sensuous hoola-hoop.

Yoda Green was just as mesmerized as his boy was, and he spoke before he realized he had opened his mouth.

"Grind it," he urged her. "Grind it down to the floor."

Both men watched silently as the gorgeous girl wiggled her ass and dipped her chips. She dropped it the right way, the way a man liked to see it fall, and both men gazing at her were biting their lips and gripping their dicks at the sight of the fresh new meat performing for them onstage.

"The pole," Yoda urged her. "Take it to the pole."

She was on it. Mami rode that pole like it was a smooth, golden dick, gripping it between her thighs and sliding her juicy breasts up and down the metal. Her nipples poked clear through her shirt and the bottom of her ass cheeks slipped from her tiny shorts, and even though both men saw much ass and twat on a regular, they had never seen it being showcased quite like this before, or from a woman who was so confident and beautiful and oozing such mad pussy appeal.

Finally, Donut couldn't take it no more.

"Aiight!" he said, grabbing his crotch and adjusting his hard dick. "Damn, if you that good with ya clothes on, I can't wait to see you get naked. Tank handles all the hiring, but he ain't here right now. I know what he likes, though, and I think I can speak for him when I say you're our type. You got a job, baby. You sho'nuff got ya self a job. Matter fact, I predict you gonna be our next mainline act, sweetie. The top stripper in our lineup. What's your name and when can you start?"

The girl standing on the stage laughed and climbed down.

She switched her gangsta hips over to them and stood with her arm resting on Yoda's strong shoulder.

"You read me wrong, Big Boy," she told Donut with a laugh. "I'm not a stripper. I'm a bartender." She gazed down into Yoda's near-empty glass. "Looks like Daddy here is ready for a refill, so how about I get started right now? And as for my name?" She giggled again. "I go by a lot of things. But you can call me Karma."

Yoda had been a major henchman for Mookie for years. He was a come-up cat who was loyal and hardbody, but who appeared to lack the cutthroat brutality needed to run a large-scale grand operation.

What almost everybody agreed Yoda was good for though, was keeping his eye on things and muscling niggahs up if they got too far outta pocket. He was big and cockstrong, and had played a little football in high school before he got kicked out for exceeding the legal age limit for a public school student.

Yoda was one of the first cats Mookie hired when he took over

```
          TRANSACTION RECORD

             ARBY'S #1576
      8201 Jefferson Davis Highway
         Richmond, 804-271-7249


CARD TYPE:VISA
No. ***********8664 EXPI.:
ENTRY:SWIPED
AUTHORIZATION:02795C
STORE #:1576
TERMINAL:2
REFERENCE:193

PURCHASE              $22    67

             THANK YOU
       APRIL  4,2019 13:24:30
       Server's name : Dorcas

          CUSTOMER COPY
```

for Capo, and he had stood in for the publicity-shy Mookie when they opened the doors on Club Humpz. His job wasn't exactly security, but it was to make sure security got to where it needed to be. If a muhfuckah got crazy and started wildin' in any of the rooms, Yoda was the first one to know it and he made sure every little spark got squashed out before it turned into a flame.

Mookie had taught Yoda the importance of keeping shit on the low. Humpz hosted high-profile, important clientele, executives, athletes, and public officials who dropped top dollars to get their fill of his stable of young, firm flesh, and the last thing they needed was some bullshit static to pull the dark curtains off their extracurricular activities.

And that's where Yoda came in. Yoda kept his finger on the pulse of the joint. He knew who was in the house, and where they were. He knew what strippers were onstage, which ones were in cages, and which ones were on their knees giving wet sloppy head in the comfortable little curtain-enclosed cubicles in the back of the club.

Yoda held shit down heavy, and when Mookie wanted to travel the country for gambling trips or to visit the racetracks or the casinos, Yoda was responsible for making sure shit was straight for those occasions too.

Today, Yoda took a nice long whiff of the sexy-ass hottie who was leaning on his shoulder and made a real quick decision. Shit, he'd seen her first. Even before Donut. There were always a bunch of paid-ass niggahs on the prowl at Humpz every night. Them ballers pushed phat whips and flashed grills and diamond pinky rings, and had mad gwap flowing from their pockets like tap water. They were wolves on the hunt, and some prime prey like sexy Karma would get snatched up in their jaws like a sweet tender calf, and then where would that leave lil old Yoda?

"Check this out," Yoda told her with a slick twinge in his

voice. "We ain't hiring right now, baby. Bartending gigs are pretty tight around here. But why'ont you come in the back and let's holla for a minute. I got something else in mind that might work for you."

Pearl grinned at the baller she was leaning on. His shoulder was rocked up with muscle and he looked just like the image in the picture she'd taken from Irish's file cabinet, only darker. Yoda Green was his name, and doing Mookie Murdock's dirt was his game. Pearl nodded, raising up, but keeping her eyes on him as he stood and raked his gaze over her body with clear appreciation.

She licked her lips then stared so deep into his eyes she could almost see straight into his empty brain. He didn't look all that sharp to be anybody's inside man, but he damn sure knew something about Mookie. Pearl flashed him a gorgeous smile and followed him away from the bar and toward a narrow stairwell along the far wall. Just looking at the back of Yoda's head made something vicious rise in Pearl's gut. Like the rest of Mookie's crew, this bastard was gonna get his, she swore inside. Yoda might not have given the orders to wreak devastation on her life, but Pearl had a feeling that his hand had helped dig the dirt and plant the seeds that made the wicked tree of her misery grow.

Yeah, Yoda seemed nice and dumb, like he couldn't hurt a fly, but Pearl had learned enough in FBI training not to let a suspect's outward persona fool her. The fact that Yoda was leading her into the private area of the club was proof that he was down in a major way, no matter how stupid he looked in the face.

In short, Pearl was gonna work Yoda's ass half to death. He might not have been the brightest bulb in the box, but Pearl had a feeling that Yoda knew a whole fuckin' lot for a dummy. Which is why Pearl decided to get a piece of his grimy ass first.

CHAPTER 21

The back rooms of Club Humpz were phat.

The décor was top-notch and no expense had been spared on the high-quality consoles, televisions, and natural-stone flooring that ran throughout the rooms. Even early on a Thursday, before any customers rolled in, Pearl could tell a lot of money flowed through the doors and shit got poppin' in this joint. In addition to the profitable number-running operation she knew Mookie had going, there was a poolroom, a movie theater, a kitchen, and a very large recreation room where about twenty card tables and chairs were arranged along the walls. Pearl knew from Cole that while card games were bet on at the tables in gambling halls like these, big time cee-low was shot in the middle of the room. There were also a bunch of tiny rooms with nothing but beds in them. Pearl could only shudder as she imagined what kind of cold fuckin' young girls subjected themselves to on those nasty sheets every night.

"You ever been here before?" Yoda asked as he showed her what Club Humpz had to offer its clients.

"Nope," Pearl answered honestly. And then she lied. "I just came up here from Atlanta, though, and we have plenty of hot spots like this in the ATL."

Yoda led Pearl through a doorway and into an area that was warm and cozy. There was a Jacuzzi, a sauna, and lots of green plants arranged in oversized brass pots positioned around the room.

"We don't allow no regular hoes back here." Yoda beamed. "This is where we bring the real special jawns. The dimes like you."

The moment Pearl entered the room, her breathing got heavy. It was like something was tightening around her throat, and standing there looking at the beautiful blue water and smelling the faint aroma of chlorine, Pearl felt herself getting dizzy.

Chill bumps broke out all over her body. Pearl felt herself trying to black out. She stumbled backward as her throat closed up and all the air in the room seemed like it was being denied to her. Pushing through the doors, Pearl flung herself out of the Jacuzzi room, and immediately sucked in deep lungfuls of cool, sweet air.

"I couldn't fuckin' breathe in there!" she gasped as Yoda joined her in the hall outside the room. Pearl bent over and swallowed hard. She was surprised to find she was clutching her own neck. "I couldn't get no air!"

Yoda shrugged. That's what he didn't like about gaming-ass chicks. If the bitch was skurred of water she should have just said so.

"Not a problem, doll. You ain't gotta go in there if you got a problem with water. I know a lot of other ways to get you wet.

How about me and you get something to drink and watch a little skin flick?"

Pearl forced herself to smile even though a chill was running through her. She didn't know what the fuck had come over her, but something had happened to her in there, for real.

She peeped the skeptical look Yoda was giving her and she couldn't blame him. But since her job was to keep Yoda interested and bust his nose wide-open, Pearl put her hand in his, and licked her lips and said in a sexy little voice, "Mami loves movies. Yeah. Let's do that."

The introductory credits and film title had barely rolled across the screen before Yoda's hands were all over Pearl. She had already prepared herself for this, and knew there was no way she could get next to street hardened ballers like these without giving up a part of herself in return. It would be hard for her, but it was a sacrifice she knew she had to make if it was going to get her closer to her father's killers. Sharing her body with these mothafuckahs would be nothing compared to losing her people. There was but one thing of true importance to Pearl right now and that was revenge. She didn't care what she had to endure, she would do any and everything to exact street justice on her family's killers.

Of course, that meant sucking strange dick and letting some of these thug-ass niggahs drill sideways in her ass, but Pearl wasn't a virgin and she wasn't sexually shy or inhibited either. It was all about the separation of mind, body, and soul. Fucking was going to be a necessity during this operation and Pearl accepted that. She had no qualms about using her prime pussy if it would dull their killer instincts and lure them into her trap. She could ride a dick physically without it affecting her emotionally, and she wasn't above opening her legs and laying on her back if it meant whoever was banging her would eventually get the ultimate fucking. Pearl knew she could get through it. All she had to do was close her eyes and pretend the dude banging her was the only man in the world that she truly loved . . .

Yoda looked okay in the face, but his body was a true masterpiece. His shoulders and arms were rocked up with muscle, and his chest was firm and his stomach cut and tight. The niggah needed to do a little something about his funky cigarette breath, but Pearl ignored that shit and set her mind to making him feel like a fresh-mouthed superhero as she pretended he was her dream lover and touched him and kissed all over his rocked chest, tight nipples, and strong stomach.

Yoda was moaning and humping halfway to heaven as she slipped her hands down the front of his pants and jacked his dick. To Pearl's surprise it had some decent weight to it and was pretty long for a man his height.

There were two Hispanic women and a low-hung brothah getting busy on the screen, and with a funky slow beat and the sounds of a three-way fucking going on in the background, Pearl and Yoda explored each other's bodies with their hands, mouths, and tongues.

Pearl could tell Yoda was hesitant about licking her pussy, which she could understand considering the line of work he was in and all the ran-through bitches he encountered every day, but if she was gonna be all up in his mix then he was gonna be all up in hers too. So when he finished sucking her nipples and tried to rise back up to her neck, Pearl was quick to grab his head and push it down between her legs.

Yoda tried to buck a little bit, but Pearl wasn't having it. And two seconds later, she couldn't have kept his face out of her snatch if she had tried. Just the sight of her juicy, caramel-colored pussy with the neat, precisely trimmed bush turned him out. The clean, fresh smell coming out of her seemed like it was a big relief to him, and he dove into that pussy like he hadn't tasted any in years.

Pearl couldn't help arching her back as Yoda sucked her clit and jabbed his hot tongue in and out of her canal. The sensations running through her were pure physical joy, and she lay back on the plush sofa and spread her legs wide, closing her eyes and pretending it was Menace who was down there lapping deliciously between her thighs.

To Pearl's surprise Yoda was a damn good fuck. He was giving and creative, and he paid attention to Pearl's nudges and directions and pleased every bit of her body before sliding on a condom and plunging up in her and battering her pussy with long, tantalizing strokes.

When they were finished, Pearl massaged his shoulders as Yoda sat between her legs smoking a blunt. He reached over his head and passed it to her a couple of times, and Pearl took a few quick pulls and then blew them right back out without inhaling.

"That was some damn good puddy," Yoda joked, reaching back to lightly pinch Pearl's naked thigh. "I don't know how them niggahs let you up outta Atlanta with ya fine-ass self, but now that I done tasted that I want you to stay right here in Harlem, you heard?"

Pearl laughed. "You dug me out real deep too, Daddy. But I can't stay in New York without no job. I been sleeping on my auntie's couch every night and both of us is getting tired of that shit. She wanted me out last week, but I can't find no place cheap to stay."

Yoda twisted around to look at her. Didn't no bitch this fine have no business sleeping on no old lady's couch.

"Well tell your auntie you just got a change of address. You can chill with me for a while if you want to. And don't worry about no job right now, neither. All the clubs in town are shutting down for the weekend and heading to Midtown for the Summer Basketball Classic."

"Basketball Classic?" Pearl asked, frowning her whole face up as she played dumb. "I don't know nothing about no sports. I don't even like to sweat."

Yoda laughed. "You don't have to know about sports to ball hard, baby. There's gonna be plenty of blow, music, and big-time partying. Whatever you into, it'll be available, trust. Come chill with me for the weekend, aiight sugar? I'll treat you right and introduce you to all the major playas in the happening town of Harlem."

Pearl shook her head quickly. "I can't be going away for the weekend just to hang out. I need to get out on the streets and hit all the clubs so I can find me a damn job and make some money."

"Relax," Yoda told her. He reached up and grabbed her chin, then urged her downward so he could kiss the worry off her lips.

"I got you, baby. My bank is long. And one weekend ain't gonna take you off the job market. Besides, all the major playas are gonna be right where I'ma be. At the Classic. So let's spend the weekend together, okay? We can use that time to get to know each other better. And if you really wanna work when we come back to Harlem then I'll see about hooking you up with a bartending spot when we get back on Monday. Cool?"

Pearl beamed and licked her lips. This niggah had been way too fuckin' easy.

"Cool!"

CHAPTER 22

Pearl was hyped as she took a taxi back to the Sunset Motel Thursday night. Yoda had taken her shopping on 125th Street, then snaked his whip down to Thirty-fourth Street so she could hit a few designer dress stores and score some fresh shit to get the Classic weekend started properly the next day.

She had shopped like a happy ho spending Yoda's cash, and even though she bought the kind of skanky clothes she would never wear in her real life, Pearl couldn't help noticing how much her new style reminded her of her sister Diamond.

"My aunt is real religious," she had told Yoda, waving off his offer of a ride home so she could get the rest of her things. "She don't believe in boyfriends and all that, only husbands. That's why I gotta get outta her crib. I'm about to go crazy up in there."

"Yo, fuck all that," Yoda said, his big hand gripping her thigh. "Look at all this fuckin' traffic, girl. It's rush hour. I already told you, you ain't gotta go back there at all. You can stay right in Harlem with me."

Pearl wasn't going for that. She didn't give a damn how much traffic was on the roads. She wanted this niggah to drive her back to Harlem so that she could catch a cab right back downtown. She had a lotta shit to do over the next two days. She had serious preparations to make.

"Nah, she's my grandmother's sister. I can't disrespect the old lady like that, and besides, I don't wanna burn no bridges 'cause I might need her again. But don't worry," she said, flashing him a dimple as she bit down sexily on her lower lip. "I'll meet you at the hotel on Friday, okay?" Pearl patted her crotch. "This thang gone stay nice and hot. I promise."

Pearl had smiled inside as Yoda gave her the name of the hotel he was staying at and the room number. "I got some business to take care of in the morning," he told her, "but I'ma leave a key card for you at the desk, aaight?"

Pearl was more than cool with that. And as she rode downtown in the backseat of the taxi she couldn't believe her luck. But Pearl also knew she had crossed the point of no return. She had made intimate contact with one of Mookie's men and set the wheels of her plan in motion. Carlita and her niece Zoe were on the ready and just standing by to help her put the people she needed in place to make her grand finale a success. There was no going back now. All Pearl had to do was stick to her plan, keep her cool, and make sure Mookie Murdock didn't peep her until she was ready to take him down on game day. And with God as her witness, and Irish as her father, Pearl was determined to do just that.

The Sunset Motel was in full swing when Pearl's taxi pulled up. Young chicks lined the streets outside, working their territory harder than most folks worked a tax-paying job. Pain pierced Pearl's heart as she looked into the faces of thirteen- and fourteen-year-old girls who all looked like they were over thirty. She wanted to take them into her arms and wipe away their misery. These poor girls had been working the track so hard that their youth had faded into the wind, and Pearl recalled seeing that same tired look of desperation in the eyes of her twin when Diamond was heavy into the street life.

Seeing the blight and smelling the odor of street sex coming off these young girls just made Pearl hate Mookie and his boyz even more. It was a man like Mookie who Pearl blamed as she watched a thick young ho in a blond wig as she walked up to a tree and spread her legs. Without hesitating, the girl pulled the crotch of her shorts aside and began peeing in a stream without wetting her clothes. No woman had taught that young chick how to do that, Pearl knew. She'd learned that move from a man.

"She must have really practiced that shit a whole lot," Pearl muttered as she climbed out of the taxi with four bags full of designer gear. She strode past the hoes and junkies just like she didn't see them. It wasn't their fault that they were out there. It was society's fault. Nobody had ever told these girls that they could do better, that they deserved better. Most of them just needed to be shown how to take a few positive steps in their lives, and then most of them would be off and running.

Pearl stiffened as they eyed her down. It was in her heart to feel for them, and under different circumstances she would have loved to stop and talk to some of the younger girls and find out what their stories were and how she could help them. But this was New York and if necessary she would fuck them up. No matter how young people were on the streets, if they smelled a weakness they exploited that shit. These little young hoes wouldn't have thought twice about running up on Pearl and shaking her down. Shit, jacking Pearl for her money would beat catching a stank ass trick by a long shot.

The male clerk at the desk was old and fat. He was reading a copy of *Tits and Ass* magazine and Pearl had to clear her throat to get his attention because his watery old eyes were glued to the young white knockers on the page.

"Hi. I'm in room two-forty-seven," Pearl said pleasantly. "Did any mail come for me today?"

The old man nodded. "Packages," he said, pointing at two large boxes that were right next to his chair. "You got two packages."

Pearl eyed the boxes and thought about how she would get them upstairs. No matter how heavy the boxes were, Pearl knew she could handle them. She was strong and fit, and could carry much more than that. The problem was, there were two boxes and she already had two handfuls of shopping bags. There was no way she could take it all up in one trip, but Pearl was hood and she knew the deal. This joint was crawling with fiends who had eyes for opportunity. If she took one package upstairs and came back to get the other, by the time she carried the second box upstairs her room would have been broken into and the first box stolen.

"Can you bring them up?" she asked the old man.

He nodded. "Yep, but I gotta charge you." He shrugged. "Labor, you know."

Pearl knew.

"No problem," she said, reaching into her back pocket and sliding him a twenty. "Just drag them both out here and I'll carry one myself."

Up in her room, Pearl set about getting things done. She turned on her laptop and slid her Internet-to-go card in the slot, then navigated to a local messenger delivery site and set up a pickup and next-day delivery for the next morning from the seedy Sunset Motel to the extravagant Primero Hotel. Once she received a confirmation, she used her FBI-issued pocketknife to slit open just the top of the larger box, then stared for a moment at the contents that had been packed within.

Carlita had done a damn good job.

Her girl was on point. She had supplied everything Pearl had asked for.

The second box was full of stuff Pearl had ordered from hunting and survival stores on the Internet, and she was impressed with the weaponry that she'd selected.

Not even the nasty long-tailed rat that had scurried under the dresser could blow Pearl's excitement that night. She took a cold shower in the crumbling little bathroom and didn't worry about the rust or the mold or the ancient germs that were surely there. As she sat in one of the folding chairs and propped her feet up in the other, Pearl covered herself with her towels and prepared to get some sleep. The only thing on her mind was getting down to business, and tomorrow couldn't come soon enough for her.

CHAPTER 23

But while Pearl was busy snoozing, the night was still young for those who ruled it. Unknown to her, somebody special had peeped her getting out of the taxicab loaded down with all those bags from Michael Kors and other New York City designer stores. Bodies were his business, and a phat physique like Pearl's was hard to miss. It was also hard to forget, and as Pearl took long strides into the Sunset Motel, Scotch Allen could only stare as he watched one of the best pieces of pussy he'd ever tasted walk through the doors of a fleabag motel.

It had been a real long time since he'd seen her. Her pops had made sure of that. Matter fact, that old fool had fucked up Scotch's whole program back in the day. And all because his twin daughters were dick freaks who liked to get fucked in wild, crazy ways.

That niggah Irish Baines had run Scotch straight up outta Harlem. All the hard work and grinding Scotch had done to establish his business had to be abandoned, and he had never forgiven Irish or Pearl for that shit.

Scotch had been back in New York for a quick little minute now, and had amassed himself a small stable of young bitches who worked the track on his behalf, but most of his drug connects had dried up while he was gone, and somebody new was slanging rock in his territory now.

Scotch narrowed his eyes as he watched Pearl switch up to the desk and say something to the clerk. She was finer than ever, and truth be told he had fucked up by boning Diamond behind her back. Scotch had dug Pearl. Dug her hard. Fucking her sister had been just like banging any other ho—something fun to do—and if Pearl had asked he could have told her without a doubt that her pussy was way better than Diamond's.

The thing was, Scotch hadn't even known Diamond was pregnant until Irish and his posse rolled up on him and tried to kill him. And even then he wasn't sure the baby was his because Diamond had been giving away free pussy out of both panty legs. The girl was a freak and she was seriously run through.

Stroking his trimmed beard and keeping one eye on his corner bitches, Scotch watched as the hotel clerk came out from behind his locked partition pushing two boxes. Pearl grabbed the bigger box and the old man took the smaller one, and both of them disappeared through the stairwell doors.

A true street hustler, Scotch always kept his ear to the ground. He didn't have no territory in Harlem anymore, but he still had a couple of manz up that way. He'd heard Irish had finally gotten his due, along with his wife and granddaughters too. The fact that both of the dead little girls could have been his daughters meant nothing at all to Scotch. He'd sampled so much young, new pussy and fucked so many bitches that he could have had hundreds of kids out there. Two less made him no difference.

What Scotch was interested in now wasn't Irish or his dead fuckin' family. Scotch was an opportunist, and right about now he saw one in the making. There could only be one reason that Pearl Baines was slumming around in a shit box on Forty-second Street. The last time he'd seen Diamond she was all fucked up. Skinny and high as fuck. She was too tore down for Scotch to even consider luring out on the track, but that didn't stop Diamond from bragging about her twin sister and all the wonderful things Pearl had done with her life.

"Yeah, my sister Pearl made it up outta here," she'd told Scotch. They were sitting in an all-night deli on Forty-fourth Street. Diamond had just turned a trick and bought a little blow, and she was hitting a few lines as she spoke.

"My sister is going places and doing shit. She's an FBI agent now, and she done made more arrests than most of these toy fuckin' cops on the streets who be so busy tryna fuck me before they cuff me!"

Is that right? Scotch thought, replaying the conversation in his mind. Pearl was a square now, and there was only one reason she would be out here slumming. Lil Mama was scheming. She had some shit on her brain, a plan for somebody. He remembered how bad she'd wilded on him and Diamond when she found out they'd been fucking. Scotch shook his head. He'd always thought Pearl was sweet and scary, but the crazy bitch had rolled up on him and slid her knife across his chest so quick he didn't know he'd been cut. She'd been aiming at his throat, intending to slit him open, but when she went back in for another swipe Scotch had jumped back, making her miss.

Man, that chick could be a monster when she was wronged.

And right about now she had been wronged royally. Pearl's entire family had been planted. And if Scotch had learned anything about the girl whose sweet little cherry he had busted when she was only thirteen years old, he knew she was all about her biz.

"Yo, Yoda!" he said after dialing a number on his cell phone. Scotch didn't have many old-school partners left in Harlem, but he did have one real important one, and since one dirty hand washed the other in the hood, he never knew when he'd need a solid from his boy. "Whattup, my nig? Check it, you remember that jawn Diamond I used to fuck, right? Yeah, y'all prolly know her as N'Vee. Irish Baines' shawty. Yep. Well, dig, I don't know if you up on this shit or what, but Diamond has a twin sister named Pearl . . ."

It was the "Yes We Can" ringtone that woke him up.

Lounging in his phat Midtown co-op, Menace had been slobbering all over his pillow, deep in sleep, and dreaming of Pearl. *Yes, we can!* he was telling her as they did a slow grind to fast music. Menace had a sweet, plump titty in his mouth and the beat of the music was almost twice as fast as their dry-fuck movements, but neither one of them really cared. *Yes we can!*

The theme music for the Obama campaign was suddenly louder than the music in his dream, and Menace opened his eyes.

"What it do?" he barked into the phone as his other hand slid under the blanket heading for his hard dick. Pearl's scent had gotten all up in his dream and it had turned him on like fuck.

"'Sup, Menace. This Lil Dray."

Menace let go of his dick and sat up. Dray was a kid that Irish had been hell-bent on saving no matter what the cost. He'd come from a rough-riding family of twelve kids, and the boy had shot and killed one of his older sisters at the age of nine for pulling a knife and stabbing their mother. He'd been in and out of shelters and foster homes, and had witnessed his brother get thrown off a roof two summers earlier. Lil Dray had come to Irish just nine months ago, right before his sixteenth birthday. He'd come to them cross-eyed and scrawny, but with a sunny smile and a killer's heart.

Dray had been special to Irish, who always reached further and dug deeper for the really lost kids, the ones that society had written off. Irish went out of his way to rehabilitate Lil Dray. He'd given him a job, got him into a regular high school, and taught him by his own example what it meant to be a real man.

And just like Menace and a whole lot of other former street thugs, Dray had blossomed under Irish's hand. The kid had resisted the lure of drugs and fast money for nine whole months, but now with Irish gone there was no street daddy left to guide him.

Menace frowned. "Lil Dray? Whattup, man? You straight?"

"Yeah, I'm good, man," Dray answered. "I'm good. I just wanted to tell you it was real cool for you to come back to Harlem, nah'mean? Cool that you back at the center now and shit. Irish woulda wanted that, man."

Menace nodded. He was back, but he couldn't promise for how long.

"Yeah. I was hoping you would show up the other day," Menace said. "I was glad when you did."

"Yo, check this out, man," Lil Dray said, his voice going deep and hard like a grown man's. "I heard you been asking around about Mookie and his manz. You and Irish did a lotta good shit for me, so fuck what anybody else think, I'ma go 'head and say what I gotta say. I ain't no fuckin' snitch, but you need to put your eye on Yoda Green, man. One of my sisters be dancing over at Humpz, and she knows all about Irish and how he used to look out for me all the time. She was tight with N'Vee too, and used to help that crazy chick hide whenever Irish sent the cops around looking for her. She could never understand why N'Vee was wildin' so hard when she had a good family who had her back. But the deal is, my sister rolled with Yoda one time when he went to meet Irish. She said them two was real friendly with each other, and shit, and they stayed behind closed doors in Irish's office for hours. My sister said when they came out they was shaking hands and grinning and shit like they was tight.

"The deal is, Yoda hates Mookie with a passion. He despises his fat ass and believes Harlem's treasures are being wasted on that ugly muhfuckah. Yoda promised my sister she's gonna be his top bitch when he pulls a takedown on Mookie, but in the meantime she can't stomach his ass 'cause he's one of the clowns who bum-rushed and smoked Irish! Him and the rest of them grimy Humpz niggahs Mookie got tied on a string. My sister said she's positive that it was Yoda and his boyz Piff, Donut, and Tang who did the kick-door, and they committed the murders too."

"Yo, man . . . Irish been gone a minute now, Dray. Why you just telling me this shit now?"

"'Cause my sister went down south the other day. I wasn't gonna say nothing while she was still in Harlem, but she's out now, man. Yoda and them can't touch her. She's out."

Menace got real quiet but he was thinking harder than fuck. He gave Lil Dray big ups for the solid, and immediately hung up and pressed Pearl's digits. He didn't know exactly what that girl was scheming on, but this kind of information was the best reason he could think of to keep her from going up in Club Humpz without him.

He was nervous as Pearl's phone rang and rang until it rolled over to voice mail. He pressed redial three times before deciding to text her and find out where she was. With his heart beating all up in his throat, Menace sent Pearl an urgent text message, then sat back to wait anxiously for her to respond.

•••

The elegant five-star Primero Hotel in Midtown Manhattan was filled to maximum capacity. Mookie Murdock had rented its biggest, most luxurious suite on the top floor with a penthouse view. Yoda had gotten a smaller suite several floors down, and while it didn't compare to Mookie's lavish weekend pad, it beat the hell outta the hot sheet fleabag joint where Pearl had been doing most of her planning and scheming.

"We gone have us a damn good fuckin' weekend!" Yoda had told Pearl on Friday when she arrived with her bags. She had one suitcase full of clothes, with her special gear hidden on the bottom, and another bag with shoes in it that also held tape, ropes, and three multiuse knives. The third bag was an oversized red Gucci purse with a thick black sweater bulging from the top. The sweater was just a prop to conceal the real deal, because the rest of the bag was packed with the miniature goodies that Carlita had helped her get through FBI supply channels. The hidden weaponry was lightweight and durable, but deadly and effective as hell.

Earlier, Pearl had waited anxiously in her filthy room until the messenger service called and said their deliveryman was downstairs and ready to pick up her packages. She'd given him a phat tip and told him to make sure her boxes got over to the Primero Hotel the next morning.

Yoda had left a key at the desk for her just like he said he would, and the moment she slid it through the lock and opened the door he pulled her close and began tickling her tongue with his.

Visualizing Menace's smooth chocolate face, Pearl sopped up that tongue like it was an Astro Pop, sucking it and licking it and going along with the program like the professional she was. She felt no guilt behind letting Yoda touch her. In her mind the pleasure he gave her came from Menace's hands, from Menace's lips, and Pearl had no problem playing this part of the game. Yoda was her key to getting in Mookie's vicinity, and if she played her hand right and didn't fold that shit too early, by this time tomorrow Mookie would have a spiked joint so deep up his rectum that his nose would be bubbling with shit.

But to her surprise Yoda flipped the tables on her.

They'd ordered a huge room-service breakfast, then fucked for about an hour until they were both exhausted. After taking a long nap they showered and headed out for lunch at an expensive Chinese restaurant around the corner from the hotel. Yoda was all smiles as he held the door open for her and pulled out her chair. Earlier, he'd offered to carry her big red Gucci bag for her as they strolled down the city streets, but Pearl had quickly said no and switched it to her other shoulder.

They ate a light lunch then walked back to the hotel, talking about everything under the sun. Pearl was surprised at Yoda's level of conversation. From what she'd read in her father's private files, he was supposed to be a mental lightweight, somebody who was dumb as fuck and could be easily flipped. But the more they talked about everything from the war in Iraq to the slaughter of Palestinians in the Gaza Strip, the more Pearl realized that not only was Yoda intelligent, he was also very cunning and conniving.

"Nah, not that one," Yoda told her, taking her hand. They were in the phat hotel lobby and Pearl was waiting for one of the five elevators to come down. She had looked up at the lighted floor indicators and saw that the last elevator was closest to the lobby and would arrive first. "That's the penthouse elevator," Yoda explained, pulling her gently back toward the first cluster of elevators. "You need a code just to get upstairs in that shit. I ain't big enough to put you in that one yet, but trust, I will be one day real soon."

There was something slick in Yoda's tone that got Pearl's attention, but the full extent of his craftiness became apparent later that night as they lounged in his suite. Yoda ordered lobster and champagne from room service and continued to treat Pearl like a beautiful black queen. He nibbled her toes and sucked her fingers, and pulled off her pants and licked all behind her knees. Pearl sighed as Yoda peeled her panties off and kissed up the back of her thighs until his nose was in her pussy. He licked her out from behind, holding her ass cheeks open with both hands as he thrust his tongue into her wetness and licked and sucked her clit.

Pearl's stomach muscles clenched as her body melted. She closed her eyes and bit down on her lip, coming up on her knees so he could reach every inch of her. She was just about to get hers, and was humping and grinding her ass all over his face when someone knocked on the door. Yoda tapped her hip and pushed her away.

"Room service!"

Pearl scooped up her panties and jeans and ran into the bathroom as Yoda answered the door. Her nipples were aching and her pussy was still popping. The enormity of what she had to accomplish over the weekend had her stress level way up there, and it only took her a minute or so to finish herself off with her fingers as Yoda took care of the waiter in the other room.

Pearl left the bathroom calm and focused.

"Yo, check it. I gotta go to a meeting in a few minutes, okay?" he said as they ate dinner.

Pearl tightened up again. She had been planning to drop a few innocent questions on him about Mookie and his gambling habits, but she wouldn't be able to find out a goddamn thing if this niggah left her in the room by herself. She forced herself to smile brightly and get herself together on the inside. No problem, she assured herself. She would simply adjust fire. She could use the time while he was in his meeting to take inventory of her attack bag and make sure everything was in order for the next morning.

"Cool, baby," Pearl said sweetly. "Just don't stay gone too long. I might miss you."

Yoda grinned and took another bite of his lobster. They ate shit up, enjoying their meal. Yoda popped tabs on the Cristal and they drank together, with Pearl being careful not to down more than one glass of bubbly.

But one glass was more than enough.

By the time they were done eating Pearl felt herself slipping.

Her left eye was acting up and the room started getting hot. Yoda was looking at her funny. Whereas he had spent the entire day serenading her with sexy looks and sweet talk, it was night-time now and Mister Yoda was talking big, stank shit.

"You know bitches these days is real slick," he said, getting up from the table. He stretched for a second and then went to sit on the edge of the sofa. "Just a bunch of gaming-ass hoes. All they want is diamonds and pearls. But you know all about that kinda shit, don't you, Karma? Diamonds and pearls?"

Pearl's stomach lurched.

"I gotta go to the bathroom . . ."

Yoda laughed as she stumbled into the beautiful bathroom with the cool marble tiles. The room was spinning in sloppy circles and she had to concentrate extra hard just to get her fingers to turn the lock.

Yoda continued to laugh on the other side of the door.

Pearl staggered to the toilet and barely got her shorts down. She was in trouble, and she knew it. She had never felt this way in her life, but it wasn't hard to figure out that "dumb-ass" Yoda had peeped her game and slipped something on her. Probably some kind of date-rape drug. Something to take her down without a fight. Her mind was working just fine but her body felt like it had been put on ice. With sweat beading on her nose and between her breasts, Pearl dug in her pocket for her cell phone. The only person she could think to call was Menace, but as soon as she flipped her phone she saw there was a new text message waiting from him.

It said: *Yoda Green murked everybody. Where r u?*

Pearl dropped her phone and almost fell off the toilet.

Every nerve in her body was on fire, and her heart pounded with rage. It took all her concentration to reach down and pick the phone up from the floor. Bracing one hand against the glass shower door, she barely managed to text Menace back. *Primero 727. Come . . .*

A deafening thud vibrated the bathroom door. The phone slipped from Pearl's hand again and sickness rose up in her with a rush. She grabbed at the toilet tissue and tried to wipe herself but her fingers wouldn't do what she told them to. Yoda kicked the door again. Her brain screamed out a warning for her body to get moving, but the drugs had her and she just couldn't. Yoda gave the door a brutal final kick, and this time that shit flew open. He charged into the bathroom like a tornado, swinging blows at her wherever he could land them.

"Yeah, trick!" Yoda yelled as he pulled her off the toilet and dragged her into the living room by her hair. Pearl tried to scream as fire bit into her scalp. Her shorts and panties were around her ankles and the skin on her legs and ass seared with friction burns as she was yanked across the carpet.

She couldn't even scream as Yoda kicked her in the stomach, then reached down and flung her up on the sofa by her neck. She landed on her stomach, her face pressed into her Gucci bag.

"Every fuckin' body thinks Yoda's stupid!" he hollered. He flung her over on her side and capped her hard in the face. "Yeah, Miss Karma! Ya fuckin' government name is *Pearl*! You's *Irish's* seed! N'Vee's sister! You thought you could catch a niggah sleeping? Man, that niggah Scotch said you and N'Vee was twins but neither one of y'all ain't no slicker than ya bitch-ass daddy was! That niggah was supposed to be hardbody but he never even saw me coming!"

Pearl lay there helpless and filled with disgust. Her father had trusted this niggah and ended up getting shit on in the ultimate way. Now he was about to shit on her too. She hadn't missed the fact that Scotch's name had come flying out of Yoda's mouth either, but she couldn't believe it. For almost eight years she'd been hoping and praying that niggah was worm food by now.

Pearl couldn't do a damn thing. She could only moan and listen as Yoda's whole personality changed and the maniac in him came out as he taunted her and described the details of how he had punked her father and banged her mother.

"That was ya shorty we put the flames on, huh? You shoulda heard how loud them little bitches screamed! And ya moms, that ho was *tight*! I dipped my dick all in that gray-haired puddy, girl! Just as hard as I banged it in yours! Yoda dee, yoda daa, yoda ah-hah! That old stuff ya moms had was so damned good! I fucked her while ya pops watched, and then I made her suck Mookie's dick! Yeah, she sucked that niggah's iron dick *clean*!"

Pearl was too sick to respond. She gagged and threw up all over the couch, her stomach wrenching violently. Dark spots were filling her left eye and her lips felt numb. She couldn't bear hearing any more about her family's torture, but Yoda wasn't finished talking shit yet. There was more he had to tell.

"I put the hammer on that old bitch, too, ya heard? Mashed them fingers so good she called me all kinds of dirty muthafuckahs! That was before I rodded her throat, tho, nah'mean? After she sucked that iron dick she wasn't tryna call on nobody but God!"

Even through the haze of drugs and the horror of hearing what had happened to her mother, Pearl's fury was ever strong. She didn't know how the hell Scotch had hipped Yoda to her game, but it didn't matter. This motherfucker wanted her dead, and he meant that shit.

"You thought you was just gonna ride up in here and put that ill na-na on me and make me bite my own nuts, right? You thought I'd bitch out my boss over your sweet little pussy, right? Oh, ya shit is good, I ain't gone lie, but it ain't good as that poison I dropped in ya drink, lil skank. I was gonna let you lick my balls one last time but that spit around ya mouth got you looking a lil raggedy. So just chill right there for a minute, okay, ma? I'ma go cancel that meeting and be right back with the posse. Wait till I tell 'em who you really is! First I'ma let my man Donut bang that sweet gushy real quick, then I'ma let Mook get hold of you. That niggah gonna crush ya neck just like he did ya sister. Bash them little short brains in. Can't no gutta bitch outslick a real hustler. Believe that!"

Yoda talked big shit as Pearl fought the sensation of suffocation. She gasped as she struggled for each breath. The room looped around her in crazy slow circles and the leftover lobster and butter clashed in her stomach and rose to the back of her throat, then came splashing out of her mouth again. Yoda had given her enough drugs to fuck her up for a minute. Pearl battled to hold on to her bowels. Drool slid from her mouth and her left eye twitched violently. She slumped over on the sofa, striking her head on something hard inside of her red bag. She closed her hand over it, feeling it on the sly.

Yoda was still laughing as he walked toward the door, and the sound seemed to come from a million miles away. He had just opened the door as Pearl slipped her hand inside of her purse and dug around sneaky-like.

"Ya daddy wasn't shit," he said over his shoulder, "ya sister wasn't shit, and you ain't shit neither, bitch. Wait till I get back and you gone see how fuckin' with me and my manz can get a ho like you planted like a flower."

Yoda turned to walk out the door and it was nothing but sheer will and determination that gave Pearl the strength to move. With the last bit of strength left in her body, and as the room grew dark and fuzzy, she reached into her Gucci bag and came out with her FBI special miniature crossbow.

With only a glancing aim, she seated her arrow and let it fly, and with fate and the ghost of her dead father's hand guiding its path, the poison-tipped arrow penetrated Yoda's back and pierced the killer's treacherous black heart.

CHAPTER 24

Sometime later—she couldn't tell how long—Pearl heard her name being called and felt herself being cradled in strong, protective arms. Her eyes fluttered open and she saw that Menace was there. He was looking down at her with deep concern as he wiped traces of dried vomit away from her mouth.

"Pearl. Open ya eyes, baby. You okay?"

Pearl struggled to sit up, thankful that at least a little bit of the fog seemed to have lifted from her brain.

"I got your text. Lil Dray was dead on it. Yoda was the inside man. He did the murders too. But you handled him, Pearl. You took that niggah down and got some for your whole family. It's done, baby. It's done."

Pearl looked around. Yoda was laying dead in the foyer, one arm sticking through the crack of the door. Menace followed her eyes, then walked briskly over to the body and dragged Yoda into the room by one foot, allowing the door to close. He locked it, then returned to Pearl and propped a pillow behind her back and covered her up with the blanket from the bed. Next he walked over to the bar and took some ice from the freezer and wrapped it in a washcloth and pressed it against her swollen jaw.

"Can you hold this while I take care of business?"

Pearl nodded, reaching for the ice and touching it to her face where Yoda had fucked her up. She watched as Menace unscrewed the long panel on the room's air-conditioning vent. The suite had its own condenser unit and at first glance it looked just like a closet, except it had a ventilation grille on the door.

She was speechless as Menace removed the grille and looked inside.

"Yeah," he said, mostly to himself. "That'll work."

Without hesitating, Menace went back to Yoda and grabbed his ankle again. He dragged the grimy bastard across the carpet on his face, handling him like the piece of shit he was. Moments later, Yoda's body had been folded and stuffed through the grille and the front panel had been screwed back in place.

For the next fifteen minutes Menace scrubbed Yoda's blood out of the carpet and cleaned up Pearl's blood from the bathroom floor.

"Aiight," he said when he was finally done. The room was pretty straight. Nobody would be able to tell what had gone down in there just by peeping in. "Time to go."

Whatever Yoda had slipped on her was beginning to wear off. Menace helped her to her feet, and Pearl did her best to stand on her own.

"Whoa—," Menace said as he reached out to steady her. Pearl was still wobbly on her feet, and she leaned into him gratefully as he propped her up. She blinked a few times, relieved that the dark spot had faded from the vision in her left eye. But with her vision clearing, Pearl was able to see something else. She saw the small vial of liquid on the coffee table. The one that Yoda had held up for her to see.

"I gotta sit down," Pearl mumbled and staggered.

Plopping on the couch, she bent over and put her head down on her knees.

"You aiight?" Menace asked, worried. "You wanna lay down for a little while?"

Pearl shook her head. Hell no. Not with Yoda's dead ass behind that vent. She was getting the fuck outta that room. Just as soon as she got what she needed.

"Nah, I'm straight. But I could use a glass of ice water, though."

The moment Menace turned his back Pearl went into action. Her hand snaked out faster than shit. She chilled as she heard Menace in the freezer getting ice again. Moments later he was standing over her, holding out the cold glass of water.

"Here, Pearl. Drink this so we can get outta here."

Pearl drank gratefully, washing away the traces of sickness from her mouth. Between sips she asked, "How'd you find out about Yoda?"

Menace grimaced. "One of your father's boyz put me down. A young kid who Irish used to look out for the same way he looked out for me. His sister used to hang with Diamond. She told him it was Yoda, Plus Piff, Tank, and Donut, three of Mookie's other right hand manz who did your family."

As weak as she was, Pearl straight-up ate the words coming out of Menace's mouth. Piff, Tank, Donut. She had it. She finished drinking the water and handed the glass to Menace. "Okay," she said. "I'm ready."

They left the hotel all hugged up, with Pearl's hair hiding the lump on her face as she stumbled beside Menace like a drunken partygoer. In his rush to get to her, Menace had parked his whip illegally on the curb and he was glad nobody had come by and towed his shit away.

"Where are we going?" Pearl asked. Somebody else had rented Menace's old room above Nastee's long ago, and Pearl sure as fuck wasn't gonna let him take her to the grimy hot-ho motel she was staying in off Forty-second Street.

"I got a little spot here in New York," Menace said as he buckled her in. "It's right here in Midtown. That's how I was able to get over here so fast."

He took her to an old clothing warehouse that had been partitioned off into lofts. His crib was a two-bedroom palace with shiny wood floors and huge windows that would have been a blast to decorate.

But Menace wasn't the decorating type. There wasn't much of anything in his crib, other than a small sofa, a folding table he used to eat off, and a big-screen television.

He led Pearl over to the sofa, which was made of soft, fine leather, and went in the kitchen to get her an ice pack. He fixed her a warm cup of herbal tea, then ran her a bath and closed the bathroom door so she could take off her clothes and get in the tub.

While Pearl soaked in the bubbly water, Menace changed the sheets on his bed and got an extra pillow from his closet. He didn't have anything decent to eat in the kitchen, so he tossed a bag of popcorn in the microwave and set the timer. He poured both of them a glass of apple juice, and was just putting a napkin by her plate when Pearl walked into the kitchen wearing a robe he'd left hanging on a hook for her.

"Hungry?" he asked.

Pearl shrugged. "I could use a little something on my stomach." She picked up a few kernels of popcorn, keeping her eyes down like she didn't want to look at him.

"You aiight?" he asked.

She nodded. "I'm good, thanks. But my head is banging. You have any Tylenol?"

"Yeah," he said, getting up. "They're in the bathroom. I'll go get 'em."

Pearl was on her feet the moment he walked out of the kitchen. Dashing into the living room, she snatched her Gucci bag and ran back to the kitchen. Her hands were trembling as she laced Menace's juice with some of the liquid from Yoda's vial. By the time he came back with the Tylenol she had stirred his juice with her finger, then wiped her hand off on his robe.

They ate in silence with Pearl pretending to doze off, nodding at the table. She was glad when Menace tossed back his apple juice and ate the last bit of popcorn from the bottom of the bowl. She thanked him as he led her to his bedroom and told her he would be right in the living room on the couch if she needed him.

"No!" Pearl said, her eyes big and wide. "I don't wanna sleep by myself, Menace. Can you stay in here with me? Please?"

He hesitated, then nodded. Menace waited until she was under the covers, then lay down beside her on the bed. Pearl listened to his breathing in the darkness, and was surprised by how fast he fell off. Her intentions were to be at the Sunset Motel by 6 a.m., but there was still work to be done before she could rest. With Menace snoring softly beside her, Pearl dug around in her bag and retrieved the folder of notes she'd taken from her father's files. She skimmed through the paragraphs, extracting info about the three murderous goonies, Piff, Tank, and Donut, and committed the details to her memory. When she was sure she knew every single thing that her father had known about them, Pearl snuggled down next to Menace in his bed. She ran the next day's plan over in her mind two and a half times before falling off to sleep.

What seemed like minutes later Pearl woke up in a panic. She'd only planned to sleep for a few hours, but after the drama and trauma of the day before, she'd slept deeply until almost noon, which was much longer than she'd wanted.

She glanced over at Menace. He was knocked out and beautiful, and snoring his ass off. After the way he put her on to Yoda then charged in to help her, Pearl felt a little guilty about dropping some of Yoda's shit in his juice.

But just a little.

She had crazy feelings for the dude, but she was working the critical parts of her plan today and she needed Menace out of her way. She figured Yoda had only given her a little bit of the date-rape drug. That niggah had wanted her conscious and aware so him and his manz could torture her ass. Pearl had no idea how much of that shit she should have given Menace, all she knew was that she wanted him knocked out. For a long time.

Pulling on her clothes, Pearl scribbled Menace a short note, then tiptoed quickly out the room. She paused in the living room and thought for a moment, then hurried back into the bedroom. With a final glance at his chocolate fineness, Pearl walked out of Menace's apartment and headed back to the Sunset Motel to finish what she had started.

CHAPTER 25

LeBron James was a king both on and off the basketball court, and gamblers, shot callers, professional athletes, and other high rollers had flocked in from all corners of the country to watch him perform in Patrick Ewing's Summer Basketball Classic.

Madison Square Garden was crawling with nigs. They were freshly dressed in the latest gear and rocking heavy bling, and no self-respecting baller could claim a legitimate game unless he had at least two fine bodied-up hotties on his arm.

Pearl had spent a couple of hours in her seedy Forty-second Street hotel room. She'd nursed her stomach and her bruises from the night before as she ran over her plan, checking and rechecking every single detail in her mind. Everything she and Carlita had ordered had been delivered and set up, and all of her FBI experience and hours of extensive training was about to pay off. She strolled into the lobby of the Garden feeling all shot out but looking like a hot summer dream. She was butter. Her hair, nails, and makeup were stunning and there wasn't a chick in the house who could go head up with her in the looks department.

Last night's battle with Yoda had left swelling and a severe bruise on her left cheekbone, but she'd applied her makeup and styled her hair in such a way that it was barely noticeable. But the shit still hurt like hell. It had her head pounding like a drum and the effects of whatever shit Yoda had put in her drink were still in her system. She was tired as fuck and would have loved to go back to Menace's crib and crawl up in his big old comfortable bed with the three hundred dollar silk sheets and sleep the rest of the weekend away, but there was work to be done, and there was no way she could lay her bones down to rest again until she'd accomplished what she had come to New York to do.

Pearl thought about Menace again and her stomach went tight. He'd looked so gorgeous sleeping his drugged-up sleep. They'd shared something special in the past, and the long-ago memory of how he'd put his sex game down on her so thoroughly and with so much tenderness and passion had her so sprung that for a quick second she had fantasized about abandoning her plans and staying right there in his bed forever, safe in his strong, protective arms.

But she'd killed those thoughts real quick.

No amount of dick whipping took precedence over taking Mookie Murdock's black ass down. Menace had rode in like a champ to save her last night, and that was cool. Yeah, Pearl felt bad again for taking him out of commission, but today was a solo day. The only thing Menace could do today was get in the way and fuck up her plans, and she couldn't have that. She couldn't have that at all.

The Garden was crazy crowded and Pearl sauntered past some of the most notorious drug dealers, organized criminals, and money launderers in the country. She peeped mad faces she recognized from FBI files and criminal reports. There were ballers galore too. The Kobe Bryants, A.I.'s, and Shaqs of the world. The Reggie Bush types, the T.I., Lil Wayne, and Jay Z set, and of course the old sports heads like Jordan, Barkley, and Magic.

Pearl's stunning beauty turned heads and rang crazy bells as she strolled through just to look around. There were thousands of other hot skirts in the joint, but Pearl was one of a kind. Her toned legs were oiled and sexy, and her hips swung wildly in a white skirt and sheath silk top that had cost Yoda a phat hunk of doe, and her backfield was fluffed and phatty. Head to toe, her shit was perfect.

Leaving the Garden and jetting across the street to the Primero Hotel, she used the key Yoda had given her and entered his suite. Everything was just as she'd left it. Menace had done a good job of cleaning up and there was no sign of the fight—or the murder—that had gone down.

Pearl closed the door behind her and locked it. Her eyes slid over to the air-conditioning panel where Yoda's body lay decomposing, and Pearl thought she heard a sound. The sound of a small girl's terrified cries for her mother.

Fuck Yoda, Pearl thought, sneering. *Right up his dead ass.*

One down, four more to go.

Setting her purse down on the bed, Pearl called down to the desk.

"Hi, this is Mrs. Yardley Green in room seven-twenty-seven. I'm expecting a delivery of packages today. Kindly have them sent up as soon as they arrive."

Opening the closet, Pearl pulled out the suitcase that she had packed especially for this weekend and spread the contents out on the bed. Her Attack Pak was stuffed with the best goodies that money could buy. Binoculars, miniature crossbows, rappel cord, blow darts with retractable tubing . . . Pearl was in possession of the most deadly and precise close-combat weaponry available from the FBI arsenal. Everything she needed was right there. She'd downloaded the Primero Hotel's blueprints from the Internet and studied them until she had them memorized and could manuever around the building with her eyes closed.

But Pearl planned on keeping her eyes open. From what she'd studied in her father's files and had been able to learn from Yoda, Donut Johnson was one of the most doggish niggahs in Mookie's posse. He kept a string of bitches on the ready at all times, and in the past couple of days Pearl had never seen him with the same girl for more than a few hours at a time.

She'd already peeped Donut's true game though, almost from the first night they'd met. Pearl had hung out in Humpz in a booth with Yoda that night, but she'd kept Donut in her sights as well. She'd found it intriguing that like most of the dudes who sat mesmerized and watched all the bumping and grinding and air-humping the strippers were doing on the stage poles, Donut was watching chicks, but he was also busy watching something else.

That niggah was watching balls.

Pearl had learned a lot in the profiling phase of her FBI training, and had become very proficient at reading people. What she'd been reading in Donut over the past few days was enough to make her laugh, but there wasn't gonna be shit funny by the time she finished laying on him exactly the kind of loving she had a feeling he was looking for.

CHAPTER 26

"Damn, baby," Donut panted as Pearl arched her back and tooted up her ass so he could go in deeper. She was giving up some back door action, and while she usually enjoyed anal sex very much, she was grateful that Donut's dick wasn't big enough to do any real damage back there.

"You got them thick booty cheeks, mami. Nice and round. Make a niggah have to drill like an oilman to get up in that hole."

Pearl moaned softly and thrashed about on the bed.

She knew damn well this niggah liked ass. He liked ass*hole*. In fact, he was a pillow biter. He was a switch-hitting bottom boy. She was sure of it. Her packages had arrived just fine from the Sunset Motel, and with her Attack Pak stocked and ready, Pearl had rung the bell to Donut's suite carrying a raincoat and the nondescript FBI bag, wearing nothing but a thong and a smile.

"Yoda sent me," she told him as he eyed her magnificent

breasts with the good-goddamn nipples. "Yoda says it's nice to share."

Pearl had run Donut a hot bath and made sure he was comfortable in it as she emptied her Attack Pak and stuck several items under his pillows.

They'd been playing sex games for over an hour now, and Donut had been down for every little freaky thing Pearl had suggested. And, Pearl had to admit, it wasn't hard to freak this fine niggah out!

Donut was the bizz. His stomach was a ninety-pack and his arms were outrageous. He had a cute smile and some pearly whites that glowed in the dark, and a head of curly hair that Pearl couldn't help running her fingers through.

Donut had eaten her pussy out so delicately that Pearl had already come twice. He'd stunned her when he'd taken ice cubes from the cooler and twirled them in his mouth and then slid one up inside her pussy, then thrust another one up her ass at the same time.

Pearl had nearly lost her mind as Donut alternated between sucking and licking out one hole and then the other. He ate pussy tossed with booty salad, and sent shivers through her body that left her hoarse from screaming. Pearl had to force herself to regroup and to remember where the fuck she was, and who the fuck she was with, and what the fuck he had done to her people.

And when she did remember, it took every ounce of control she had for her not to kill that grimy muthafucker right then and there.

"Yeah." She humped and urged him on as he lapped her nookie juice with a soft tongue that felt as big as a washcloth. Donut's face was buried deep in her pussy and Pearl had his head on lock. Somewhere off in the distance Pearl smelled smoke and heard a child's cries. A little girl screamed for her mother to help her, and a cold tremor replaced the steamy trails of passion that ran through Pearl's blood. Her long legs were clamped around Donut's neck, her muscular thighs were ready to squeeze.

Still humping, Pearl maneuvered her body until Donut's lips broke contact with her pussy. He'd been sucking so deep it sounded like a suction cup popping off of her. She twisted until she was behind him and had his face gripped in the crook of her leg, behind her knee, and her calf was pressed against the side of his throat. Curling her toes back, she braced them behind her free leg as it completed the encircling of Donut's neck and trapped him in a headlock.

"Hey, yo!" he protested, raising his hands to claw at her legs.

I could snap this muthafucka's neck right now . . .

Pearl contracted her muscular thighs until she felt Donut suck in a deep breath, then she suddenly relaxed and giggled, raising her long legs above her in the air.

This wasn't part of her plan . . .

"Sorry," she said, laughing. "I get carried away when I nut real hard like that."

Donut sat up grilling her and rubbing his neck.

"Yo, bitch! That fuckin' shit hurt!"

Pearl pouted, then flashed him a sweet look that begged for forgiveness.

"I didn't mean to hurt you, Daddy. It's just that your tongue had me going crazy. You shouldn't do me so good! I get like that when my pussy gets licked so deliciously."

She put her arm around him and eased him back down on the bed. "I'm sorry. Let mami make it up to you," Pearl whispered, sitting behind him and planting kisses on Donut's monster shoulders. They looked like sides of beef and were rock-hard beneath her lips.

She reached around in front of him with both hands and found his tight nipples and pinched them between her fingers. They stiffened immediately, and twirling them gently, Pearl went to work kissing and licking up and down Donut's back and murmuring sweet nasty shit to him at the same time.

She traced small circles on his skin with her tongue, then blew on the wetness before moving downward and sucking until small hickeys bulged and appeared red and prominent.

"Ah, shit," Donut moaned, leaning back. "That shit feels good baby . . ."

Pearl teased and stroked his nipples, all the while planting soft, wet kisses and sucking up hickeys on his back in a trail that lead down to his ass as Donut gasped air through his teeth and started jacking his dick to a nice slow rhythm.

"Lay down," Pearl told him when she had reached his waistline and could go no farther. Donut lay on his back with his dick pointed at the ceiling, thinking he was about to get some neck pussy, but Pearl had another trick for him instead.

"Uh-uh," she said, tapping his thigh lightly. "Turn over, Daddy. On your stomach. I got a game I wanna play with you. You do like to play games, don't you?"

Getting up in Donut's shit was easier than Pearl had imagined. She'd reached under his pillow where she had stashed all of her toys and came out with her prober. It was a six-inch rigid green plastic tube that fit over her finger with soft padded rubber on the outside.

"Just relax," she whispered as she licked and nibbled on Donut's muscular ass cheeks. They were firm and sweet, just like Menace's, and Pearl wasn't acting at all when she moaned with pleasure and the sound vibrated on her lips.

Wetting her toy with the saliva in her mouth, she probed between his legs with her finger and pushed gently at his back door.

Donut buried his face in the bedsheets but didn't protest, and Pearl slid the toy into him gently, finger-fucking him and sucking and licking the mound of his ass at the same time.

Donut gave it up to her. Spreading his legs wider, he arched his back and let her dig him out as he gasped softly and gyrated on the bed. Pearl kept on whispering and licking and sucking, making him comfortable and giving him pleasure for long minutes until his movements became more frantic and she knew her finger was simply not enough.

"Hold on, Daddy," she told him in a low, seductive voice. Her hand went under the pillows once more and this time she came out with the bizzness. Donut lay still, his face pressed into the covers as Pearl quickly strapped up and mounted him, her thighs gripped on either side of his hips.

"Relax," she whispered again, her hand pressing down on the flat of his spine as she guided the head of her nice-sized rubber dick and inched it between Donut's cheeks. He accepted what she was offering with a loud moan, then shuddered as she penetrated him fully.

Pearl lay down on him, her erect nipples pressing into his muscular back. She held his hips and thrust deeply, pushing into him, then withdrew slowly, fucking him like she was a man.

They rocked together, with Donut reaching back and rubbing Pearl's ass as she drooled on his neck and gyrated her hips, pushing hard rubber into him from behind.

"Come up on your knees," Pearl told him as she came up on hers. She pressed her thighs together and sat back on her ankles. Donut backed toward her until his ass was above the dildo pointing in the air, then he bent his knees and lowered his body while Pearl helped guide him down until he was impaled on her rubber dick and nearly sitting in her lap. Pearl grabbed his waist as he raised and lowered himself, slamming himself down over and over again on that plastic dick as Pearl pounded, going hard and tagging his ass the way she knew he wanted it.

And his dick was rock hard too.

She reached in front of him and stroked and squeezed it, sending loud moans falling from his lips. It jerked and spasmed in her hand and Pearl could tell he was about to shoot one off.

Quickly, she released him with one hand and searched under the pillow for the special toy she had brought with her. Her right hand closed over it and Pearl dropped her left hand down and scooped up Donut's big bulging balls and gripped the base of his dick all at once.

Fingering his own nipples, Donut was busy moaning and cumming and slamming his ass down in her lap, and by the time he realized what had happened Pearl was holding his dick and both of his severed nuts up in the air.

The sound he made was a half shriek, half yelp, and then Pearl's right hand moved again, a lightning-fast blur over his shoulder as her fish-gutting blade sliced a second time, this time higher and deadlier as she opened up his throat and cut off his cries.

And as Donut pitched forward on the bed dislodging himself from the plastic dick he'd just been riding, Pearl gazed at her left hand, still held high in the air, as the grimy blood of her daughter's killer ran down her arm and dripped from her elbow.

CHAPTER 27

Game time was approaching and Pearl knew she'd have to move quickly. Nigs were probably already blowing up Yoda's phone and banging on the door to his suite trying to figure out where he'd dipped to. When Donut turned up missing too, it was sure to make Mookie suspicious and get him to tightening up his net, and that was the last thing Pearl wanted him to do.

Killing Donut had been a messy affair, and with no Menace around to help her get rid of the body, Pearl had been forced to handle her business on her own. She had run up and down the hotel stairs searching the hallways furtively but diligently until she found what she was looking for, and if cleaning Donut's bathroom, putting fresh sheets and blankets on his bed, and emptying his trash was the price she had to pay to buy herself some time, then it was a small price indeed.

Right now, Donut's body was wrapped in his bloody sheets and cooling at the bottom of an industrial laundry bin that Pearl had stolen from an unlocked third-floor housekeeping closet. She'd taken clean sheets, a comforter, disinfectant, towels, and garbage bags, and made his room up neatly, then stashed the laundry bin in the rear of the large housekeeping closet where other used bins were waiting to be emptied.

Fifteen minutes later she was back in Yoda's corner suite, preparing to implement the rest of her plan. She would have preferred to stay in Donut's room but she didn't want to risk getting peeped going in and out of there. Besides, a niggah called Piff was next on her list and she looked forward to sending him on a ride. She wasn't sure how she would handle him, but she had more than enough toys in her bag of tricks to give her plenty of options.

After taking a quick shower and swallowing four Tylenols, Pearl changed into a pair of black shorts and some fresh black Timbs. She put on a white belly shirt and covered it with a long-sleeved black hoody, then took an inventory of everything in one of the smaller boxes that had been delivered, laying all the items on the floor to be sure all the essentials were there.

She had just counted out everything she would need when she heard a fuck-noise ringtone cut into the silence. She recognized it as coming from Yoda's cell phone, which was in the pocket of the pants his dead ass was still wearing. Pearl's eyes snaked over to the air-conditioning duct where his body was hidden, and for a moment she thought she could smell his ass, already beginning to rot behind the panel.

She'd have to move fast.

Flipping open her own phone, Pearl sent a simple text message to a woman she had a lot in common with, but had only recently met.

2:30 p.m. Party in the Penthouse. Decorations ready?
Seconds later she had a response.

Cake already baked. Can't wait.

Minutes later she was outside on the large balcony where she spent some time tying and securing the rope she'd brought to the right side of the railing and around the metal frame of the round lawn table that was bolted to the cement deck.

She planned to rappel near the corner edge of the building where she would avoid being seen by the guests in other rooms. Of course, anyone who bothered to look out from the buildings across the way might peep her, but by the time they made any noise or raised any alarms her dirt would be long done and she'd be long gone.

Pearl slipped her arms through her backpack, then strapped up and fastened the harness around her thighs. Using her muscular arms, she hoisted herself easily over the ledge and ran the rope between her legs then tested it briefly. With her left hand on the rope in front of her, and her right hand holding the other end behind her snug in the crack of her ass, Pearl bounded off the balcony and rappelled three floors down until she reached the railing of the balcony on the fourth floor.

Once there, she quickly climbed over the railing and stripped off her hoody, then took off her small backpack, and pulled out the red satin ribbon. She wrapped it around her tight waist, crisscrossed it between her breasts, and tied a big bow at the top of her head.

Nipples erect, pumped-up and smiling, Pearl let her vicious hips sway as she walked the length of the balcony until she was standing before the sparkling glass doors. She peered inside, then knocked and stepped back as Piff Walker opened the sliding glass doors. He stood there in hot leather pants and dirty socks, with a grin on his face and a frosty beer in his hand.

His designer shirt was unbuttoned, showing a pale, scrawny body with wiry black hair sprouting on his sunken chest.

Pearl gave him a huge, dimpled smile, but on the inside she was grimacing at the nasty sight of his man titties and acne-flared skin.

"Who dis?" he said, his lips spread wide in a crooked grin.

He was a pathetic muthafucker, Pearl thought. Skinny, yellow, and stank looking. She would have to make quick, easy work of his ass because there was no way she could bring herself to lure, bait, or fuck him.

"Yo, who is you? Who the fuck sent me a present?"

According to Irish's files, Piff's goofy looks were deceiving. He had a rep for being a brutal gangsta who liked to inflict pain. He was quick on the trigger and had a string of dead bodies to his credit. Pearl knew she had to be slick and careful. Piff was one of them sleepers the FBI always warned them about. Criminals who looked harmless, even pitiful, but were the coldest, most vicious killers you ever wanted to run into.

Pearl wasn't taking any chances. She was still a little weak from the ass-kicking and drugs Yoda had put on her the night before, so she knew she had to get this niggah quick and dirty before he could get her.

"How you get out there?" Piff asked, looking up and down the balcony as Pearl giggled and backed up toward the railing.

"Mookie sent me," Pearl said sexily. She slipped the bow off her head and let the ribbon fall at her feet, then shrugged out of her tank top until her bold, sweat-dotted titties were pointing at Piff like double bazookas.

"He said I'm yours for the weekend!"

Piff grinned and followed Pearl outside onto the balcony. A suspicious glint shone in his eyes but Pearl went to work providing the ultimate distraction.

She licked her lips and let her gaze drop down to his crotch, then put her fingers on her waistband. She unbuttoned her shorts and began zipping them down.

Piff smelled pussy and he was on it.

He opened his arms and took two steps toward her, and that's when Pearl let him have it. She kicked out with amazing speed and power, turning her ankle just before she connected with him. The flat edge of her Tims cracked his shin and made him scream. Piff pitched forward, his bone splintered. Pearl struck again as he was on his way down, jabbing four fingers deep into the meaty part of his yellow neck, paralyzing him before he could recover.

She caught him before he hit the ground, thrusting her knee into his soft, nasty stomach, and hoisting him under his arms. Bending slightly, Pearl clutched Piff's leather-covered crotch with her right hand and lifted him until his back was on the railing, then tipped his head and neck backward and flipped him right over, sending his body, wide-eyed and wide-mouthed, flying down to the roof of the empty dance hall below.

A dull thump resounded as his body landed and lay motionless and still. Pearl watched coldly as a puddle of blood spread beneath him in a slow-moving circle. And somewhere in the distance, a burning child cried for her mother.

CHAPTER 28

Tank Parker had overindulged.

After drinking, smoking, and partying to excess the night before, he had lounged in the bed snoring and farting until nearly 3 p.m., and if the stupid-ass maid hadn't been banging down his door he could have slept all fucking day.

But that would have been defeating the whole purpose of being on the scene, Tank told himself as he rolled his bulky frame out of bed, pulled on his pants, and let the maid inside his room.

The pregame party last night had been the shit. He'd hit at least forty lines of fish scales and sucked down every drop of Krug the waitresses could carry. He wouldn't even talk about the sticky. Nig had smoked till he couldn't smoke no fuckin' more. Smoked till he couldn't fuckin' see. His manz had to bring him to his room and toss him on the bed—that's how fucked up his head had been.

And now his head was banging and his stomach was hollering.

Tank wanted some food and some weed, and not necessarily in that order.

"Hey," he said, walking into the bathroom and barking at the skinny little Asian girl who had already started stripping the sheets off his bed. Bitch was titty-less and flat-assed. He left the door open as he took his dick out his boxers and leaned one hand against the wall and started pissing as hard as a bull.

"Call down to room service and tell them to send me up a couple of steaks and some other good shit. Make sure my meat is rare. I want that shit bleeding like a bitch needing a tampon. Throw in some potatoes and runny eggs. And get me a bottle of wine."

Tank shook his dick off, then reached into his back pocket and pulled out a phat knot of bills. He peeled off two fifties and tossed them at the maid.

"Tell them to hurry up with that shit too."

He picked up a Black & Mild off the top of the television and lit it, then went back inside the bathroom and stopped the tub up and started running the hot water. As the sweet smell of strawberry sticky filled the air, he poured the tiny bottle of bubble bath into the stream and cursed.

"Why y'all muthafuckahs only give a niggah this much soap? Who ass this s'posed to wash? Some lil itty-bitty tiny Chinese ass? Ain't no niggah got a ass this little! Man, get me some real fuckin' bubbles for my bath, shit!"

The maid nodded and smiled, and went to hop to it.

"Sir, you want me to clean your bathroom first, sir?"

Tank toked his blunt. "Nah, I want you to get me some food and some fuckin' bubble bath!"

The maid gave Tank about ten tiny bottles of shower gel from her cart, then walked over to the phone to place his food order.

Tank slammed the bathroom door and stripped out of his

clothes and sank his fat ashy butt down into the hot water. He dumped five bottles of gel in and let the water run until he had a tub full of bubbles.

Closing his eyes, Tank lay back and relaxed, puffing his green and thinking about all the after parties he planned to hit later on that evening. The main one was gonna take place in a penthouse suite right after the game, and everybody in the world who claimed any kind of street cred would be there. Pimps, capos, kingpins, fine-ass whores. There'd be plenty of lap dances, neck pussy, titties, and big, round asses: whatever a niggah's sexual thang was, he could get it off at one of Mookie's joints.

Just thinking like that made Tank's dick wake up under the water, and he reached through the bubbles and squeezed the head, then stroked the shaft with the rich, soapy suds. He'd been with a fine ho last night, a bitch with titties so damn plump and round they looked like little softballs.

Tank had been feeling all over them firm, round things, and planning on ramming his long dick up her cleavage and getting him a nice little titty fuck, but all that liquor and blow had gotten to him and he couldn't remember what the fuck had happened to him or where the chick had gone. All he knew is that he didn't get none last night, or he wouldn't have been as horny as he was right now, and that was straight truth.

He let the water out of the tub and refilled it again, dumping three more bottles of gel in and foaming up the suds. He tried to take his mind off sex, but his dick was still hard and his fingers found his balls and squeezed them gently.

Pussy was as plentiful as air at the hotel this weekend, and Tank knew he could get some ass with just a quick phone call. But his hand was already on his dick again and he didn't wanna wait for his nut.

Tank closed his eyes and relaxed as he masturbated for long

minutes into the warm, soapy water. He fantasized about the unknown ho with the big fluffy titties from the night before, yanking his dick with expert strokes.

He was breathing hard and almost there, his lips slack, his tongue between his teeth, when the bathroom door opened and Tank saw something that brought a big smile to his face.

It wasn't the skinny little Asian maid and it wasn't the steaming platter of steak and eggs he had ordered that had him going neither. It was something much better than that, and Tank's dick nearly leaped out the tub at the sight.

"Room service," she said, stepping into the bathroom on the sexiest legs he had ever seen in his life.

The bitch was stacked. Thick too. Hips like a muhfuckah. Her stomach was sexy as fuck with a deep-ass navel, her titties were bolder than any he could have imagined in his fantasies, and she was gorgeous in the face, with dimples and pretty honey-colored skin that just glowed under the lights.

She had on a short red skirt and a red bra top, and she didn't look like no room-service waitress Tank had ever seen, but what the fuck. It was the Classic weekend and Mookie could be a high-rolling muhfuckah when he poked his fat head out the box. No telling what kinda shit that niggah had lined up for his homeys! Tank was just glad he was down with the click, 'cause steak and eggs had never looked so fuckin' good in his life.

She smiled and sat down on the edge of the tub, balancing the tray on her lap.

"Hungry, Daddy?" she cooed, cutting up hunks of meat and grinning at Tank like he was the meal. "Let mami help you put a little something in your belly."

Tank was grinning his head off as she cut and slid chunks of steak, eggs, and potatoes into his mouth. She laughed and cooed like he was a big baby, even playing that stupid-ass airport game, talking about picking up the passengers from the terminal on his plate, and dropping them off at the airport in his mouth.

Tank was getting more turned on by the minute. Every time she leaned over to place a forkful of food into his mouth, her cleavage screamed and her big titties almost fell out of her bra and into his bathwater.

By the time his plate was empty his dick was extra long.

He reached up and squeezed one of her titties and flicked her hard nipple with his thumb.

"What's your name, ma? Who sent you down here?"

She smiled, then moaned as he fingered her stiff nipple.

"I'm Karma. Mookie sent me."

Tank nodded. He'd figured that. His niggah was just paid like that.

"Take off some of that shit, girl. Get up in this water with me."

Tank stood up in the tub and motioned to her as the soapy water cascaded down his big brown body. The girl set the tray on the floor, then stood up too and began to unzip her skirt. Tank fondled her breasts as she inched her skirt down her hips and his breath caught in his throat when he saw she had nothing but a neatly trimmed pussy and naked hips underneath her clothes.

"Goddamn, baby," he said as she stood before him in her red bodice. "You could kill a niggah with those hips."

Pearl laughed and stepped into the water with him. Tank took her into his arms and buried his face in her neck as he cupped her phat, meaty ass.

"Did you get enough to eat?" she asked softly. "Are you full?"

"Yeah," he muttered, massaging her ass and grinding his dick into her stomach. "Poppa's full."

"Let me see," she said. She lifted her arm and reached into her bra.

Pearl's hand moved like a breeze as she flicked open a small fillet knife and plunged the blade into Tank's stomach right above his groin. She thrust upward, slitting him like a cow, gutting his stomach and spilling its contents into the soapy bathwater at their feet.

Tank stood there in complete shock, but Pearl moved lickety-split.

She hopped out of the water the moment his blood splashed in.

Tank's lips moved and he balled up his fists to swing on her, but the gaping slit in his center checked him.

"Bitch beater," Pearl taunted. She had studied her father's notes very carefully. Tank was one of the niggahs Irish had had to get with for kicking Diamond's ass in the street like she was a man.

Tank took an involuntary step and lost more of himself to the tub, then clutched both hands to his stomach in a vain attempt to hold his middle together.

Giggling, Pearl pulled her skirt back on and zipped it up, but not before showing Tank her crazy little birthmark, the one she shared with her twin.

"That's for N'Vee, you bitch-ass punk! Now you and my sister are EVEN!"

Deep realization was in Tank's eyes as his life slid down his legs and into the foamy bathtub. His eyes darted around the room, but there was no hope and no salvation. He was too weak to yell for help, and his pants, with his cell phone in the pocket, were too far away to reach.

Pearl Baines watched as Big Tank grew weaker with each passing second. Moments later, he bent at the knee and plopped down heavily in the bloody water, his mouth wide but mute, his disbelieving eyes glazed with pain.

A tear slipped from Pearl's eye as she thought about what

Diamond had been through at the hands of men like Tank, and then another rolled down her cheek as she thought about what she had been through too.

Sure, sisters were tight, but twins were eternal.

Diamond and Pearl, two hearts, one world.
I love you my Diamond.
I love you my Pearl.

CHAPTER 29

Menace was just a little kid in his dream.

He had snuck into Six Flags and was riding a Ferris wheel that was spinning fast. Too damn fast. So fast that people were being flung from their compartments and falling forty feet to the ground.

Menace was screaming along with the other riders, and holding on to the safety rail for all he was worth. The wheel was turning so fast that he flipped head over feet in his metal cage, banging his shoulders, knees, and arms, and flinging bile and acid into his throat, making him throw up.

The wheel slowed slightly, and Menace clenched his stomach muscles and tried to fight the wave of dizziness that gripped him, but just when he thought shit was under control, two things happened: the Ferris wheel picked up speed again and the door to his compartment flew open.

Screaming, Menace went sailing out into the warm summer

air, and as his body tumbled in a free fall toward the ground, there was only one thing on his mind.

Pearl!

He sat up in the bed before he could hit the ground.

Pearl. Goddamn Pearl.

A wave of nausea gripped him. His stomach heaved, the bile rising in his mouth really real, not a dream. He stumbled into the bathroom and hugged the toilet, and when there was nothing left inside him, he pulled himself to his feet and looked in the mirror and immediately he knew.

Slick-ass Pearl. She had fucked him up.

The details of the night before came back to him. Menace had never felt so sick or slept so deep in his life. He didn't know what she'd given him, but he knew she'd given him something strong.

And he knew why too.

Splashing cold water on his face, Menace rinsed his mouth with Listerine and took a piss. He was gonna get that damned girl. For real. It was Saturday, and he could pretty much figure out where she was and what she was doing. And ten minutes after waking up with Pearl's name on his lips, he jumped in his whip and once again headed over to the Primero Hotel to find her.

■■■

So far revenge was feeling sweet as hell to Pearl, and very soon her mission would be complete and the souls of her people could finally rest. The satisfaction she felt just from knowing that Mookie's henchmen would never break down another door and terrorize another innocent family was like a ton of boulders being lifted from her heart. But there was still a small, or rather a large matter that had to be attended to.

Although Pearl had annihilated four of Mookie's main manz with her very own hands, the ultimate satisfaction would come when she'd taken it to the head with the capo who had actually ordered the hits.

Losing her father and her daughter and her sister and her niece was horrific, but it was the brutal shit that had been done to her mother that had Pearl crying oceans. Zeta had been a beautiful woman who Mookie had used to break Irish's spirit before taking his life. The degrading shit that Mookie ordered inflicted on Zeta with spiked metal dicks and hammers let it be known that shit was personal between him and Irish. Dicking his woman in the mouth had made it so, and Pearl was about to make sure shit got real personal for Mookie too.

See, some years earlier another New York City family had been victimized in a crime that had a very similar MO as the one Mookie had perpetrated on Pearl's family. Before she left D.C., Pearl had asked Carlita to search the FBI's crime database for any home invasions that came close in scope to the one that took her family. Together they located the unsolved case of Marlo and Tricia Honore, an East Harlem couple who had been the victims of an assault with details that were very similar to those in the murder of Pearl's family.

In the Honore murders, Marlo had been an assistant prosecutor who was working on a number of cases involving gambling, drugs, and prostitution in East Harlem. He was working with an unknown informant and on the verge of obtaining some solid information that would take down an empire, when a crew of goonies pulled a kick-door on his family.

Marlo's five-year-old daughter had been having a birthday sleepover that night, and somehow he had heard them coming and managed to hold the goonies off with a small caliber pistol while his wife hid their daughter and four of her young cousins. The girls were stuffed under the subfloor in various rooms of the

Honore house, as Marlo and his wife were bum-rushed and attacked.

All kinds of unmentionable shit had been done to the Honores as their girls cowered out of sight under the wooden floorboards shaking in horror and fear. As in the Baines case, Marlo's wife had been tortured and sexually violated, her mouth brutally torn apart with a jagged metal object. The murderous thugs had poured gasoline everywhere and set the house on fire before leaving, and all five of the poor babies hiding under the floorboards had either burned to a crisp or suffocated to death.

The more Pearl learned about Mookie Murdock and compared the two cases, the more she was convinced that, like her family, the couple and their girls had been killed by his order. Mookie was running shit from one end of Harlem to the other, and the details of both cases had his personal stamp of sadism all over them. Pearl was almost sure that Mookie had put a hit out on both families.

It had taken quite a bit of work, but hunkered down in her room a few mornings earlier at the Sunset Motel, Pearl had gone through the Honore file and called the mothers of those four little girls. Nobody had ever been brought to justice for murdering their little girls, and the families had never gotten any retribution or any closure. Even after three years, the four mothers were still grieving, and sitting on the dirty floor of her motel room, Pearl didn't have to do a whole lot of talking to convince them that Mookie had burned and killed their precious babies, or to persuade them to get on board with her program to take him down for good.

Carlita's niece Zoe was working as the trainer for the East Coast basketball team playing in the Classic, and she was more than willing to help out too. Pearl would need a couple of solids from Zoe to pull this thing off, and Zoe was more than down to help her out. At Pearl's request she had arranged a car and driver to get the Honores to the Primero Hotel when shit popped off, and then to get them back to East Harlem again. All Pearl had to do was set shit up lovely and make sure the timing was just right.

As with everything else, Pearl had planned her details down to a tee, but where Yoda, Donut, Tank, and Piff had been relatively easy to get next to, nobody got close to Mookie Murdock without his permission.

Mookie had rented himself a penthouse suite, and according to Yoda, Mookie was the only one with the elevator code, and he changed it each time he let someone up. Pearl had thought about rappelling in off the roof, but the penthouse had no balcony, and all that swinging on a rope and breaking through a glass window shit only went right half the time. There was a real risk that both her damn legs woulda been broken trying to bust through all that thick-ass Plexiglas, and she would have probably ended up dangling outside his suite bleeding and cracked all the hell up.

She'd also considered posing as room service again or maybe even housekeeping, but Mookie was a highly suspicious niggah, and if he didn't order it or ask for it, he'd smell a rat if you tried to force it on him.

It was the smelling of a rat that gave Pearl an idea. Just thinking about it was nasty and it damn sure wasn't something she had planned on doing, but if this was the only way she could get up in Mookie's suite, then the foul deed just had to be done.

Pearl tried to keep her mind blank as she slid her card key through the slot and reentered Yoda's room. For a moment she swore she could smell that niggah rotting behind the wall, but her experience told her that Yoda hadn't been dead long enough to put out no real funk.

Pearl's hands were steady as she used a small pocket tool to loosen the screws on the condenser grating. She kept her focus strictly on what she was doing and why she was doing it, and refused to think about what was there on the other side of the grille.

Digging around in a dead man's pockets wasn't something Pearl was anxious to do, but thankfully she didn't have to. Yoda's phone was attached to his belt, and Pearl braced herself before rolling his dead ass to the right, then felt around on his waistband and unsnapped his clip.

Minutes later the grille panel was screwed back in place, Yoda was once again out of sight, and Pearl had exactly what she needed to get next to Mookie. Of course the niggah's cell phone was just as dead as he was, but the charger was still plugged in near the nightstand where Yoda had left it, and she waited patiently until there was enough life in the battery to process a call and access the contact list.

Back now. What's the code.

Is what she texted to Mookie once Yoda's phone went live, and to her relief she got a text back almost right away.

87352 Hurrup.

Pearl hurried all right. With her Attack Pak stuffed with handy shit, she took the main elevator to the lobby and pressed the button for the penthouse elevator. She used the code Mookie had texted her to gain access to the private elevator, and once she was inside and the doors had closed she immediately sent Mookie another text.

Wait. 4got my shit. Be a minnit.

Then Pearl went to work. It was an easy jump to reach the emergency exit panel overhead, and Pearl lifted herself through the small passageway with no problem. The elevator shaft was dark and drafty, and the cables creaked as the car skipped past the other floors and rose steadily toward the penthouse.

The elevator came to a stop, and crouched on top of the dusty car Pearl held her breath as the doors opened directly into the living room of Mookie's phat penthouse suite.

"Fuckin' stupid Yoda . . . dumb ass musta got off the elevator . ..." Pearl heard a big voice say as the empty elevator stood open on Mookie's suite. Game time was approaching and Pearl figured Mookie had been waiting for Yoda to show up so they could roll out to the Garden, but of course he hadn't heard from his manz. 'Cause Yoda was downstairs in his room dead as fuck. Pearl glanced down as a text came over Yoda's phone.

Where da fuck u at? Ball is bouncin. Get up here.

Pearl texted right back.

My bad. Be a minnit.

"Where that niggah at?" Pearl heard one of Mookie's bodyguards say. It was that country niggah Ransom. Her and Yoda had run into him the day before on their way to the Chinese restaurant. Pearl had stood by listening as the two men talked shit about opposing teams in the Classic, and now she recognized his drawling voice. "Muhfuckah been chasing pussy and missing in action ever since we rolled in."

"Yeah," Mookie said quietly, and Pearl could actually feel the suspicion in his voice. Mookie was a swift nig who wasn't about to be caught sleeping. He was a psychopath but he hadn't reigned this long or this large by being slow. "I'm about to switch up that code, though. Let that niggah ask for it again when he gets back."

Pearl moved quietly from her perch on top of the elevator and grabbed on to the railing along the shaft's perimeter. It was dark and scary in the shaft, but Pearl had been in this type of environment plenty of times while on the job. Instead of being afraid she kept her focus on getting Mookie. She crept along a dusty beam until she found what she was looking for, and minutes later she slid back a cover that led to the industrial air duct right above Mookie's kitchen.

Music thumped from the living room, and peering through the vent Pearl looked down at the empty gourmet kitchen complete with granite counters and high-tech appliances.

The grate was slick with accumulated grease and dust, and Pearl's hand slipped several times before she was able to pry the screws off and swing the grille downward on its hinges. Squeezing her toned body through the narrow opening, Pearl dropped into the kitchen like a cat, silent and on the balls of her feet.

Ransom was in the living room rapping to Robb Hawk's latest cut. Pearl didn't have no beef with Ransom, but he was in her way, so he had to go. She could have bust on both of them at once, but that would have ruined the little party she had planned, so she decided to lure Ransom into the kitchen and knock him out the box real quick.

She listened as he spit over Hawk's track. Ransom had a dope bass voice and sounded pretty good, but little did he know he was rapping his last song. Getting him in the kitchen by himself was gonna take some work, but there was a carton of Chinese food on the counter with a plastic fork stuck inside of it, and Pearl decided to use what was available.

Turning a front burner on high, she laid the plastic fork on top of the coil, then unclipped her Attack Pak. She took out a blow dart and extended the narrow plastic tubing. Checking the mosquito needle at the end, Pearl flipped off the cork, priming the dart and shaking poison into its tip.

As the plastic fork smoldered and melted on the stove, Pearl ducked behind the small island and waited. And she waited, and waited.

Dumb asses, Pearl thought, rolling her eyes as she crouched on the floor. That was just like a bunch of men. They didn't even notice the smell. Tiptoeing back to the stove, Pearl pulled the entire carton of food onto the cherry-red burner, and watched briefly until the cardboard caught a spark, and then a flame.

Back behind the island she crouched in wait again, hoping like hell Ransom came in to put the fire out before shit got bad and she had to put it out herself. But just then she heard Mookie yell, "Yo niggah, get me a Yellow Boy," and Pearl grinned. That would work too.

She braced herself as Ransom entered the kitchen, and without even glancing at the stove, he opened the refrigerator and took out a Corona.

Pearl moved quick.

Jumping to her feet she blew the FBI-designed dart at that niggah and hit him in the back of the neck, then yanked the dart back as he slapped his neck like he was killing a mosquito.

Pearl crouched back down for just a second, and listened as Ransom started stumbling.

"Oh . . . shit . . ." he yelled as he dropped the beer and his body hit the floor with a thud.

Pearl froze. The glass bottle had shattered on the porcelain-tiled floor and that niggah had yelled so loud Mookie woulda had to be dead not to hear him.

"Yo, whattup?" Mookie called from the living room. Pearl heard his heavy footsteps nearing, and thinking faster than a mother, she snatched a Taser from her attack bag and ran toward Ransom, who had landed on his back and was thrashing his limbs around on the beer-soaked floor.

Pearl threw herself on top of him, face up, and reached for his massive left arm and crooked it around her own neck. Holding the Taser, she pressed her right fist into Ransom's right palm, and started wiggling like a dying roach, flinging both of them around on the floor like it was a life-or-death struggle for real.

And this was the scene Mookie discovered when he walked into his penthouse kitchen. Pearl slobbering and gasping for breath as Ransom gripped her in a headlock and choked the shit out of her.

"Who dis bitch?" Mookie shrieked. "Yeah! Choke her monkey ass! Fuck that troll up!"

Pearl faked like a pro. She dug her heels into the floor and flopped around on top of Ransom slinging both of them from side to side and waiting for Mookie to come just a little bit closer.

And when he did, stomping his sloppy fat ass into the kitchen with glee in his eyes and rage in his grin, Pearl zapped that motherfucker with fifty thousand volts of electricity that made him hit the floor hard enough to cave that shit in.

It was Mookie who was stiff and doing the dying roach dance now, as Pearl jumped to her feet and zapped him again.

"Yeah, muthafucker!" Pearl yelled as she looked down into the contorted face of her daughter's killer. "You about to get yours, you grimy black bitch. You's about to get it real good."

CHAPTER 30

Pearl was a strong girl, but lifting Mookie's three-hundred-pound ass was out of the question.

Slicing the cord off the suite's venetian blinds, Pearl tied Mookie at the hands and the feet. She tied another length of cord around his neck, then used all her strength to drag him into the living room.

"Bitch, is you crazy?" the monstrous niggah sputtered as soon as he was able to speak. "How'd you get up in here? Do you know who the fuck I am?"

Pearl walked over and buried her boot in Mookie's gut, but otherwise ignored his noise. There would be plenty of time for the two of them to catch up on shit later. Right now she needed to get the new code for the elevator so she could put the next phase of her plan into motion.

"Okay," Mookie gasped. "This is about bank, I know. Tell me how much you want." Mookie's words were even-toned but there was a calculating fury in his eyes that Pearl recognized well. She'd seen it in the eyes of serial killers and mass murderers. If Mookie ever made it out of this he would kill her real slow. Twice.

"There ain't enough money in the world to pay for what you did, Mookie."

Mookie laughed. "Everybody got a price, sweetheart. Yours is prolly pretty cheap. Lay it on me."

"Shit," Pearl said, glancing at her cell phone as it vibrated on her hip. She frowned. "You are one arrogant niggah, ain't you, Mookie? Well, we've got company, baby. Give me the new code for the elevator and then we can talk about how much this is gonna cost you."

Mookie laughed his ass off.

"Oh, so now you need something from Big Mook? Well bitch you betta fuckin' get down here and take it!"

Pearl sighed and looked down at the fat ugly beast that lay tied up on the floor at her feet. She wasn't about to play no games with him. At least not yet. The Classic basketball game was already in progress and time was getting short. The Honore women were downstairs just itching to come up, and Justine Honore had already texted Pearl twice to get the correct elevator code.

"You better do what you can do to me," Mookie warned coldly, his dark eyes sinister and deadly. " 'Cause when I get loose . . ."

"Niggah *please*," Pearl smirked. "Be careful what you ask for. What's the goddamn elevator code?"

"Word is bond," Mookie said, quietly ignoring her request. "I'ma *eat* ya ass when I get loose. I can promise you that."

And Pearl believed him too.

She reached for her Taser and zapped his fuckin' ass again, letting his evil black ass have it until he passed out.

After making sure he was unconscious, Pearl strode calmly

into the kitchen and got the dishrag she had used to put out the
fire she'd started on the stove. Back in the living room she planted
her left foot hard on Mookie's forehead, then scrunched the rag
up into a ball and shoved it deep in his mouth.

Mookie's mouth and body were slack and motionless, but to
Pearl's surprise she heard some kind of movement coming from
the kitchen. She ran back in again and stepped around the island
and stared at Ransom. The poisonous dart had taken him down,
but he wasn't dead. His body was shuddering and convulsing as
he tried to pull himself into a sitting position.

There had been no info on this country cat in her father's files,
and as far as Pearl knew he hadn't taken part in the murders of her
family. She thought about it for a quick second, then moved deliberately. Ransom might not have killed her people but he damn
sure would have if Mookie had told him to.

Sliding a Slim Jim out of her Attack Pak, Pearl bent down and
gave Ransom a real quick and merciful smiley face. She didn't
hang around long enough to watch the blood spread out on the
floor under his body.

Back in the living room she rolled Mookie over and positioned
him so that he was splayed out on his stomach with his arms
stretched over his head. She used another stretch of cord to secure
his tied hands to the footrest on the wet bar, and his feet to one
leg of the plush sofa. Then she lit a Philly blunt she'd found on
the living-room table and sat down on the floor next to Mookie
so they could have that little conversation he had requested.

Turning his head to the side, Pearl punched him in his nose
until he was conscious. Then she pulled up the back of his shirt
and placed a pen in his hand, and a slip of paper close enough for
him to write on.

"What's the elevator code?"

For a hardbody street niggah who had terrorized an entire community and deaded countless rivals in the cruelest of ways, Mookie was a big bitch at heart. Do what she could do to him? Sheeiit. It took less than twenty deep cigar burns on Mookie's naked back before he scribbled a six-digit number with an asterisk at the beginning and at the end.

Satisfied, Pearl rolled the big niggah over till he was once again on his back, then texted the code to Justine Honore. Minutes later four furious mamas, who were burning with grief and starving for vengeance, stepped off the elevator and into Mookie's grand suite.

Mookie looked like a big rusty-ass whale as he lay flat on the floor with his arms stretched over his head.

Vickie, the youngest of the sisters, moved in on him first.

Before Pearl could say a word the chick strode over to Mookie and sliced him. Her sparkling blade slashed deep into his fat armpits, severing the tendons that connected his pecs to his biceps, and Mookie screamed into his gag as his shoulders separated from his ligaments and fell back on the floor.

Vickie got him at the feet next, grabbing his legs and slicing the Achilles tendons behind his ankles. Mookie shrieked into his gag as he lay helpless, unable to move a goddamn thing.

"Niggahs ain't the only ones who can get medieval!" Vickie yelled, and Pearl stood back as the Honore chicks went to work. Justine turned up the music and the rest of them got ready to party.

Pearl didn't even flinch as one of the sisters pulled out a hammer and they took turns pounding Mookie's fingertips. His wrists were tied tightly and he tried his best to curl his hands into fists, but he was no match for the mothers of the four innocent little girls he'd had murdered. They bent his fingers back until the bones popped, then hammered every one of his nails until his hands were straight bloody.

But those grieving chicks had waited a long time to get their get back and they weren't finished yet.

They flopped Mookie over onto his stomach and pulled down his pants. Big bad Mookie had shit on himself from fear and pain, and Pearl sneered at the sight of his gigantic ashy ass and stank, shit-stained drawers.

Sitting on the sofa, Pearl watched the women do unto Mookie as he had done unto those who they'd loved. She thought about her sister Diamond and how men like Mookie had used and abused her and planted their poison inside her head. She also thought about her father Irish Baines who had devoted his life to helping young black men escape the trappings of hood life. Him and Zeta had been parents to their children and grandchildren, and to all the children of their community.

But gazing at Mookie's flabby black ass as the Honore women took turns rodding him with a foot-long spiked metal dick, it was the thought of Chante and Sasha that hurt Pearl the most.

If they had lived, those two little girls would have grown into two special young ladies, Pearl knew. Both of them had been brilliant and loving, talented and beautiful, and it was the snuffing out of their lives and the brutal manner in which they had met their deaths, without even the benefit of holding each other's hands, that completely iced Pearl's heart as Mookie squealed and moaned and took a hurting that was far less than what his murderous ass had put on those children.

The Honore women were thorough and efficient. They were finished dicking Mookie and now they commenced to whipping his big fat ass.

"This is for Monique!" Justine spat, and swung a piece of plastic clothesline at Mookie's gigantic butt. A long welt rose on Mookie's flank immediately, and he clenched his ass cheeks together and moaned.

Vickie was up next. She wrapped her white plastic cord around her fist and Pearl saw it was the same kind of clothesline that used to bite and sting her legs when her and Diamond jumped Double Dutch with it when they were kids.

"This is for Fatima!" Vickie swung so hard that the rope cut into Mookie's ass and bright blood seeped through his skin.

"This is for Jaqueline!"

"This is for Nae-Nae!"

"This is for Cynthia!"

"This is for Tricia!"

"This is for Marlo!"

Pearl closed her eyes as the Honores took turns whipping Mookie and shredding his ass for all the suffering him and his boyz had brought into their lives.

The sound of the ropes zipping through the air and cutting into his flesh became more and more frantic and frenzied, and Pearl couldn't help chanting along with the Honore sisters, and whispering the names of her own dead loved ones.

"This is for Daddy! This is for Mama! This is for Diamond! This is for Chante! This is for Sasha!"

Pearl didn't open her eyes until she smelled the fumes, and by then it was just about over for Mookie. She watched as they poured a deadly mixture of rubbing alcohol and slow-burning fuel all over Mookie's naked body. The gangsta screamed into his gag and bucked his torn bulk around on the floor as the toxic liquid seeped into his cuts and seared his raw flesh. One of the sisters stood near Mookie's head and waited patiently until he had stopped raging and flopping around, then she poured her portion carefully into his hair and around his mouth, soaking liquid into the dishrag that Pearl had stuffed deeply in his mouth.

Mookie moaned and gagged, panicking as the toxic fuel slid down his throat and burned its way into his stomach. He gagged and hissed, the poisonous chemicals creating chaos in his tortured esophagus.

Pearl rose from her seat on the couch and stood over Mookie as he lay there unable to scream anymore, but still bucking and writhing in pain.

"Do you know who I am?" she asked him.

Mookie's eyes bulged with fear and he shrieked terror from his throat like a petrified little bitch.

Pearl held a box of matchsticks high in the air. She took one out and pretended to strike it, and that got Mookie's full attention.

"I said, do you know who the fuck *I am*?"

Fear multiplied in Mookie's eyes as he stared at the matches. Pearl saw him desperately searching his memory and coming up blank, and she wasn't surprised when Mookie blinked rapidly then shook his head slightly, no.

"Nah, you wouldn't know me, would you. We don't run in the same circles, so it's cool. But just so you understand, my name is Pearl," she said, lifting the edge of her shirt and revealing the birthmark she shared with her twin.

"Pearl Baines. I'm the sister of the chick you strangled. I'm the pride of the good woman you had tortured, and I'm the joy of that fearless black man you got your boys to murder. And yeah, I'm also the mother and the aunt of those two sweet little girls you had tied to their beds screaming and crying before they lit that gasoline and left those poor babies there to burn. The same way you're about to burn. So do you know me now?"

Realization was all over Mookie's face, and with it came the sure knowledge of Pearl's incredible wrath. His eyes bulged with the force of this knowledge and Pearl smiled as she heard her father's voice in her ear.

Don't get mad, Daddy's Pearl! Get even!

Pearl glanced at her watch.

She was certain that Zoe had already done her thing, and right about now the East Coast Classic team that Mookie had bet a stack of money on shoulda been walking off the basketball court dripping in defeat. Pearl almost laughed as she thought about the mild sedative and strong laxative that Zoe had slipped into the point guard's water bottle. He was a hotheaded baller who had fast feet and could pound the rock, but he was arrogant and grimy as fuck too, and had been on the take for Mookie ever since he'd been in the league. Zoe hadn't juiced him with enough drugs to take him completely out of commission, but she had damn sure given him enough to slow him down and throw him way off his usual smoking game.

"And guess what?" Pearl said as she rose to her feet and prepared to leave Mookie to die the horrible death that he so justly deserved. "That phat hunk of gwap you dropped on your little loudmouthed point guard from Philly? You can chalk that shit up as a loss, baby. Right about now he's probably either passed out or shitting his lungs out. Either way, you lost your last bet, Mookie. Your odds just got evened, you fat ugly bastard, and this time you lost for good!"

Waving the Honore women toward the elevator, Pearl stepped back and swiped a matchstick across the outside of the box. Staring into Mookie's enraged eyes and seeing all that fear . . . it did something to her. Pearl held the burning matchstick over him then tossed it down on his chest. A tremendous weight was lifted from her as the flaming tip rolled down to his stomach and ignited the fuel that had pooled on his skin.

All five women stepped into the penthouse elevator and

watched in silence as Mookie shrieked and brayed and burned slowly on the floor. By the time Pearl punched in the code, his skin was bubbling and scorching and Mookie was rocking from side to side and bucking around like a chained bull. A horrible sound came from deep in his chest as he shrieked with indescribable pain, and Pearl could only imagine that those were the same sounds her niece and daughter had made before they died.

"Hold up!" Vickie Honore stuck her hand out of the elevator before the doors could close. She darted back into the suite. "I'ma turn the music up a little louder, Mookie!" she said as she ran past him and over to the boom box. "You just keep hollering and making that ugly-ass noise! You got some nice sounds going, dude. This must be your beat!"

The women rode down to the second floor of the hotel in a satisfied silence, each of them engrossed in their own thoughts as they rejoiced in the aftertaste of their bitter revenge.

Stepping off lively on the second floor, they found the stairwell. As the penthouse elevator closed and rose up the shaft, Pearl and the Honore sisters silently composed themselves, then walked briskly down one flight to the lobby where they'd already arranged to split up and leave the hotel through four different exits. They would disperse into the crowded city streets to be picked up by the driver Carlita had already arranged for.

But shit doesn't always go as planned.

Pearl had just walked past the bank of elevators and was heading down a carpeted hallway that was lined with ground-floor guestrooms on both sides. Her destination was an exit sign at the end of the corridor, and she knew the rest of her life was waiting on the other side of that door.

She had only gone a few steps when he grabbed her.

Rough hands gripped her from behind, catching her by surprise and lifting her from her feet.

"Yeah, bitch!" Krazy Kevvie, the bodyguard she'd cursed out at Club Humpz, roared in her ear as he choked the shit outta her. "You thought you was slick, yo! I know who you is now! We was on the look-out for ya ass! My man Scotch put Yoda down on you *and* your slimy-ho sister! You thought nobody peeped ya grimy game? Well we did, bitch! We *did*!"

Pearl went into fight mode. She had forgotten all about this psycho-looking niggah with the one big eye, but here he was now, cock-strong and crazy with fury. Kevvie's breath was hot and stank on her skin as he tried to strangle the life from her body. Pearl sucked for air as she clawed at her neck, instinctively seeking to break his death grip.

"You coming upstairs, bitch! Mookie's gonna *kill* you . . . " Kevvie grunted as Pearl elbowed wildly from behind, catching him in the solar plexus. There was no way in hell he was gonna get her back in that penthouse elevator. She took advantage of his momentary stunning and slammed her heel down on his instep, then she reached between their bodies and grabbed his nuts.

Black spots appeared before Pearl's eyes and she knew she couldn't survive much longer. Her brain was begging for oxygen yet she forced herself not to panic. Using every bit of her strength and will, she choked his crotch with the same fury that he choked her neck, and it was Krazy Kevvie who let go first.

"Bitch!" he shrieked, flinging her to the floor as he reached for his nuts and grimaced. "I'ma kill ya fuckin' ass!"

Pearl scooted backward on the carpet, gasping and choking, trying to get some air and get away from him at the same time.

"You done, bitch," Kevvie said, advancing on her like a big black nightmare. A switchblade glinted in his hand. "You done."

Kevvie wasn't just krazy. He was a psycho. The niggah was way off. Pearl looked into his eyes and saw her death waiting there.

She scooted backward even faster, then turned on her stomach and tried to climb to her feet.

"Help!" Pearl rasped, her voice not much more than a whisper. "Help!" she cried out again, and this time it came out a little louder as she got her footing and started staggering back toward the lobby as fast as she could.

CHAPTER 31

But that maniac was on her.

She had only taken three or four steps when he slammed into her from behind, knocking her through the air with brute force.

"Where the fuck you think you goin'? Huh? Where the fuck you goin'?"

Pearl crawled on her belly. All the wind had gone out of her and her back hurt so bad it felt like an eighteen-wheeler had hit her. Getting to the hotel's lobby was the only chance she had of surviving Kevvie's wrath, but Pearl doubted if she could make it that far.

Especially when she felt something wet trickling down her back. Pearl reached around with her right hand. She felt a warm dampness below her bra strap on her right side, and when she brought her hand to her face it was covered in bright red blood.

"Yeah! That's right, ho!" Kevvie shrieked as he stomped down the hall behind her. "I stuck you! I stuck you! Bleed slow, jawn! Bleed slow so Mookie can get a piece of ya ass!"

Pearl tried to climb to her feet, but that krazy niggah just wanted to play with her. Every time she made it up on her knees and crawled a few steps he would laugh and shriek and grab her ankle and snatch her back down to the floor again.

With blood running from her body and her face pressed into the carpet, Pearl thought about her father.

One day you're gonna be proud of me, Daddy. One day I'm gonna make you proud.

She knew that no matter what happened now, Irish really was proud of her. She had handled the family business. She'd taken down the scumlords who had decimated her family. She had exacted street justice for the Baines blood that had been spilled. She had gotten hers.

Daddy's Pearl had gotten even.

Krazy Kevvie could be as psycho as he wanted to, but Pearl wasn't going down without a fight. She pretended to crawl toward the lobby again, and this time when he grabbed hold of her ankle, Pearl kicked out sharply with her other foot, snapping it from a bent knee and cracking him square in the face.

Kevvie buckled. That niggah grabbed at the bone she'd popped in his nose with one hand, and reached over and capped Pearl in the face with the other.

"Bitch!" he screamed, then let go of his nose and released a flurry of furious blows that sent Pearl to the carpet for good. He beat her down like she was a niggah who owed him money, slamming his fists anywhere he could get them.

Through the haze of pain and punches Pearl heard several room doors open, then close quickly again, like whoever had peeked out knew better than to get involved in somebody else's ass-kicking.

She managed to roll over and protect her face while giving Kevvie her knifed and bloody back as a target. His fists felt like hammers, and Pearl cried out in pain. She wished he would just stab her again so that death would come quickly. Pearl was preparing herself to leave this world and join her family in the next one when the blows suddenly stopped and she sensed something leap over her and slam into Kevvie.

It was Menace.

Once again he'd found her, and instead of helping her stuff dead bodies in air-conditioner vents, this time he was going toe to toe with Krazy Kevvie and fucking him up like a wild gorilla.

Menace moved with strength, grace, and speed.

He was a street fighter and a martial artist too. There was brute power and precision in his blows, and Kevvie went down to his knees as Menace snapped his wrist, breaking bone, then slammed the psycho's face into his bended knee.

It was a mismatch and all three of them knew it. Pearl could only watch in relief as Menace broke Kevvie up in pieces. But when Kevvie tried to reach into his pocket, Pearl found the strength to call out.

"He's got a knife!"

Life moved in slow motion as Menace reached back and slid a gat from his waistband. His arm came straight up as he aimed the tool at Kevvie's head, then swung back and bitch-cracked him across the face with the chrome weapon, denting Kevvie's skull and sending him down to the ground with a thud.

Quick as shit, Pearl scurried over to the downed man. Once again Menace had galloped in right on time, but Pearl had started this shit by herself and she was determined to finish it by herself too. Fighting the pain lancing her back, she grabbed Kevvie by his chin and the top of his head. With one swift motion she twisted sharply, breaking his neck.

Long seconds passed in silence, and it wasn't until they heard another room door open then quickly slam shut, did either one of them move.

"Owww . . ." Pearl moaned as she tried to stand up.

"Damn, girl," Menace said as he ran over and cradled her in his arms. "You slumped him, baby. Straight slumped him! Yo! I told you to stay ya ass at my crib! You so damn hardheaded, Pearl!"

She frowned up at him for a moment, then smiled as he kissed her forehead, her nose, and then finally, her lips.

"Goddamn, your head is hard!"

Pearl winced as he helped her to her feet.

"Lemme carry you," Menace said, and lifted her easily in his big, muscular arms. He held her like she was no more than baby weight as he hurried toward the front lobby where his whip waited at the curb. "Just relax. I'ma get you to the hospital, baby girl. I got you."

But Pearl couldn't relax. Precious minutes had passed since Kevvie had jumped her, and it wouldn't be long before Mookie's entire penthouse suite was up in flames.

Menace's route out of the hotel took them in the opposite direction from where Pearl had been heading. He carried her past a restaurant and the indoor pool where families were lounging on deck chairs and children were splashing and playing in water that was so full of chlorine it stung her nose. A few passersby glanced curiously at Menace as he carried a full-grown woman in his arms, but after one look at his killer face, none dared stare too long.

Pearl lay weakly in his arms as he hurried past the indoor swimming pool. The sound of laughing children met her ears, a sound that she would never again hear without reliving the pain of her loss.

But nobody else should have to feel that pain.

Pearl knew it was already too late for Mookie. By the time they found him he'd be good and crunchy. Burnt to a crisp.

But every precious child on every floor in that hotel deserved to live a beautiful life.

"Hold up," she demanded, squeezing Menace's shoulder to make him stop. "Go that way, baby," Pearl said, nodding toward a small corridor that was right near the pool.

"Yo, my car is in the front, Pearl. I gotta get you to a hospital, baby."

But Pearl knew what she had to do, and it was no less important than everything else she had already done.

"Please! Go that way!" she insisted, struggling to get out of his arms.

Menace looked into her eyes and saw something that made him comply. He turned down the small corridor as she'd demanded, and he hadn't gone very far when Pearl saw what she was looking for.

A small red plaque mounted on the wall read: IN CASE OF FIRE BREAK GLASS.

With thoughts of happy little girls on her mind, Pearl smiled as Menace lowered her gently to her feet and watched as she broke the glass.

And two seconds after the alarm was pulled, the man she loved gathered her up in his big strong arms again and they broke the hell out.

CHAPTER 32

It was hard for Pearl to believe that a whole month had passed since she'd taken down Mookie's crew, but the days had flown past before her eyes. She had chilled with Menace in Midtown for two weeks, resting and healing in his phat little crib, and thinking about what she wanted to do with the rest of her life. They'd gone to the morgue together and claimed Diamond's remains, then had a small ceremony at a funeral home in Midtown, where they had her body cremated and her ashes placed in a beautiful, diamond-studded urn.

At Pearl's request, Menace had accompanied her to the cemetery. They stood quietly before the small plot where the rest of her family was buried and Pearl talked to God and confessed her hopes that her people hadn't suffered too badly, and offered her prayers that they were in a better place.

"Love doesn't die, Pearl," Menace told her gently as she cried.

Pearl knew he was remembering his mother, who he'd lost so long ago and at a very tender and vulnerable age. "It never dies. They can still feel us, just like we can feel them," he said as he kissed her forehead and wiped away her tears.

Pearl snuggled closer to him as she gazed over her shoulder at the grave that held the bodies of her family members. She knew then that Menace spoke the truth because she actually felt her father's love in Menace's protective embrace. There was no doubt that Irish had raised his young pup to be the kind of man that Pearl could trust with her love and with her life.

Just being in the presence of so much death drove home the reality of the tragedy, but Pearl managed to hold herself together much better than the last time she was there. The pain of her loss was still immeasurable, and the urge to be with her family still persisted, but she was getting stronger each day and better able to deal with her grief.

That didn't mean she had gotten over the ache of their murders, though. Pearl still had some really bad episodes where the reality of how she had come so thoroughly unzipped and of what she had done to avenge their murders came down on her. Sometimes it hit her so hard she got sick.

During these dark moments Pearl reminded herself that it was Mookie Murdock, not her, who had brought destruction down on all of them. Mookie Murdock had started it. Pearl had only finished it. But it still hurt. She reminded herself that it was okay to miss her daughter and to grieve about not being there with her more while she was alive, but Pearl also acknowledged that even from a distance she had built a wonderful relationship with her baby girl. There had been nothing selfish about leaving Harlem to establish a better life for herself and her child. Her parents had wanted her to leave. They had encouraged her to go as far as she could in her career, and they were proud that one of their daughters had escaped the brutal streets and become progressive and accomplished in life.

And it wasn't like she had abandoned Sasha or left her with just anybody, Pearl reminded herself. She had left her baby in the most capable hands in the world, hands that were far more capable than her own. Irish and Zeta had given Sasha and Chante all the love they could have ever wanted in their short lives, and Pearl knew that even if she had stayed put right there at home, she couldn't have loved her daughter any better than that.

But she *had* loved her daughter. Loved her more than she loved her own life. Sasha had been happy, indulged, and surrounded with affection. There was no way Pearl was gonna let Mookie Murdock and the terror of what he'd done rob her of those beautiful memories. She was working toward putting the blame for her daughter's death squarely where it belonged—on the treacherous crew who had killed her. Instead of bearing their burden, Pearl was slowly letting go of the guilt and pain that allowed Mookie and his boyz to continue wielding power over her from the grave. Instead of covering her ears from the phantom sound of her daughter's cries, Pearl was learning to embrace the memories of her family's special love. She was paying tribute to them by living a life that would make each of them proud.

And there was something else Pearl was doing that she knew would have made her parents proud. There had been a few things that she just couldn't shake from her heart and mind, and Pearl had made quite a few trips back downtown to the Sunset Motel to see what she could do about that.

In the blighted area around Forty-second Street, Pearl had run across many young girls who were out there hustling on the track. Some of them were busy fucking like grown women all day and all night when they were barely twelve and thirteen!

For days Pearl sat on an abandoned stoop and watched as the young girls picked up tricks and rode off down the block with them. She knew the customers would pull over on a dark street or even lean up against the side of a building and get their trick on, using the young girls like they were nothing but disposable pieces of meat to be pinched, rubbed, and fucked at any man's whim.

There was one street chick in particular who caught Pearl's attention because she stood out from all the rest. The girl had something about her that struck Pearl's heart, and it wasn't just because she was gorgeous and had a body that kept men rolling up and down the streets eager to buy what she was selling. The young ho looked like she was about fifteen, right about the age that Pearl and Diamond were when they gave birth to their daughters. She didn't laugh and joke around with the other girls between customers the way normal teenagers did, and she didn't crack a smile when a john pulled up and invited her to climb into his whip, neither.

In fact, the girl looked dead as hell to Pearl. Like she was there in body, but definitely not in spirit. Her street name was Cookie and she reminded Pearl of Diamond. She wore the same haunted look of hopelessness that Pearl had so often seen in her sister's eyes, and her heart went out to the child who was busy selling the only thing she thought she had of value. The girl had just taken care of a john and was walking slowly back to her designated spot on the track when Pearl saw something that fucked her straight up.

It was a ghost from her past. A too-pretty niggah whose dieseled-up body was draped in fine rags from head to toe.

Scotch Allen hadn't changed much over the years. He was still a gorgeous no-good hustler who used young girls any which way he could. Irish would never tell Pearl exactly what he had done to

Scotch to keep him out of Harlem, and secretly, Pearl had hoped his gaming ass was dead and buried.

Pearl had gazed at Scotch for long moments as he barked in the face of the young girl Pearl had been watching. This muh-fuckah had fathered and lost two daughters by her and Diamond, yet Pearl felt absolutely nothing except disgust toward him.

She started feeling way more than that when he pushed up on Cookie and snatched her by the arm and slung her down into a row of metal garbage cans that rattled loudly on the street. Pearl jumped to her feet, pumped. She felt herself going into fight mode and had to check herself. There was nothing to be gained by fucking Scotch up out on the streets. Even though she was more than capable of putting him on his ass, Pearl forced herself to stand down as she thought about how good it would feel to serve that muthafuckah up! But there was more than one way to kill a sewer rat, she thought, as she whipped out her cell phone and chose Carlita's name from her list of favorite numbers.

"Slimy ass!" Pearl muttered as she waited for her call to be answered. Scotch would get his, Pearl vowed. All in due time.

In the safe haven of the bedroom they shared, Pearl and Menace had spent a lot of time just talking. They put their fears and their dreams out there, as well as their hopes for the future. They put their love out there too. The love they had always felt for each other.

"I never fucked with your sister," Menace told her. Pearl believed him because she could see the integrity in his eyes. "You were wrong about what you thought you saw in the bathroom that day. Nothing ever happened between us. I never touched her."

"But still," Pearl countered, "even if nothing did happen, you kicked me outta your room that night, remember? I was real young, Menace. That shit really hurt."

He nodded. "I know and I'm sorry. It hurt me too. I just didn't have shit to offer you, Pearl. I had too much respect for your father to be messing with you like that. What we were doing felt real good, it just didn't feel *right*."

That young love was in the past, and both of them were fully grown now. Menace was man enough to put his shit out there first.

"I love you, Pearl. I been loving on you for years, girl. Probably since the first day I saw you. I was just a pup back then. A scared kid who was trying to find his way. But I'm ready now. I'm ready to love you the right way now. But I need to know what you got for me."

Pearl had nothing but love for him and she told him that. The same love she'd always had, but only now it was stronger and much more mature.

Menace made it clear that even though his business was in Philly, his heart was in Harlem. He wanted to stay connected to the streets of his youth and to continue the work that Irish had started at No Limitz.

Pearl had found her heart in some unexpected places too. She couldn't get those young streetwalkers out of her mind. She spent a lot of time downtown just chillin' with them. Finding out what wound was causing them to sell their bodies to strangers and what she could offer them that would help them heal.

It was beginning to become a personal mission for Pearl. A mission of giving back some of what had been given to her. Talking to the young girls, she saw Diamond's eyes, and sometimes even her own, in almost all of their faces. Their stories weren't that different from Diamond's or Pearl's. They'd walked the same streets and breathed the same air. There but for the grace of God

went Pearl, and she understood that the only real difference between her and these young girls was the guidance and influence
that had been so unselfishly given to her. Harlem had never called
out to Pearl before. But it was damn sure calling her now.

"I made my decision," Menace had announced a week earlier.
They were sprawled across his bed eating Chinese food and
watching an episode of *The First 48*. A nineteen-year-old man
had been gunned down while holding his infant daughter in his
arms.

"I'ma go 'head and work here," Menace said firmly. "Right
here in New York. I'ma go back to Philly and shut everything
down, then look around for some office space somewhere up-
town. That way, I can run my biz and still run your father's center too. You feel me?"

Pearl was feeling him all right. Feeling him hard. Menace had
taken her under his wing and provided the same kind of love,
protection, and high hopes for her future that her father once
had. It was so easy for her to see why out of the thousands of
young thugs that had flowed through No Limitz over the years,
Irish had chosen only one to bring into his home and into their
lives. He had chosen Malik "Menace" Brown for all the right reasons.

"You sure?" Pearl had asked. She knew he wasn't the type of
man to just say shit off the cuff, but she had to ask anyway.

"Yeah," he'd answered. "I'm sure."

Pearl had lain beside him quietly. It didn't really matter if he
was in Philly or in Harlem. She lived and worked in D.C., and
there was no way they could be together every day. And that was
what Pearl wanted. To be with this man every single goddamn
day.

The last few weeks had been a period of joy and healing for
Pearl. She'd done a whole lot of crying, but she'd done a lot of

laughing too. No longer was she afraid to close her eyes at night. The nightmares had vanished, and even though the grief and sorrow would always be with her, Pearl had discovered that love and happiness could actually cure a broken heart.

Sex helped too. Lots of good, hot, tender sex with a dark-skinned cutie who had a monster dick and knew how to stroke it with love. Even though they slept in the same bed, during the first two weeks she was there Menace had refused to touch her. It had taken twelve stitches to close the knife wound that Krazy Kevvie had left in her back. The doctors had assured them that no vital organs or nerves had been damaged, but Menace was scared he'd hurt her and he fought like hell trying to make Pearl keep her hands to herself.

Of course she snuck him.

Shit, Pearl liked to get her gushy on and it had been almost ten long years since she'd had the dick of her dreams. She'd woken up real early one morning while Menace was still sleeping, and she'd sucked his soft dick into her mouth while he was weak and defenseless. By the time he opened his eyes his package was hard and wet, and Pearl was giving him the juiciest dome he had ever had.

They flowed naturally in bed after that, and it wasn't hard to pick up right where they'd left off all those years ago. Of course, Pearl was more experienced now and her sex game was nothing to sleep on.

They'd had their quiet moments too. Times when they talked in soft tones about their families and what their losses meant to them, and about how they wanted to live the rest of their lives in a way that would always make their parents proud.

"I gotta tell you something," Pearl said the next Monday night as they were eating dinner. Menace had already found a prime spot for office space and had met with his attorney, a realtor, and the building management and signed the contract that would make the space his. He'd been running around handling his biz all day long, and Pearl had been up in his apartment by herself.

"Whassup?" he'd asked, getting down on some chicken wings Pearl had baked. She couldn't cook shit else, so if Menace wanted to be with her he was gonna have to either take her out all the time, or get used to eating a whole lot of chicken.

"Remember when we talked about finding a zone of purpose and doing big things in our own little sector of that zone?"

Menace licked his fingers and nodded.

"Well, I think I found mine. I've been making calls all day, and there's a position open in a field office on the Lower East Side. My lead instructor from the Academy is running things down there, and he said the job is mine if I want it."

The room went quiet, then Menace said, "Do you?"

Pearl shrugged. She had been expecting him to jump up and down at the idea of her taking a job in New York, but he was playing it cool.

"It's a decent job." Pearl shrugged again. "So I might." She had never shown much interest in her father's outreach center in the past, but a whole lot of things had changed in her life and she wanted Menace to know she was sincere. "I've been thinking a lot about No Limitz."

Menace didn't say anything, but looking into his eyes Pearl could see she had his full attention.

"I know my father felt it was important to save young boys from the trappings of the street, but I'd like to do a little expanding to the programming. Open it up to young girls. You know, girls like Diamond who have a better chance of getting swallowed up by the streets than of graduating from high school. I can relate to girls like that," Pearl said, her words coming out eagerly. "I've been out on these streets, Menace. I came up in

Harlem and ran around with thugs and got pregnant when I was fourteen. If it wasn't for my parents I wouldn't have made it. These girls out here need them an Irish and a Zeta. Between you and me, if we work hard enough, I think we could be that."

Menace stared at her for a long moment, then nodded and took her in his big, strong arms.

"Damn, girl. You don't know how glad I am to hear you say that. I'm feeling that shit, Pearl. Our young sisters need saving just as bad as our brothers do. But you hate Harlem. You think you got what it takes to live here?"

Pearl shrugged. She had what it took to do whatever she had to do.

"I ain't gotta live with you or nothing. I mean, I'll find my own crib and stuff, but yeah. New York is in my blood, and Harlem is home. Dead or alive, everybody I love is here."

Menace grinned. "That's what's real, baby. I think I'm the shit, but a brothah was gonna have to turn into Superman to get back and forth from D.C. to New York every day, nah'mean?"

"No," Pearl said, sitting up straight, a slight smile spreading across her face. "I don't know what the hell you mean!"

"I told you I was gonna keep the center open and *work* in New York. I didn't say nothing about living here. For the last week I been talking to a realtor in D.C.," Menace said quietly. "I couldn't see myself letting you go back there without me. I was willing to commit to a big-time commute every day because I believe you're worth it, Pearl. I didn't give a fuck how early I had to leave the crib or how late I got back, I just know I wanna go to sleep holding you every night, Pearl. Every fuckin' night."

Pearl melted in his arms, she couldn't believe what she was hearing. She couldn't believe how far Menace had been willing to go just to be with her. Her man wanted to be with her just as bad as she wanted to be with him.

Later that night, after they talked and dreamed about plans for the future they wanted to build together, Pearl unbuttoned Menace's pants and went down on him with all the love in her heart. She gave that neck pussy up to him without hesitation, and Menace took everything she offered and threw more back at her. He planned to take his time with her and was nowhere near ready to bust yet, so he pulled her up and smiled as she lay on top of him. He massaged her ass and eased her into a sitting position. Sucking her tongue, Menace slid his legs off the bed until his feet were touching the floor.

He stood up swiftly, holding Pearl in his strong arms. His muscles were rigid as he cupped her hips and licked her breasts.

"Put it in," Pearl had moaned, eager to feel his thickness inside of her. "Come on, baby. Put that thang in."

"Gotta wrap it up," Menace whispered, walking toward his dresser holding her in his muscular arms.

"Do me a favor," he said, turning his back on the dresser. "Reach in the top drawer and open up that box."

Pearl did what he asked. She smiled as she pulled out an unopened box of condoms from his dresser drawer.

Menace carried her back to the bed and sat down. Still gripping her ass, he leaned back to create some distance between them, and sighed as Pearl cracked open the pack of Rough Riders and slid one over his rigid shaft.

He stood up again, balancing Pearl's frame perfectly. With his six-pack clenched, Menace lifted Pearl in the air and impaled her on his joint. Both of them moaned as he lifted and lowered her, thrusting into her with long hard strokes.

Pearl rode her man hard, timing his thrusts and clenching her pelvic muscles on each downstroke. The loving was long and strong, and by the time Menace lay her on the bed and began pounding on top of her, Pearl was ready to cum.

"Yeah!" she panted. She spread her legs wider and gripped his ass, pulling him deeper into her slit. "Just like that, baby! I love this shit! Just like that!"

Menace went to town in that pussy.

He dug her out, pelvic bone to pelvic bone, with Pearl's body stretching to accommodate his length and his width.

Pearl ran her hands all over him, like she had never touched him before. His strong back, his hard ass, his muscled-up shoulders and chest. He was everything she had ever wanted, and the memory of every other sex partner she had known was completely erased from her body and from her mind as Menace made love to her like it was their very first time.

Displaying his incredible dick control by holding out as Pearl came twice back to back, Menace withdrew from her hot, clenching tunnel and delved into that pussy with his tongue. He nibbled on her clit, applying pressure with his lips until Pearl began thrashing around on the bed, snatching at the sheets as she gapped her wide legs open and gave him access to every inch of her womanhood.

"My ass . . . ," she whispered as Menace lapped her out, and she only had to say it once, too. Menace massaged her sweet tight hole with his finger and probed it with gentle pressure as he sucked and licked her softness. He didn't stop until Pearl had come again and was beating on his shoulders, begging him for the dick.

And boy, did he give it to her. They damn near broke the bed down as their bodies rocked and collided in heat and passion, Pearl's enormous stamina no match for the amazing power and control of her man's. There was an explosion in the room as they hit the top of that wave at the same time, and rode it out together. Menace pressed his face into her hair and breathed deeply as he tried to catch his breath, feeling physically and emotionally complete for the first time in almost ten years.

He rolled off Pearl and held her in his arms for long minutes before finally stroking her hair and speaking.

"Ain't no limitz on a soul emboldened and a mind inspired, right?"

Pearl grinned. She loved the way her father's motto sounded coming out of her man's mouth.

"No limitz, baby," she said softly. "No limitz."

CHAPTER 33

Leaving her job in D.C. was an emotional experience. Pearl had made a lot of friends and earned a lot of respect for her work ethic, her tactical expertise, and her warm, outgoing personality. She was gonna miss a whole lot of people, but she'd miss Carlita the most.

"Harlem ain't but two hops away," her friend had said, hugging her tightly. Carlita had visited her in New York when she was laid up recuperating from her stabbing, and she'd given Menace his props right away. "Trust, Pearl. There comes a time when everybody moves on to bigger and better things. The time for you and Menace is right now. He's the one, chica. I can feel it."

Carlita had offered Pearl her guest bedroom for her short stay in D.C., and as they sat up talking that first night the older woman had taken Pearl's hand and said something that really fucked her up.

"You know, Pearl, I wasn't gonna hit you with this while you were in New York trying to heal and get your head right, but I think its good that you're not coming back here to stay."

Pearl had the confused look going, so Carlita laid it all the way out.

"Look, after what happened to your family, everybody in the office was praying for you and hoping you would be okay. We all missed you and wanted you to take time to feel better, but Lance still believed in you. He had a welcome-back surprise just waiting for you. A great promotion to a field office in Los Angeles. But your boy Cole blocked it. He told Lance you was too shot out to handle that kind of responsibility, and pulled some strings to get one of his buddies the job. I thought that was real grimy of him, but I wasn't surprised. I told you from the gate Cole was a control freak. His whole game was about keeping you in his grip, and that's the only reason he shot down your promotion. He wanted to make sure that when you finally came off leave you'd have to come right back to D.C. and be with him."

Pearl was heated. Cole deserved to get fucked up good for all the shit he'd done to her. From blocking the truth about her sister's murder, to blocking her out of a lucrative promotion, that niggah was one item on her agenda that still needed handling.

Pearl had spent the next day in her office clearing out her files and tying up loose ends. Her department was in the midst of a huge annual inspection, and the regional commissioner was on-site and being escorted through the facilities by several section chiefs. Every agent in the office had been working overtime to make sure that their shit was above standards, and when Pearl's supervisor asked if she would mind running a target test before their inspection at the indoor range, Pearl saw an opportunity to kill two birds with one bullet.

She had been ducking Cole in the two days since she'd been

back, and Carlita said as far as she knew Cole didn't have a clue that she'd been stabbed, or that she planned to transfer to a position in New York.

The indoor target range was scheduled for inspection in a little over an hour, and Pearl was about to put her plan in action. She called Cole's cell phone and for the first time in weeks, she heard his voice.

"Hey, baby!" Pearl said brightly. "It's me. Pearl. I'm in D.C.—back to work! Did you miss me?"

That twisted niggah was full of himself.

"Yeah, I missed you, Pearl. I was the one who told you not to go in the first place, remember?"

"Don't be mad, Cole. I'm back now."

"So, did you find yourself?" he asked, whining like a little bitch. "Or did you find somebody else?"

Pearl was hot, but she kept her voice light and sweet.

"I wasn't looking for nobody, Cole. I told you, I had to take care of business, and that's what I did. It's a wrap now. I'm back, so when can I see you?"

He was still a little stiff, and Pearl could tell he had his lips poked out.

"When you wanna see me?"

"How about later on tonight?" Pearl said, dropping her voice.

"Why I gotta wait until tonight?" Cole bitched, just like she knew he would. "Why you can't make time for me right now?"

Pearl giggled. This cat was just too predictable.

"Okay," she agreed. "I need to make a little run across the quad and take care of something for our inspection. Give me a walk. I'm coming right past your building. Meet me outside in ten minutes."

•••

Fifteen minutes later Pearl was unlocking the maintenance door at the rear of their live shooting range. There was a huge multi-function stage inside that had only recently been constructed. One side had been built to reflect an urban setting, with fake brownstones, tenements, and alleyways. The other side was set up to look like a business district where a hostage scene might play out. The range was state-of-the-art and an effective training aid. There were a variety of cut-out targets depicting various ordinary, law-abiding citizens mixed in with dangerous criminals. There were gangsters, good guys, killers, kids, and of course innocent little old ladies carrying their groceries. Agents from D.C. and its surrounding communities in Maryland and Virginia signed up to use the range for live firing on a regular basis, and it was one of the primary areas to be inspected during this cycle.

"Why'd they ask *you* to test the range?" Cole complained as Pearl unlocked the door. "*My* boss is escorting the commissioner through here. They should have asked me."

"Come on," Pearl giggled, grabbing him by the hand and pulling him through the maintenance door. His ass had gotten fat. His stomach was pudged out and his cheeks looked like he was storing munchies in them. "All I know is they want a target test. You can help me."

Cole reached under her skirt and pinched her ass, then followed behind her like a puppy. They entered the range from the rear and maneuvered around a few targets as they headed toward the control panel.

"Remember that time we did it outside under that pavillion?" Cole whispered. He grabbed Pearl's hand and pressed it to his swollen crotch. "That was some good shit, baby. Some real good shit."

Pearl grinned under the dim lights and turned to face him. She pressed her body to his, pushing against him until his back was up against a target pole. She closed her eyes and forced herself to suck his bottom lip into her mouth.

"It was good as hell," she whispered truthfully, nibbling and rubbing against him until his breathing got heavy. "But I know how to make it even better."

"How?" Cole asked, and gripped her hips. He slid his hands down her thighs and reached under her short skirt. Pearl giggled and backed away as Cole tried to dig his fingers in her pussy.

"I used to fantasize about fucking in front of a lot of people," she confided. "It was just a secret fantasy, though. I never really thought I'd experience it."

Cole laughed, leaning back on the target pole and waving toward the endless life-sized cardboard cutouts. "Well, there's about a hundred muhfuckahs up in here with us right now, girl! We can get busy right here. I can make that fantasy come true."

Pearl jumped bold and grabbed his thickening dick. Tonguing him down, she unbuckled his pants and inched his zipper down. She stuck her hand into his boxers and squeezed. His dick was hard and had drops of pre-cum on the head. She rubbed his wetness all over him then tugged at his pants and moaned in his ear, "Take 'em off."

Cole kicked off his expensive leather shoes and let his pants fall around his ankles. He yanked down his drawers and stepped out of everything, panting as Pearl kicked his discarded clothes behind him and moved in closer.

He reached for the bottom edge of her shirt and Pearl raised her arms and let him slip it over her head. He unsnapped her bra like an expert, and flung it on the floor, leaving her breasts naked and beautiful before his eyes.

"Damn, girl," he said thickly. "You still got it."

Pearl giggled again and moved closer to him. "I got it and now I wanna give it to you."

Cole took off his shirt and flung it over by her bra. Pearl jacked his dick and sucked on his neck. Cole put his head back and moaned, closing his eyes as he fucked into her palm. Keeping her hand rhythm steady, Pearl moved behind him and bit down on the back of his shoulder. He reached back and rubbed her bare thigh. She nibbled his neck and licked up and down his spine.

"Goddamn that feels good!" Cole whispered.

Pearl laughed, stroking him harder. She reached into the back pocket of her skirt and pulled out her service cuffs and clicked one end onto the target pole, masking the sound as she said, "Well, relax, baby. I'm about to make you feel even better!"

Lightning fast, she let go of his dick and grabbed his right hand. Pinning it to the pole, she clicked the other end of the cuff around his wrist.

Pearl stepped in front of Cole and narrowed her eyes.

He looked down at his handcuffed wrist and laughed. "Ahh, shit! You got a little freak in ya, huh? Well, come on over here and freak daddy out, girl!"

Pearl freaked the *shit* outta him.

She punched him in his grill so hard his head snapped back against the pole.

"Bitch!" he shrieked, grabbing his nose with his free hand. "What the fuck you do that for?"

He moved toward her and swung his arm in an arc, trying to backhand her.

Pearl caught his thumb and bent that shit way back.

She jerked it outward, dislocating it from the joint, and Cole screeched as a sharp bolt of heat shot up his arm.

"That one was for not telling me about my sister," she said. "And this one"—she lifted her leg and kicked him deep in his pudgy gut—"is for trying to fuck me out of a promotion!"

Cole coughed and dropped to his knees, his metal bracelet sliding down the target pole.

"Girl, you wrong," he moaned as he squatted there naked. His dick had shriveled up and was now hiding somewhere under his pregnant belly. "I love you, Pearl. Why you do some shit like this to me? I love you!"

"You don't love nobody but your damned self, Cole. I heard all about how you tried to stop me from finding out that my sister was dead. My own sister! And then you tried to cheat me out of a promotion you knew I had earned." Pearl picked up her bra and shirt from the floor where Cole had tossed them and put them on quickly. Cole's gear was far enough away that both his arms would have to grow another foot before he could reach it.

"I could stay here and kick your punk ass all day, but I got some targets to test."

He broke. "Yo! You ain't gonna leave me in here, are you? Come on, Pearl! Don't play me like that!"

Pearl ignored him and walked up the aisle past the colorful cutouts of thugs in street clothing, businessmen carrying brief-cases, and terrorists hiding bombs. The range was full of targets. The ones mounted on poles moved back and forth, and the lay-down type popped up and down.

Moving over to the wall, Pearl opened the control panel and flicked on every switch. She giggled like hell as multiple targets popped up and down and slid across the floor.

"Yo! What the fuck you doing?" Cole yelled.

Pearl cracked up as she watched him running naked in his socks, back and forth across the range stage as he tried to keep up with his moving pole. She killed the switch when Cole's pole was dead center on the stage, and tears rolled from her eyes at the sight of his ridiculous-looking ass standing there in his socks look-ing panicked and shook.

"Yo, Pearl," Cole begged. "Don't do this shit! The commissioner is about to come through here. With my boss! At least gimme my clothes!"

She smirked. "Don't worry about your clothes, Cole. What you need to be worried about is the hurting I'm gonna put on your ass if I ever lay eyes on you again."

Pearl headed toward the front exit. She igged the shit out of Cole as he begged and hollered behind her. She flipped off all the lights on her way out, and that's when Cole really broke.

"Wait! They gonna be firing up in here in a minute, Pearl! You can't leave me in the fuckin' dark!"

Pearl didn't even miss a beat.

"You left me in the fuckin' dark about my sister, Cole. Just holler when they get here and you'll be all right. Don't worry," Pearl said as she dismissed Cole's faggot ass and anticipated getting back to New York to see Menace, her strong and loving man. "If you holler loud enough they'll hear you."

Getting back in the New York groove had been a lot easier than Pearl had thought it would be. There was something about being back on the streets of Harlem that made her walk different, talk different, and definitely look at the world in a totally different way.

New Yorkers had some bad-ass swagger, Pearl realized. There was something about this city that was colorful and moved to a funky rhythm that felt like the beat of congas and steel drums and maracas all in one.

Pearl was a little nervous about the huge task she had bitten off, but she knew she could handle it. Giving back to the community ran in her blood, and she shook off her old fears and dug deep inside for the confidence that was her birthright.

She had been up half the night making sure everything was set for this day. Menace had brought in a team of contractors to put up a Sheetrock wall and partition off one side of No Limitz so that her girls could have their own space. They would have their own computers and their own bathroom too. In fact, they'd have everything they needed to help them gain the confidence and self-esteem to get back on their feet and recognize their human value and intrinsic worth.

Pearl had invited over twenty girls from Forty-second Street to the grand opening of the women's center at No Limitz. She had no idea how many would actually come, but several seemed excited when she told them what she was doing and promised they would do their best to swing by.

Although she would have been happy just to have at least ten girls show up, Pearl was prepared for all twenty. She had ordered bomb turkey-and-cheese heros and macaroni salad from the deli up the street and decorated the room with colorful balloons and streamers that said WELCOME, BEAUTIFUL BLACK QUEENS! She had stuffed bright yellow folders with information about welfare and food stamps, alternative high schools, emergency shelters, domestic violence centers, drug abuse and rehabilitation hotlines, and any other information she thought might help these girls get their feet up under them.

Pearl had done everything she could think of to provide the young girls with information on services that were readily accessible to them and that would meet their most immediate needs. She was confident that those who really wanted help and were willing to take that first step could definitely be helped.

Pearl had done something else for the girls at the Sunset Motel too.

Something they had no idea she was doing for them.

Just two days earlier a scuffle had gone down on the street outside of the Sunset Hotel. Somebody had dropped a dime, and the local police department had been alerted to the presence of a twice-convicted felon who was wanted on numerous major outstanding warrants. They'd rolled up with guns drawn and dropped one Tony "Scotch" Allen to the ground with a series of blows from their nightsticks that should have knocked him straight the fuck out.

But Scotch was a two-time felon and going to jail on a third major charge wasn't something he was gonna just lay down for easily. He'd fought like a muthafucka, and when the cops got tired of tussling with him they Tasered his ass right into submission.

Pearl had stood across the street watching and laughing inside as Scotch got his. She'd showed up to drop some positive words on the young chicks before the next pimp moved in on Scotch's action, and she ended up sticking around to enjoy the show. Good for that niggah!

She had to give it to them Blue Boys of NYPD. They wasn't no joke. They were serving Scotch's ass good, but Pearl knew that niggah still had a lot more payback to get. His real punishment would come when he went to trial and got sentenced for human trafficking for the purpose of prostitution. The smooth-talking two-time felon was about to become a three-time loser, and even the squarest cat in town knew what that meant. Scotch had fucked over his last young girl! Thanks to Pearl he now had three strikes against his black ass and he was going upstate to be a pretty boy for life!

Pearl ran around No Limitz putting the last-minute touches down. The floors had been mopped and waxed, there was plenty of food and cold juice and sodas, and there were fresh towels, robes, and even unopened packs of panties and bras stacked in the ladies' room.

She'd asked the girls to come by at 2 p.m., and after helping her clean up and making sure she was straight, Menace had left the center at 1:30. They'd closed the doors to their male clients, even though Saturday was their busiest day, because they both thought the young girls would be more comfortable if there were no men hanging around.

At 2:15 Pearl was sweating. She went outside and looked up and down the street, but all she saw were the regular folks from the Harlem neighborhood, shopping, playing, and generally enjoying the sunshine and the beautiful weather.

By 2:30 Pearl was officially worried, and by three o'clock her ass was sick.

It wasn't until 3:30 that Pearl allowed the blanket of disappointment to fall fully around her shoulders. She tried not to feel too bad, but it was hard not to. Maybe she didn't have that thing that Irish and Zeta had had, she thought. Maybe she hadn't given the girls enough motivation, or radiated that confidence that made people place their trust in a stranger.

Pearl wasn't stupid and she wasn't naïve. If she wasn't able to rescue her own twin from the grips of the street life, what in the world made her think she could rescue a bunch of perfect strangers? Hell, Irish got most of the boys in his program because the judge mandated them to be there. Not because they walked in on their own. None of the girls Pearl had picked up off the strip had any special reason to allow her access into their lives or to trust her. This was New York. That's just the way shit was.

Reaching for the cell phone clipped to her jeans, Pearl called Menace and gave him a quick rundown.

"It didn't work," she told him, fighting hard to keep the disappointment out of her voice. "I guess they wasn't feeling me, 'cause nobody showed up. You can come on back now, and bring the boys with you so they can eat up some of this food."

Menace wasn't feeling that.

"Just because they didn't come today doesn't mean they won't come *one* day," he reassured her. "People don't heal and grow on somebody else's schedule, Pearl. They can only do that shit when they're ready. Those girls know where you are. And they know who you are too. They'll find you when they need you. It might not happen today and it might not happen tomorrow, neither. But if you keep your heart open, Pearl, some of them will definitely come."

The turkey-and-cheese heroes were all that. There was nothing like that long New York Italian bread to make a sistah feel good. It was crusty on the outside and soft on the inside. It wasn't a sub and it damn sure wasn't a hoagie. In New York it was a hero, and it had its own distinct taste and flava, just like everything else in the naked city.

Pearl sat down in one of the chairs she'd arranged in a semicircle around a podium and took a big bite of the sumptuous sandwich. She swigged some cold vanilla cream soda straight from the can and thought about her sister.

Both her and Diamond had loved eating heros when they were growing up, which was one of the reasons Pearl had decided to serve them to the girls on the track today. She had ordered way more than enough because she knew that no matter how much bank a prostitute made on her back each night, almost all of it went to her pimp. A lot of those girls barely got enough to eat on a daily basis, and she figured some of them might want to take some food back with them.

With Menace and some of their male clients on the way down, Pearl knew the food wouldn't go to waste, though. She finished eating slowly, glancing around the room at her carefully placed decorations with more than a little sadness in her heart.

She had just gotten up to throw her napkin in the trash when she heard the front door open. Pearl turned around with a wry smile, expecting to see her man's handsome chocolate face, but instead she was treated to several pairs of street-worn eyes and uncertain smiles.

"Sorry we so late," said a girl that Pearl had come to know as Uniqua. "You know niggahs and bitches can't be on time for shit!"

All Pearl could do was grin. Uniqua was a beautiful dark-skinned girl of about sixteen who had the prettiest smile that Pearl had ever seen. Uniqua had told Pearl bits and pieces of her personal story, and the fact that the young girl still had the strength to smile after all she had gone through in her short life seemed like a miracle to Pearl.

And Uniqua hadn't come by herself, either.

Pearl's smile got big as shit as almost all twenty girls she had invited filed into the room, plus over twenty more! Most of them were dressed in their hoochie hooker street clothes, and there were mad juicy titties and phat asses hanging out galore.

"You said we could bring some of our friends," a young Hispanic girl said, sashaying up to Pearl for a hug. Her name was Juliana and she was from Spanish Harlem. She had big hips and a bright attitude, and Pearl had grown to really like her. Juliana was thirteen.

Pearl stood in the middle of the room watching as the girls came in and rushed straight over to the long table that was stacked with food. Some of them were wrapping heros and chicken wings in napkins and sticking them in their purses and all up under their clothes, but Pearl didn't care. They could have any damn thing they wanted today. She hoped and prayed that they'd strive for everything they *needed* tomorrow.

Menace showed up just as the girls had finished grubbing.

They were laughing and talking and clowning around just like kids taking a break from their grown-woman duties.

Go away! Pearl mouthed and waved Menace away from the door with a big grin. *Come back later!* Him and the boys started acting up, pointing at the food table and making eating motions as Pearl shooed them away.

It took more than twenty minutes to take the girls on a tour of the center. They were crazy and wild and running their hands all over the computers and printers and touching everything that looked high-tech and wasn't a part of their normal world.

A lot of them freaked out when they saw the brand-new bathroom and the five big, clean shower stalls. It seemed like Pearl had only blinked twice and in a flash all the towels, bathrobes, and endless packs of panties and bras she had filled the room with had disappeared. These girls were desperate and resourceful. Like scavengers, they were out to get any and everything they could.

"Oh, I'ma be first in one of those big-old showers and then I'ma put me on two pairs of these clean drawers," one girl announced, causing everybody else to bust out laughing.

Pearl turned toward the voice and was astounded to see it was Cookie, the beautiful young girl with the dead-looking eyes. The girl who reminded her so much of Diamond. Pearl smiled at the girl and got a shitty twisted lip in return.

Cookie turned to her friend and muttered, "I don't know what the hell she looking at. Only reason I came was to get something to eat. After I get in that shower and wash my ass, I'm out."

Yeah, Pearl said to herself. This one was gonna need a whole lot of time and attention. But she was capable of being helped, Pearl knew. It was just a matter of offering herself and her love, and putting in the work.

"Okay, ladies," Pearl said loudly as she shuttled the girls back into the main room and encouraged them to take a seat. There weren't enough chairs so some of them sat together, half of somebody's ass hanging off the side of each seat.

Pearl looked out into the sea of worn, but innocent and expectant faces. She saw possibilities in each of them. She saw possibilities in herself.

"Y'all know I asked you to come down here because I see hope and promise in each of you. Some of y'all probably came just to get off the track for a quick minute, others might have come because I promised to hook y'all up with some free food." Pearl waited as they laughed and dapped each other, covering their mouths like the joke was on her.

"But I want you to know," she held up her hand and continued, "that it really doesn't matter why you came. The important thing is that you made it here."

Pearl paused and took a deep breath. She felt the blood of her father coursing through her veins and it felt so damned good. Pearl was starting to believe that if she opened up her arms wide enough some of the girls would walk into them on their own.

"Check it out. I've heard it said that every journey begins with just one step, and I believe that. But before we can walk we have to crawl. And before we can crawl, we have to first believe. Belief begins with the words we tell ourselves. It begins with a single sentence."

Pearl came from behind her podium and stood before the girls, the light in their expectant eyes warming her soul until there was no room in her heart for selfishness anymore.

"I'd like you to turn around, ladies. Turn around and read that sentence written on the wall behind you. Let's say the words out loud together as we begin a journey into the possibility of a new life."

"There are no limitz on a soul emboldened and a mind inspired."

•••

Pearl smiled. Every one of them, even her tough little Cookie had spoken the words out loud. And really, Pearl knew, that was all it took. Speaking could lead to believing, and believing could lead to changing.

Pearl looked out at the young prostitutes and sighed deeply. Grief tried to sneak up on her and shut her down, but she wouldn't let it. She might not be Daddy's Pearl anymore, but these young girls needed her, and from now on she would always be Harlem's Pearl.

I can change! was something Pearl had heard her twin sister say over and over throughout the years. *I can change!*

Yes, Diamond. Pearl whispered a few silent words of love to her twin.

There are no limitz in this life, my sister, but with a soul emboldened and a mind inspired, all of us can change. Even me.

She's Harlem's Pearl and she's here to stay
She cut down the thugs who took her family away!
She found room in her heart for the girls on the track
Now she's helping little sisters get their precious souls back
There's no place like Harlem so she stayed and flipped the script
'Cause hell has no fury like a chick who comes unzipped!